LOVE and VANDALISM

LAURIE BOYLE CROMPTON

sourcebooks
fire

Published by Sourcebooks Fire, an imprint of Sourcebooks, Inc.
P.O. Box 4410, Naperville, Illinois 60567-4410
(630) 961-3900
Fax: (630) 961-2168
www.sourcebooks.com

Library of Congress Cataloging-in-Publication data is on file with the publisher.

Printed and bound in the United States of America.
VP 10 9 8 7 6 5 4 3 2 1

To Mom—for teaching me that mountains
are best moved with mustard seed faith.

Thank you for appreciating the irony
that this is the book dedicated to you.

CHAPTER ONE

My can of spray paint rips into the gentle night, releasing a loud *psssht* into an open mouth of fangs.

I shove a dreadlock away from my face and pull down the handkerchief mask I've been breathing through. The thin material hangs lightly around my neck as if it's still holding my breath for me.

I take a few steps back from the wall and consider my work.

In the circle of my lantern's light, a ferocious blue lion roars in my direction. Streaks of teal and turquoise slice through his mane in an exhilarating way, but I'm not loving the flatness in his yellow eyes.

I'm startled by the growl of a car approaching, and the underpass I'm standing in lights up from headlights rounding the distant bend. *Shit.*

I fling a long, black tarp over all my supplies and hiss, "*Rory's sorry,*" to the cans that clatter and clink together in response.

The car's high beams grow steadily brighter as I run from

the scene. The second I reach the end of the cement wall, I recklessly launch myself headfirst into the bushes beside the road.

I hear the car slow to a crawl as I lie facedown in the underbrush and pray to whatever graffiti gods are within earshot, *Please don't be a police cruiser. Or my dad. Or I'm-begging-you-oh-pleasepleaseplease, not my dad driving his police cruiser.*

The car lingers. My lion has been spotted. I lift my head and see a mild-mannered Jeep Wrangler stopped just inside the underpass. The top is down, but the thing is on spring lifts, and from my position on the ground I can't see over the Jeep's massive tires.

I will the driver to leave my cans alone and pull away. Maybe I should've joined Kat at her weird Jedi Mind Trick training workshop after all. I'm not really clear on what she and her Star Wars groupies do together, but I think it has something to do with trying to channel The Force to make shit happen with their minds. Also, they like to wave around flashlight lightsabers while dressed in bathrobes.

Desperately, I whisper at the driver, "Move-your-vehicle's-ass-you-need-to-go-go-go-far-away-now-please-thanks."

A camera's flash lights up the underpass for an instant before the Jeep jumps forward and roars away.

So I guess that's how Jedi Mind Tricks work. I sigh with relief. The driver just wanted a photo of the newest lion in New Paltz. Probably didn't even realize the paint's still wet.

It was a fluke that anyone came down this deserted road in the first place, but I stay on the ground a few minutes, breathing hard as I imagine all the horrible ways that scenario could've gone.

The local police department is on a campaign to rid the town of graffiti art, and according to an article in *The New Paltz Times*, the police sergeant was quoted as saying he considers each new lion painting a "personal offense."

The New Paltz police sergeant also happens to be my dad, but of course, he has no idea the paintings are mine—or that his being *personally* offended makes them so much more fun for me to paint.

I fling the tarp back off my supplies, and my spray cans rattle with relief.

The lantern illuminates the wall, and I lock eyes with the newest member of the carousing graffiti pride I've created throughout our rural upstate town.

So far, I've been painting my lions in out-of-the-way places, but I hope to change that very soon.

Everybody is going to notice the lion I'm planning next.

I used one of my custom stencils on this one's body, so it shares the same stance as all the others, but with my special spray techniques, I've made his face one of a kind.

I'm convinced the only way to capture each lion's unique rage-y-ness is by going freehand.

The rough texture of the wall gives this particular fellow a snarly quality, and the idea of his roar echoing through the underpass makes me smile.

Somewhat satisfied, I pack my workspace into a long,

plastic crate, shove the rolled-up tarp on top, and drag the clink-ing heap through the weeds to where my hatchback waits.

With a grunt, I toss everything in the back, jump into the driver's seat, and, after a churn and a shift, I'm zipping down the road.

I notice a splotch of blue paint on my wrist and lick my finger to rub at it. The dashboard's weak glow shows the blue spot spreading ominously as I speed through the winding woods, leaving my lion to say…

everything I can't.

My head snaps up at the chime of the brass bell over the art store door. From behind the counter, I watch a gang of teenagers each hold the door for one another as they walk in. They're laughing together as they head for the project supplies section, and I recognize them from school.

None of them are actual art people.

One of the girls glances my way, and her laugh slices in half when she recognizes me. She is wearing head-to-toe white, and her blond head bows toward a darker-haired version of herself who's wearing pink.

The two of them act as if I can't see them whispering about me from ten feet away.

I moan inwardly and turn back to the fashion mag lying open on the counter. Someone left it tucked underneath the inventory clipboard, and it's okay that I'm reading it because

I'm reading it ironically. Nobody would ever mistake me for caring about style and makeup and diets and shit.

"You could be one of those models, you know."

I slam the magazine closed and fling it deep under the counter. "Can I help you?"

A tall guy with curly hair stands in front of me. He asks, "Got any one-inch brushes?"

"Sure, follow me." I hop over the counter and keep my head down as I stride along the aisle, toward the front windows. Thankfully, the brushes are in the opposite direction of the poster supplies, where the gaggle of besties is still quacking.

When I reach the brushes, I cup my palm and slide it along the shelf dramatically. With phony politeness, I ask, "Anything else I can help you with?"

When I glance up, the guy's intense brown eyes are studying mine. He drags them away to consult the list he's holding, and I admire his messy curls.

Without thinking, I reach out, pinch a curl, and pull it straight. His eyes jump back to mine as I let go and say, "Boing," with half a smile.

His dark eyes wander down and back up, taking in my height. He's around six three, so he has an inch or two on me. Finally, he smirks and reaches over, gently tugging one of my dreadlocks. "Smoke a *bong*?" he asks.

I decide to forgive him for his stupid model comment.

"Love to." I grin. "Although I'm curious: Did you assume I'm a pothead just because I dread my hair?"

I'm not really curious at all, just messing with him, but his face flushes and I wonder if he's going to bail on our banter. This could be a nice distraction from being whispered about, but I know that not all guys who come in here can handle me.

After a beat, he says, "Who said anything about a pothead? You just seem like a really cool chick to hang out with."

I smile, showing him all my teeth. "I *am* a really cool chick to hang out with."

"So then, what time do you get off work?"

The curly-haired guy's studio apartment is small and stiflingly hot, but fairly tidy for a guy's place.

I've seen enough of them to know that stoner art students who live off campus generally prefer more of a "clothing on the floor and dishes congealing in the sink" habitat. But this guy has actual furniture I can see, and his dinnerware seems to be put away. He may even own a mop.

He asks, "How long have you been working at Danny's art shop?"

"This is my second summer, but I'm only part-time. I lifeguard too, so my hours are pretty all over the place."

"I'm a sophomore, but I've never been to the public pool. How is it?"

I glance at him. Swimming in a blue chlorine box isn't really my style, but I just say, "I guard up at the lake."

"Oh, yeah, I guess that's a little easier to picture." He's obviously picturing me in a swimsuit.

"Heh." I glance pointedly around the room. "We discussed the partaking of some weed?"

"Right." He turns his head, and his curls ricochet back and forth. "I think I left it under the bed." A rare bedframe spotted in the wild. Most art students I've known have their mattresses lying directly on the floor. He gestures for me to sit on the mostly made bed, but I plop myself on the tiny sofa instead.

"So, what's with all the beer posters? Shy about displaying your own artwork?" I'd love to get a sense of his talent and style, since I'm actually here on a serious mission. I need to find an assistant for the big graffiti project I'm planning, but my hunt so far has been unproductive.

This guy doesn't even have a sketchbook lying around for me to flip through. "Let me guess," I say. "You're a sculptor?" I eye a glazed clay ashtray sitting in the center of the coffee table. It looks pretty ordinary.

"This is the only sculpture I've ever made." He rises from under the bed holding up what appears to be a crude, windowless skyscraper made from kid's building blocks. The colorful structure has a small pipe angled out at the bottom.

I laugh. "Lego bong. Nice."

He opens his end table drawer, pulls out a Tupperware container filled with buds, and starts packing the pipe. "I'm just taking a summer watercolor class to fill a requirement. I know fuck-all about art, and everything I paint runs together, but it's better than studying a foreign language or computer science over the summer."

I should leave now. My leg actually gives a few involuntary twitches, as if it's already heading back down the steps. I'm here to find an assistant, not to make time with some basic frat boy.

"But right this moment," he says, "we've got this weed to study. This shit is guaranteed to get you *stupid* high."

Then again, it has been a while since I've been stupid high. I smile. "I'm up for a quick study session."

With a grin, he carries his Lego tower to the sofa and sits down beside me.

Handing me the sculpture, he leans back to dig into his front pocket and pulls out a plastic lighter. The Lego tower in my hands isn't even well crafted. The blue bricks are all clumped together at the bottom and the other primary colors are a haphazard mess, like he started off making the bong solid blue, then realized he didn't have enough blue bricks and said the hell with it.

He says, "Ladies first," and dramatically flicks the lighter. It just sparks and we both laugh. With a grunt, he shakes it and continues flicking until the cheap thing finally lights. He repeats, "Ladies first."

I fit my mouth into the square hole at the top of the Legos and take a few small pulls to light the bong before drawing in as much smoke as my lungs can hold.

Passing the tower over, I sit back and continue holding in my smoke. He takes a full inhale and covers the mouth of the bong with his palm. After a few involuntary coughs, he exhales.

The smoke is clawing at my lips, but I hang on to it a moment longer.

Finally, when a wave of lightness nudges the front of my skull, I let out a smooth stream of air that turns into a laugh at the way he's watching me.

"Not a bad bong you've constructed there." I take it back from him and draw another deep hit.

"And you clearly know your way around a bong." He raises his eyebrows in a way that says he's genuinely impressed.

I tell him about a recent run-in I had with the law, a.k.a. my father and his crazy intuition, and the reason why I don't carry my own stash.

My new frat-boy friend says, "Oh, I see how it is. So you only like me for my pot?"

"Who said that I like you at all?"

"Touché," he says and takes another drag.

I give him a few tips on getting past the local law enforcement if he ever gets stopped. "If the officer is anyone who looks middle-aged, just confess and say you're sorry and new in town. The oldies are the softies on the force. That is," I say, "besides my dad. If you have a run-in with the guy who looks like a balding, fifty-year-old linebacker, lie like your life depends on it. Same goes for the younger guys on the force: all a bunch of ballbusters."

"What if I get caught holding?"

"Toss the stuff as far as you can and then deny, deny, deny."

He hugs his bong lightly, looking like I've spooked him.

"That there is some valuable insider advice," I say. "You're welcome."

I lie back on the sofa as my mind skips off to painted lions with colors so bright they can't be seen with the naked eye.

I envision a giant pride of Rory lions, slowly closing in.

They snarl and yowl until their open mouths turn into yawns. One by one, they lie down in the grass. Release all their rage. I feel myself smiling stupidly at the light beam streaming through the window.

Something brushes against my arm, sliding up to my shoulder, and when I move to swipe it away, I realize it's frat boy's hand. His fingers walk toward my neck as he watches me with amusement.

I'm happy enough to just sit here grooving this buzz, but this guy clearly has some expectations. In all fairness, when I thought he was an artist, I imagined he might have some potential, so there's a chance I may have been leading him on.

I ask, "What's your major anyway?"

He grins. "Finance."

I try to keep my expression neutral, but it isn't easy. "So, you want to…?"

"Make lots and lots of money when I graduate," he says. "Preferably on Wall Street." Which is exactly the wrong answer to give if he wanted to impress me.

Not being an artist is one thing but a *finance* major? That's the literal study of money.

My mom lived in downtown Manhattan before marrying

my dad and has always referred to Wall Street as the "Valley of Lost Souls."

Mr. Finance Major leans forward to kiss me, and I put a hand on his chest, holding him back and closing my eyes as I try to make a decision. But my decision-maker seems to be acting fuzzy at the moment.

I assess the situation.

Messing around with him right now would represent a new personal low. But when I open my eyes, he is giving me the cutest grin. I can tell he's used to getting the girl, and his curls are practically begging me to play with them. He wasn't kidding about this weed being quality.

But I don't owe him anything.

I'm the one in control and I don't—

His lips are on mine. After an awkward moment of me not kissing him back, he finally pulls back. "You're not into this?"

We watch each other for one beat...two beats...three beats...and I force my face into a grin. "I just like it more like this." I push him back on the couch and position myself on top of him seductively.

The surprised happiness on his face is so rewarding, I lean down and give him a deep kiss.

He grunts with pleasure and wraps a hand around my waist as we continue making out. I feel as if I'm outside myself, sitting on the floor and watching this erotic scene unfold on the small sofa.

He's too good-looking for anyone to have ever corrected

his kissing, so I guide him, gently illustrating the concept that less is more, especially when it comes to tongue. He's a fast learner, and before long, I'm feeling a little turned on. Acting as if I'm really into this helps.

Things continue heating up between us, and when his hand slides from my waist to my side boob, I don't stop him.

The lions in my head rouse from their rest, but I hush them all. Tell them that everything's okay. That I'm the one in control here.

I'm always the one in control.

"When you're working on a special piece, it's important to access your every raw emotion," Mom tells me in the kitchen. I'm sitting on the swivel stool by the counter, eating sherbet and mulling over the problems I'm having with my big lion project.

I really need to snag an assistant to help me pull it off, and frat boy is just the most recent in a series of very disappointing dead ends.

My dad hates it when Mom and I discuss art. In fact, he's tried to forbid it, but it's our deepest soul connection. All my talent comes from her, and he can't find a way to relate to any of it. So he tries to squash it.

"You *must* listen to your inner voice," Mom's saying. "It took me weeks to finally be somewhat content with the twisted yellow vase on the mantle. At least it should still be there." She looks perplexed for a moment, closes her eyes, and takes a deep breath.

I wish I could reach over and put a comforting hand on her arm, but we just sit together silently.

Finally, she continues, "Getting that dappled effect took so much planning. Of course, there's always an element of surprise and discovery with glassblowing. With any art. And with life too, I suppose."

My mother is the most amazing artist I've ever known, and I mean that as an art lover, not just as her daughter. I swear, her way of seeing the world is so unique and deep, it's like I'm getting one-on-one, free art lessons from a master every time we chat.

We're breaking Dad's number-one rule right now with this discussion, but if there's one thing I've learned from her, it's that art has nothing to do with rules. It jumps beyond the neat and tidy boundaries of order and discipline.

Art that matters is some scary shit.

We're both smiling as Mom goes on. "Art is our way of expressing our true selves. And the most interesting art comes from our darkest places. You are an artist, Rory, and as an artist, you must not be afraid of your pain. *Use* it."

I allow my mind to dip into my chest and consider the dark places. In addition to the myriad feelings of regret and loneliness, there is a black pocket of tender ache trapped just underneath my ribs.

It waits there, always, but I'm not disrupting it now. I save it for when I'm painting. When my lions are wide-awake and out on the prowl.

Mom begins telling me the story about when she was a little girl coming home from kindergarten and she got off the bus one stop too early. I've heard this before but lean forward to listen, wishing I could comfort that little girl now, almost forty years too late.

Her expression is one of wide-eyed innocence as she describes that agony of feeling hopelessly lost. My heart breaks for her as she talks about reopening the wound again and again as she paints, tapping into that dark place.

"Every brushstroke is like a step in those stiff, new school shoes that had already bloodied my feet with blisters. I couldn't know if each painful stride was bringing me closer to home or farther away." She mimes holding a paintbrush and dabs the air as she clicks her tongue in time with her strokes. She stops and looks around as if she's just woken up. "I should really be painting right now."

Finished with my sherbet, I scrape the rest of it into the garbage and quickly rinse my bowl before putting it in the dishwasher. Dad has banned me from art, but Mom is free to do what she wants.

"That's it for tonight. Love you, Mom." I head up the stairs to get ready for bed.

I pause when I hear the faint strains of her voice as she continues talking to herself. I waver on the steps a moment, sensing the pull to go back downstairs to her.

But I'm too exhausted to take in anymore. I continue climbing slowly up to my room as I imagine broken blown glass scattered across each step.

The next morning, I stand at the front door and call up to Dad, "I'm heading out." He immediately comes thundering down the stairs with Kelly at his heels.

Kelly is a retired police dog who's been busy patrolling our home for the past two years. Supposedly, she's the family pet, but she hasn't quite mastered the concept of being off-duty.

"Where are you headed today, Rory?" Dad asks with false casualness.

I give him a mock salute. "Guarding at the lake. Double shift." As it happens, there is no such thing as a double shift up at the lake.

"So, you have your bathing suit in your knapsack?"

With a sigh, I pull one of my red straps from the neck hole of my T-shirt to show him. "Come on, Dad. I've been good all summer."

"*Summer* just started last week, Rory, and I thought we talked about you getting a job someplace other than that art store."

"*You* discussed that. *I've* explained that it's just a job. It's not like I can make art when I'm working." His gaze on me is so steady, I feel a growl growing inside. "You won't let me visit the art studio at school. You monitor what I do when I'm home and in my room. Dad, stop worrying. I've quit making art."

"I really don't want to catch you again." Dad suddenly looks very, very old and tired. "Rory—"

The two of us are the same height, and I place my hands on both his shoulders as I look him in the eye and swallow down my anger. "Don't worry. I'm just working there because I'd make a terrible waitress and Danny's pays better than the bookstore."

"I'm sorry, Rory. I just worry about you."

"Well, stop worrying," I say. "None of that stuff is a part of my life anymore."

Dad tries a smile, but it's so forced he looks constipated.

His phone sounds with a *ping* and I ask, "You on your way to work?"

"No. I'm on the later shift today." He pulls his phone from his back pocket, glances at it, and quickly puts it away. My dad schedules everything in such detail, that alert may've been telling him to go use the bathroom.

I point my thumb toward the door. "I'm heading out."

"Oh wait, your new AAA card came yesterday." He pulls out his wallet and starts flipping through credit cards.

I say, "You know one of your patrol guys always comes to my rescue before the automotive alcoholics can get there." My hatchback isn't particularly reliable, but our police force is.

Dad gives a chuckle. "It's always good to have backup." He hands me a gold card.

I shove the card into the front pocket of my backpack. "You cops and your obsession with backup. You really should trust that I know how to take care of myself."

He shrugs and says, "A little trust goes a long way…"

Together we finish his favorite mantra: "*And the less trust you use, the further you go.*"

I notice a shadow pass over his expression as he glances at my bag.

My breathing slows and I look at the ground. Right now, his words are telling me he'll see me tonight and that I should have a good day and please check in later, but I know he's wondering if I'm carrying any drugs.

Clearing my throat, I call, "Hey, Kelly." When the dog moves in front of me with her ears tuned for orders, I lift my backpack by the strap and hold it out toward her. Glaring at my dad for a moment, my jaw clenched, I turn to Kelly and command, "Find it!"

She digs her nose into the side of my bag with her tail wagging, checking for drugs. Dad's eyes are filled with emotion as he watches her work.

I let Kelly sniff all over the bag from every angle. She was the top K9 on the force before she retired, and she clearly misses being on the job.

Our shepherd goes over every inch so thoroughly I start to get nervous and second-guess whether there was ever pot stashed in this backpack.

To cover up my nervousness, I snipe at Dad, "Did you train her to sniff out art supplies now too?"

His eyes don't move from the dog as he reads her every move.

His worry that I've gotten back into art is almost as strong as his fear that I'm carrying narcotics. He was horrified when he checked in with my art teacher back in May and found out I'd been spending all my spare time at the school's art studio.

Finally, Kelly sits down and looks up at my dad, giving me the all clear. If she'd detected any drugs, she'd be scratching at my bag right now, and despite the beginnings of tears in his eyes, I have no doubt Dad would be putting me in cuffs.

"You didn't have to do that." His voice cracks, but there's relief in it too.

I open the front door and leave without making eye contact with him again.

CHAPTER TWO

Speeding through the woods on the road that winds up the mountain, I try to outrun my anger with my car. I'm just rounding the second switchback when I give an involuntary gasp of surprise.

What the hell? Some asshole with slicked-back black hair is wandering along the shoulder of the road like he's just arrived on earth and has no idea how roads work. I resist the urge to blast the horn as I swerve around him.

But I cannot be expected to stop myself from flipping him the bird as I zoom by.

He doesn't seem to notice as he continues walking in his high-end activewear. I hate freaking weekenders. This guy probably just took the tags off his hiking shorts this morning.

Just one of the *many* reasons I prefer sticking to my out-of-the-way places. Unfortunately, there's only one entrance to the lake where I lifeguard, but once I'm inside the park, I head straight to my private little section of wilderness. The area doesn't even need a "keep out" sign to discourage visitors. It's completely overgrown and it's all mine.

A long time ago, there was a boys' camp in these woods with about two dozen cabins that have been mostly reclaimed by nature. Nature is insatiable. I once read someplace that a parking lot left abandoned will return to forest within twenty years. Only a handful of cabins remain, and the way the trees have pierced the rotting floors and shredded the roofs with their branches make me believe they won't last much longer.

I drive toward the one cabin that I've managed to wrestle back from the forest.

My lair.

It's well hidden along an overgrown path and—thanks to pure determination, plus a hacksaw and a few odd tools that my dad will hopefully never miss—the thing is still standing on its shaky struts. Just barely.

It's the place where I plan my paintings and store all my graffiti supplies.

Parking my hatchback as close as I can, I swing my backpack over my shoulder and hike the rest of the way through the less-traveled woods to my illicit hideout.

I feel a rush of excitement as I open the splintering door and see a piece of my oversize stencil spread out on the wooden floorboards. I only have a few hours before I need to hit the nearby lake for my *single* shift, so I immediately kneel down and get to work.

Sliding long pieces around, I carefully trim edges with my

box cutter as I line up the negative space that will eventually reveal my greatest lion, roaring for all to see.

I lose myself in creative flow, curious paws in my mind batting at ideas.

The lion I'm planning has a purpose, and the location I've picked out is perfect. Radically public. My ambitious eye is set on a surface that overlooks the whole valley: the town water tower.

The tower was recently painted with a giant, obnoxious ad for Sparkle Soda. The thing has been taunting all of New Paltz's residents with its ecstatically happy blond and her perfect skin, smiling manically from above. She commands us all to "Submit to the Sparkle," as if Sparkle is some sort of divine god who we all must serve.

I'm determined to transform that blasphemous ad.

I gloss over the irrational size of the equipment packs I'll need and deny just how high the ladder affixed to the leg of the tower goes. (Hint: it goes *all* the way up.) I ignore the ridiculous amount of work and skip straight to the image of my huge, majestic lion pouring out his roar over this whole valley.

He is going to devour the model, with her perfect skin and phony grin, like a big-cat circus act that will change everything.

I envision my lion getting discovered that very first morning. He'll be bursting with wild color in the glow of that early dawn.

Waking everyone up.

I fall into the rhythm of mapping out my stencils as my

X-ACTO knife slices into a new sheet of card stock. The mental image of my growling lion rises into sharper focus, and it's as if the razor-sharp blade is leading my hand where it wants to go.

I get so absorbed in my project, the next thing I know, I've ignored several reminders from my phone and have told myself, *I'll leave in just one more minute*, so many times I'm already late for my shift.

The pull to stay and work feels almost physical, and I release a grunt as I grab my bag and shoot through the cabin's weathered door.

I'm already looking forward to the few solid hours I'll have alone with my lion after lifeguarding.

I sprint down the path leading to the lake and pass my car. When I reach the turn onto the public trail, I start undoing my shorts. I'm still a half mile or so away, but I need to be ready to jump right in the canoe as soon as I get to the beach.

Barely slowing down my momentum, I lean forward and step my right leg out of my shorts. It's a learned skill.

I go for the left side and find myself hopping around with my foot awkwardly in the air as I reach a bend in the trail. I hop faster when I spot the jerk with the slicked-back hair that I passed on the road. He's straight ahead of me, sitting on a rock and reading a book as he bites into a protein bar.

I finish pulling my wadded shorts off my ankle, and my toe catches the leg hole, bungling my balance.

I flail as I'm pitched into the underbrush.

"Are you okay?" The guy seems more amused than

concerned. He's about my age and height, but he's super pale and his black hair has way more product and style than mine. Plus, I can smell his cologne from here.

I stumble out of the bushes, pulling a leafy branch from my hair, and snap, "You might want to watch your ass when you're walking on the road. I nearly ran over it this morning."

"I'm not from around here," he calls after me as I continue moving down the trail.

"Yeah, no shit." I spin around quickly, catching him by surprise as he ogles my butt. Of course, I realize it's a very fine butt in a red bathing suit, but still. "I said watch *your* ass, not mine."

He tips his head to one side, but his hair doesn't move. "Who *are* you?"

Clutching my shorts, I jog away calling, "Nobody you'll ever get to know."

By the time I reach the lake, my fellow lifeguard, Scott, is already pushing the canoe from the beach into the water.

"My turn to do the first sweep," I huff as I enter the pebbled clearing. The two of us always take turns paddling the canoe around the lake, and I'm up first today.

He doesn't look back at me. "You should've been here on time."

"I ran into someone along the path." I drop my backpack and shorts, arching my back as I smoothly take off my T-shirt.

"It's always something with you, Rory." Scott keeps one

foot on shore and one foot in the canoe but stands upright, watching me. His eyes are like two pale-blue moths attracted to the light that is my cleavage.

I don't want to take advantage of his obvious fascination with my assets, but I desperately need the dose of inner peace that comes from a solo cruise around the lake. I don't quite aim my tatas in his direction, but I do let my shoulders drop.

The poor guy actually licks his lips as he says, "I guess you can get this round. I'll do the checklist."

Doing a safety check on all the equipment is like the opposite chore to gliding freely around the lake in the canoe. After a moment of guilty hesitation, I grab the oar.

Small clouds of fog still cling to the lake's surface as I float peacefully along.

I get that surreal sense of connection to all the people who have visited this spot over hundreds of years.

The original lodge burned down a long time ago, but visitors still come from all over the world to ooh and aah over the views. And, of course, they go absolutely apeshit over the colorful dead leaves in the fall.

I imagine what it must've been like to be the very first adventurer to discover this place while exploring. A sky lake, fed purely by rainwater, here at the top of the mountain. Stumbling upon it must've felt like a miracle.

I like to imagine the person pulled out pen and ink or charcoals or some ground-up pigment or a chisel and stone and started drawing like mad.

Folding the oar over my lap, I breathe in the raw air, taking my time.

I know it was a sacrifice for Scott to give this up. He loves coming back to the beach to announce, "All clear," as if we're under siege and he's just risked his life.

When I reach the far end, I allow the boat to drift smoothly along the edge of the lake. My dreads shift back off my face as I lift my chin, scanning the trees.

I'm halfway back to the beach when my reflexes curl and my gaze springs like a cat on *the thing that doesn't belong in the woods.*

It's that damn guy again. The walking perfume department just standing among the pines by the shore, watching me. When he sees me looking, he smiles and gives a casual wave. Like we're friends now or something.

He's not exactly trespassing. I'm here to patrol the woods for illegal activity and to check the water for swimmers outside the swim area.

But right now, I want to chase this intruder from my woods.

I shake my head no to him and dig my oar into the water, expertly aiming the canoe back toward the main beach.

He calls a loud, "Yo!" after me, but I don't give the guy another look.

When I get back to the swim area, I climb the wooden lifeguard ladder and scoot onto the seat beside Scott. He's focused on the water. The beach officially opened twenty minutes ago, and there are half a dozen people of various ages milling about in the lake.

I sit, watching as a petite mother tries to wrangle her toddler into submission. The toddler is repeatedly calling out, "Duck!" while pointing to a sweet mallard family swimming by.

My instincts flip to high alert, since the toddler's older sister is treading water in the deeper section alone. The girl is only about nine or so, but her mom seems overly absorbed with the offspring that's still sporting a swim diaper.

"Yes, ducks!" she says to the toddler as if he's just discovered a renewable energy source. "And what sound does the duck make?"

The toddler goes into an admittedly adorable imitation of a duck, waddling in the shallow water and quacking while he flaps his little elbows like chubby wings. His mother's laugh rings out.

I wonder if his older sister feels as abandoned as she looks. I call to her, "How about coming a little closer to shore, honey?"

The mother snaps her head up and shrills, "Kendra, get over here. I can't keep an eye on you too." She glances at me. "Sorry about her."

I clutch my whistle. "She's fine. Just starting to look tired is all." It's too bad not everyone gets a mom as great as mine.

As Kendra carefully doggie-paddles back toward shore, I relax a bit.

Scott grins at me. "Nice lifeguarding."

I hold my hands out. "It's what I do."

"It's *one* thing you do." He gives me a smile. "Any progress with the sergeant?"

I shake my head. "Lost cause." Scott doesn't know about my lions or my cabin, but my dad showed up here one day to check that I wasn't sneaking in some creative activity. I had to fling my sketchbook into Scott's arms and explain the whole crazy no-art policy to him after my dad left.

I turn in my seat now to scan the beach. The mother is rubbing the toddler dry with a towel as her daughter sits wrapped in a hooded, pink beach towel, eyes closed, and face tilted to the sun. She's smiling and holding a large, clouded baggie filled with some form of trail mix.

There's no eating allowed on the beach, but I don't usually enforce that rule unless people are being disruptive. Mothers are supposed to give their kids healthy snacks. The nine-year-old opens her eyes and pops a raisin in her mouth, looking as if she might not be plagued with mommy issues her whole life after all.

My bag hangs on the back of the lifeguard chair, and from its pocket, I hear the muffled notes of Dad's ominous ringtone. It's the theme song from the TV show *Cops*.

"Whatcha gonna do when they come for you?" I sing along with the tune as I dig out my phone.

Scott says, "Tell Sarge I say hi."

Dad was pretty suspicious of Scott's drawing talent when he busted me, so he's not exactly on my father's good side. Not that many people are.

I give Scott a light punch and hit Answer as I jump down from the chair. We're not allowed to use our phones while on duty, but he can handle the solitary couple kissing in the deep end without me. Better I answer than have Dad showing up here to check on me again.

"Hello?" I say, but all I can hear is a scraping noise and a muffled conversation on the other end.

"Hello!" I call into the phone, but there's no response beyond the continued scraping. I yell, "Great job dialing me with your *butt*, Dad!" but he can't hear me. He just told me this morning his shift at the station starts later this afternoon, so I wonder who he's talking to.

And then I hear it. The lilt of an unfamiliar female voice. She's telling him to "behave" in a way that implies he doesn't really need to.

My insides drop to the pebbled beach.

"Hell no." I clutch the phone closer to my ear. I'm trying to make out the words they're saying, but the conversation sounds like it's happening underwater.

"Is everything okay?" Scott is watching my face as he leans down from his seat.

I point to the lake, even though the couple's already moved to the ladder that leads up to the dock. I turn and walk toward the back of the beach.

Listening as hard as I can, it becomes clear that what I am hearing is a flirtatious exchange between my father and a woman who is not my mother. It doesn't sound like a casual exchange between strangers either. In fact, I hear what sounds like the scraping of silverware on plates.

"I've really missed you this week," the woman says.

My dad's voice streams through the phone. "I know. I wish we could meet more often."

I press the phone closer to my ear but can't make out what she's saying now. Something about being together. My heart beats against my eardrums.

The next thing I can decipher is my dad saying, "I'm sorry. She's just not ready."

What the hell?

The conversation goes quiet and the clanging of dinnerware is all I can hear. Finally, my dad asks, "How're your eggs?"

He is literally asking another woman about her eggs. *How could he do this to Mom?*

It feels as if the fog is back, and instead of hanging in wisps over the lake, it is clogging up my lungs and making it hard for me to breathe.

When I can't stand listening for another second, I end the one-way call and climb back onto the lifeguard bench beside Scott. He watches me so intently, I instinctively check the lake for swimmers. The water's empty now.

Still, I don't look back at him when I say, "I think my dad is having a fucking affair."

I think back to the worst things I remember my dad ever doing:

Drop-kicking the neighbor's basset hound into the snow after the dog ate half of our linoleum kitchen floor.

Backing over my bicycle in the driveway to teach me a lesson about putting things away.

Shoving all my art supplies into a giant, black waste bag and flinging them directly into the open mouth of a garbage truck in a fit of rage.

And now. I didn't think it was possible, but Dad has managed to top himself.

His new worst thing is cheating on Mom.

By the time my shift ends and I've hiked all the way back to the door of my cabin, the fog in my lungs has turned into searing-hot steam. I know I won't be able to focus on organizing my big project plans.

My lions are agitated and restless and murderously hungry.

I need to paint. Now.

Hurriedly, I stuff painting supplies into an empty rucksack. I know just the spot for this lion, and the excitement of imagining it releases a tiny bit of the pressure in my lungs. I actually let out a grunt as I prepare to go.

Throwing my faded black baseball cap over my dreads, I head off in the direction opposite the lake. The path grows increasingly windy and overgrown, and the thorns claw at my legs.

I wish I weren't wearing shorts, but my journey feels vital.

Like the lions are prowling alongside me.

I'm trying not to think about the phone call, but sound bites from the underwater flirting keep rising to the surface.

I need to catch my fraud of a father in the act. Too bad Kelly isn't trained to sniff out cheating rat bastards.

I'd bet anything Dad's marking his meetings with his mistress in his smartphone's calendar. Although he's probably using some sort of code, since I doubt he'd label his datebook, "Event title: *Cheat on my wife.*"

I command my brain to stop thinking. I'm heading to paint, and everything will be okay for a few hours.

Stopping for a moment, I lick my finger to rub a deep scratch on my leg where the thorns have drawn blood. The sting helps me focus as I press on, toward my waiting stone canvas. I move faster as I get closer.

With a grunt, I toss my bag over my shoulder and climb a tall, rattling fence. Last year some corporate assholes put this metal eyesore up to protect us all from the awesome swim hole inside. As if that would stop kids from swimming here.

I climb past the sign that says something about the place being one huge safety hazard. Meanwhile, this spot should've been zoned as sacred ground.

Over to the right, a rough wall of rock sports a few amateur tags. Before the fence, nobody would've even thought of painting graffiti here. It was too perfect and beautiful. I walk over and run my fingers across the crude white letters.

Damn vandals.

I'm glad I have a can of white because zero effort was

put into these letters and my lion will be absorbing these ugly initials. It's not that art can't be ugly, but as Mom says, it should display signs of effort and thought and purpose—evidence of giving a shit.

These letters are just some kid pissing his name in the snow, but my design will transform the scrawls into something magnificent.

It's important to be flexible when your canvas is shared public space.

I lay down my thick tarp, empty my duffel bag, and stand, staring at the rock face. I imagine the way the planes of this lion's mouth will best fit into the craggy surface.

I usually paint exclusively at night, but this swim hole is completely secluded. And the type of locals who do come here to swim would probably cheer me on once they saw what I'm doing.

I have a number of fans who post photos of my lions on social media, and I have to admit, it's pretty damn awesome.

There's a folded-up stencil in my bag, but as I replay the mystery woman's voice cooing at my dad, I decide I don't need it.

I keep watching the wall until the lion's open mouth reveals itself in a wicked 3-D effect. I smile, and excitement pumps through my limbs.

Holding back for that extra minute, I savor the moment of being about to begin until I can't resist anymore. With a stretch and a few deep breaths, I tie my mask around my neck and pull it up to cover my mouth.

I grab a can of spray paint in each hand and pounce on the rock face.

I'm using five different tips, plus a loose flap of cardboard to help direct the paint streams and define the edges. But from tail to mane, this wild beast is all freehand.

My cans chant purposeful sounds as I *sssspray* and stop and *shake, shake, shake*, creating metallic giggles that ring out through the woods.

Their giddy echo lulls me into a trance as I make this small section of beautiful nature my own.

If it wasn't for the fence already wrecking the view, this isn't a spot I would normally choose. I love and respect these woods. But the area has been caged in anyway, so the way I see it, this space could use a lion's roar. Climbing over the fence for an illegal swim will seem more adventuresome once this guy's complete.

I hum as I think about the reactions he'll get. When I take a step back for perspective, I notice his proportions seem to be running a little larger than my stenciled ones.

I wonder if anyone will notice the lions have started to grow.

CHAPTER THREE

I hear the fence behind me give a distinct rattle.

Deep-fried crap balls.

I stop spraying midstroke and spin around. I'm trapped like an animal, and I half expect my dad to be standing there in full uniform with his gun drawn and aimed at my head.

Instead, it's that damn cologne-ad model again. He looks at me with his eyes so wide I can see the whites all around. "*You're* the one painting those lions?"

Pushing a dreadlock off my face, I calmly make my way to the fence where he's standing. Ignoring him is suddenly much less of an option.

I say, "I don't know what you've been doing here all afternoon, but camping inside the state park isn't allowed."

"Oh, like you're not breaking any laws." His eyes are locked onto my lion. "And besides, do I look like a camper to you?"

"No." I resist the urge to ask what hiking catalog he just stepped out of. "But you do seem to be occupying the woods pretty hard. Are you staying up at Mohonk or something?"

Mohonk is the expensive resort that sits at the top of the adjacent mountain. We get a lot of their guests "slumming it" here on the public-state-park side.

This guy's face is pressed against the fence, and the way he's staring at my lion is making me nervous. "I can't believe you're the actual artist." He finally looks at me.

I hold my paint-stained palms up. I was supposed to be in planning mode all day today, so I didn't grab rubber gloves.

I say, "Guilty. You caught me red-handed. And orange handed and purple handed..." I let my voice fade and rub my palms together, hating the fact that I need him to be cool about all this.

His eyes sparkle. "Running into you must be fate."

I cross my arms. "I don't exactly believe in fate. I believe in *shit happens*."

"'Shit happens' *is* fate." He grins at me. "Well, maybe more 'shit happens *for a reason*.'"

"I see. So you've recently converted to some religion or cult or whatever, and now you've decided New Paltz is your new mecca. Of course." The town naturally draws spiritual seekers, along with its fair share of wackadoos.

"I'm staying here with my aunt for the summer," he says. "Getting away from Long Island to figure a few things out with my life."

36

I laugh. "Why do people always think they need to leave home to find themselves?"

He ignores my comment. "I've been studying these lions of yours around town, and they're saying something. They're not just roaring. These guys are *raging*." He tilts his head as he studies my work. "Is this one bigger than the others?"

I turn away and start collecting my supplies. "Listen, I just need you to be chill about this. Getting busted would be pretty messy for me."

"I know what that's like," he says. "Are you on probation too?"

"No." My turned back hides my surprise. He doesn't strike me as the "on probation too" type, a.k.a. my type. "I have a family member in law enforcement and let's just say things could get very bad *very* quickly."

I turn at the rattling sound of the fence and see he's climbing over to my side.

"By all means, do join me," I say sarcastically as he moves in front of my face.

"I'm Hayes." He reaches out to shake my hand like we're here for a formal business meeting in some sort of outdoor conference room.

"Hello, Hayes." I ignore his hand. "Welcome to the lion's den." I try to look menacing, but he just responds with another easy grin. I notice his lips are the tiniest bit lopsided in a way that tries to draw me in. I look away.

He moves closer to the lion's face, and I will the thing to spring to life and swallow him up.

"This fellow seems especially angry." Hayes turns to me. "Where is all this rage coming from?"

I laugh. "Maybe I'm just a good artist."

"You're an amazing artist." His intensity makes me blush. "But this anguish can't come from nothing."

I consider the lion's drawn snarl. He's right. Pain and rage shade every groove.

I angle my body away from him. "Listen, I just need you to not tell anyone about this. About me. Okay?"

He watches me silently, as if deciding something. My heart beats harder and harder until I turn around and start shoving spray cans into my backpack.

I was an idiot to pick a spot where I couldn't make a fast escape. I've always been so careful, but I let my anger toward Dad interfere with my judgment.

Finally, Hayes says, "I'll make you a deal. Let me take you out to lunch. I want to talk with you about your lions."

"I never talk about my lions. Ever." I glance at him over my shoulder. "And I do *not* go on dates with guys from Lawng Eyeland."

The grin is back. "So it's not a date then. Let's just think of it as an exchange. I'll keep silent about your identity if you shed a little light on the meaning of your lions. Also, I'm starving, so we should maybe get a bite to eat while we talk."

"You're seriously going to blackmail me into going out with you?"

"Don't make it sound so creepy." He moves to climb back over the chain-link fence. "I just want to take you to a casual lunch. And in exchange, I won't alert the authorities to your identity."

He has to be bluffing. "You have no idea who I am." I crane my neck to look at him since he's already reached the top of the fence.

He grabs the bar with one flexed arm, pulls himself up, and flings a leg over before peering down at me.

"Oh, I think I have a pretty good sense of who you are." He jumps to the ground. "And I know what you drive. And I know where you work."

Shit. "Guess you found your true self here in New Paltz after all," I call out. "You're a creepy *stalker* blackmailer!"

Laughing, he says, "I'll wait for you out by the park entrance." He doesn't even look back as he adjusts his pack and walks away. He's the one in control now.

Impulsively, I pick up a nearly empty spray can, and with a few quick flips of my wrist, my lion's eyes go red with fury.

Sitting at my favorite place to eat, the Main Street Bistro, has never felt so confining. My leg shakes with impatience as Hayes pores over the menu. I say, "Just order the Fifty-Nine Main Express breakfast burrito. Unless you're a *vegetarian*." It's an accusation. "Then get the Veggie X."

He gives an easy grin as he closes his menu. "Fifty-Nine Main Express burrito it is. You know, trusting a stranger can feel really good sometimes."

"Yeah, well, forgive me, but I'm a little too busy being blackmailed to focus on *trust* at the moment."

"Ice water?" he asks pleasantly, and picks up the sweaty pitcher sitting between us. My buddy John is our waiter, so instead of plastic cups, we have nice glass steins with lemon slices perched on the rims. I hold mine toward Hayes.

As he pours, one of the ice cubes leaps onto the table. Scooping it up neatly, he pops it in his mouth. The bistro often has a line of people out the door, but it's the middle of the week and most of the college students are tucked away in their assorted hometowns for the summer, so the place is semiquiet.

Hayes slides our waters to the side along with the pitcher, so there's nothing between us. When he leans forward, I grab the handle of my glass and quickly toss back an icy-cold gulp.

He looks at me as he slides the lump of ice back and forth in his mouth. Finally, he crushes it between his molars with a loud crunch. When he's finished chewing, he asks, "Do you believe in signs?"

My water glass clinks down in front of me. "Yeah, sure. The big red ones that say *stop* are my favorite."

"Very funny." His forehead pulls up as if drawn by elastic. "I'm talking about the divine, meaningful sort. The kind that give guidance."

There it is. "No, I do not. Sorry, I should've mentioned

I'm not a flake. And I'm not really interested in learning about Allah or Buddha or accepting Jesus-as-my-personal-lord-and-savior-thanks." I reach over and pat his arm. "But you've come to the right place. New Paltz should offer its own welcome packet and walking tour for people on *spiritual pilgrimages*."

Hayes laughs and we're interrupted by John asking if we're ready to order. We each get the Fifty-Nine Main Express and John gives me a knowing wink as if he can see what this is.

Except even I don't know what the hell this is.

Hayes says, "Ever since I was a kid, I've always had this thing for lions."

I pick up my fork and press the tines into my thumb. "Yeah, well, with the name Rory, I guess I could say the same thing."

"Makes sense," he says with a grin.

I cringe inwardly at my oversharing. Now he has my name too.

"Lions aren't just my favorite animal. It's like I'm drawn to them," he says. "Every time I see one, it feels like a message for me to pay attention."

"So lions are your *spirit animal*?" I mock.

"Funny." He doesn't laugh.

Hayes is a fast talker and launches into a story about how, a few years ago, he saw a whole pride of lions in the wild while on safari in Africa. Apparently, going on safari in Africa isn't a big deal to his family because Hayes mentions it like it was a road trip to Pittsburgh or something.

But when he describes seeing those lions, he makes it sound like a holy experience.

"One of them looked directly at me, and even though I knew we were relatively safe in our tour jeep, I've never felt more scared in my life." His eyes shine. "But it was an uplifting sort of terror. Like, the lion probably wanted to attack me, but being *seen* by him was worth the danger."

Before deciding to, I tell him about the time my mother took me to the Bronx Zoo when I was seven years old and I got lost. I'd followed the signs leading to the Lion House, and when she found me an hour later, I was standing in front of the glass, having a staring contest with a young lion.

"She still repeats the story that the poor thing seemed to be losing his confidence under my glare," I say, "like he couldn't decide if I was the prey or if he was supposed to be the prey. I'm pretty sure he was thinking I'd make a nice snack, but I have to confess, I vaguely remember feeling thrilled as I looked into those big amber eyes."

I realize Hayes has been listening to me with an unnerving amount of focus, and I look down at my still-stained hands, wondering what got me babbling on.

He holds up his water glass and declares a toast. "To the mighty lion, king of the beasts."

His lopsided grin draws me in and the moment feels heavy. I lift my glass, and before I can stop myself, I countertoast, "To being seen."

Hayes and I stare at each other. His voice is rough as

he repeats my toast. "To being seen." He clinks his glass to mine.

We watch each other drink and place our glasses back on the table between us without breaking eye contact.

Finally, I look down and mumble, "Or something corny like that."

"Sorry to interrupt you two, but here you go." It's John bringing us our food.

We thank him, and after Hayes bows his head silently for a moment, he digs in. He displays an appropriate level of awe over the utter deliciousness of the Fifty-Nine X.

"Now, *this* is what I'm talking about," he says between bites. "It might have taken me a month to try this if we never met. Or I could've missed out altogether."

"Glad to be your resident burrito guru," I say. "Now you can head back to Long Island utterly fulfilled."

"Oh, no. You're not getting rid of me that easy."

"Um, I'm pretty sure I am. I mean, I'll let you pay for my meal and all because you seem sort of rich." I lower my voice to a whisper. "But I don't actually believe you would turn me in for *vandalism*." I dig a forkful of potatoes from my burrito.

"Not reporting you makes me an obstructer of the law. And I've recently become more conscious of respecting each and every facet of our fine legal system."

"Yeah, well, being on probation can do that to a person."

"Tell me about it." He starts to give me the story of how he ended up getting busted for drunk driving back in Queens. Twice.

I eat slowly as he talks quickly, describing the first time he snuck a drink from his parent's liquor cabinet. He liked the dizzy feeling it gave him. He was twelve. "It wasn't long before I was sneaking whatever alcohol I could find. My parents keep a fully stocked bar for social occasions. Well, I mean, they used to."

He tells me how his drinking escalated until one year when he showed up drunk to his mother's formal spring tea. He tried to hide how blitzed he was, but his loud talking gave him away and his mother was mortified.

"I felt terrible and tried to stop drinking after that." He looks down at his hands. "But quitting was harder than I thought it would be."

"And you were how old?"

"I was fourteen by then, but it was like I'd been missing this puzzle piece all my life and the alcohol fit perfectly in that empty hole. Or at least, it nearly fit. And gradually, it started taking more and more liquor to get the same feeling of wholeness."

"You must've been dealing with some pretty heavy stuff to need to escape that bad." I chew a bite of my burrito slowly.

He puts down his fork and knife. "Actually, I grew up in a loving family in a stable home in a really good neighborhood. My turmoil was all internal."

I'm ashamed to realize Hayes has been growing more appealing to me as he's shared the shitstorm he made of his once-perfect life. My dad would hate the idea of me being with this guy. Maybe I wrote him off too quickly.

"Staying here with my aunt for the summer is my final big shot for a do-over," Hayes says. "I'm lucky to get a third chance, and now I'm paying closer attention to *everything*."

"So you need me to show you where all the hot parties are?"

"Very funny. I've been sober three months now."

"You mean, like, with AA?"

He blushes. "That second A is supposed to stand for *anonymous*. But it's been good. The meetings here seem…deeper than the ones I was going to back home."

"New Paltz certainly has her charms—the views, the trails, our recovering alcoholics."

"So, what about you?"

"Do I party?"

"No, I mean…what about *you*? What's with all the angry lions? When did you start painting them?"

I hold up my steak knife as if I can physically slice the memory that tries to rush toward me. "You could say it all started with something I like to call *none of your damn business*."

Hayes laughs and swallows the bite he's chewing. "This is going to sound a bit out there, but it *can't* be a coincidence that I caught you painting. I feel like your lions led me right to you." I look around with alarm and he lowers his voice. "How many other people know you're the artist?"

I squeeze the handle of my knife as I saw a large hunk off my burrito. "Nobody," I admit and continue cutting the bite into smaller and smaller bits.

"I was hoping you'd at least give me a tour of the town.

Sort of an insider's view. Those places only the locals know about. My aunt is cool, but she works a lot, and she's not real big on hiking or exploring."

"I'm sorry, but my obligation begins and ends with these fabulous burritos." I stab what's left of mine and leave the knife sticking straight up. "You seem nice enough. And I'm glad you appreciate my lions, but I'm not the sort of tour guide you're looking for."

"But I believe *fate* brought us together."

"And now, my undying *free will* shall be splitting us apart."

Hayes laughs as if I'm joking. "Are you honestly going to try to tell me you're not dealing with something pretty intense right now? That you have *no idea* what I'm talking about when I tell you that I see rage in your work?"

I just stare at him for a moment before mumbling something about needing to use the ladies' room. As I stand up from the table, I add, "And then I really need to get going."

Who the hell talks like this with someone they've just met?

Once the bathroom door is locked, I run the water until it's liquid ice that I splash on the blotches rising up my neck.

When I close my eyes, the memories try to muscle their way into my head. Pure-white tiles. The bathwater. All that blood.

Stop it, Rory!

Yanking a strip of paper towel from the roll, I dry my neck and face, avoiding eye contact with the mirror.

When I get back to the table, Hayes has already paid the bill, plus he's apparently made friends with my buddy John. The two of them are talking by the register counter where shelves of baked goods peer out from behind the glass.

When I walk up, Hayes pulls a giant peanut butter cookie wrapped in plastic out of the paper bag he's holding. I don't want to ask if he just magically guessed my favorite or if John told him.

I take the cookie. "Well, thank you. This has been... different." I want to turn and walk away, but something keeps me standing there.

John tells Hayes, "Good luck," and says to me, "See you, Rory," as he turns back to the coffee machines.

Hayes crosses his arms and bumps me with one elbow. "So listen. I've been wrestling with this whole *one day at a time* sobriety challenge and can really use some sort of release."

"I'm not getting drunk with you," I say. "And from your story, it sounds to me like you really shouldn't be going out drinking."

He laughs. "That's not what I'm saying. I was just asking John about things the locals like to do around here and he mentioned a place called Stony Kill Falls?"

I throw a glare at John, but it is deflected off his back. I say, "Yeah, it's a secluded waterfall that we try to keep private. We don't need a bunch of out-of-towners knowing about it."

"So, I was thinking, maybe if you weren't doing anything special tomorrow, we could head up there. You could show me around."

I shake my head. "I'm working my other job tomorrow."

47

"What time do you start? I can do early morning."

I look out the window as my mind cranks its gears. If I get out of the house first thing, I'll avoid seeing my dad. *But is it really a good idea to connect with Hayes again?* I don't like how exposed this guy makes me feel.

Unwrapping a corner of my cookie, I take a bite and chew slowly as I turn toward the door.

Hayes lunges to hold it open for me.

"Thanks," I say. Once we're out on the sidewalk together, I hold my cookie toward him. He breaks off a piece and pops it into his mouth. After a beat, he pretends he's about to pass out from ecstasy.

"Mmm," he says. "Come on. This is *delicious*! The Fifty-Nine Express was delicious. You *have* to help me find more local hidden gems. One lion lover to another?"

His face is so open and innocent, I can almost picture him as that twelve-year-old boy taking his first drink and liking the fuzzy feeling it gave him.

Finally, I say, "Meet me in front of the Mud Puddle on Water Street at 7:00 a.m. tomorrow."

He snags another piece of my cookie and gives me a lopsided grin.

"Don't give me that cocky grin. I'm showing you the falls and then we're done." I turn and walk away, resisting the urge to check if he's watching me go.

CHAPTER FOUR

"Your father was like a knight in shining armor who came barreling into my life in his big, black Camaro to rescue me from my parents' home."

I'm sitting in the kitchen listening to Mom and can't even bear to think about that accidental phone call that I got from Dad earlier.

"My mother and father weren't terrible, mind you," Mom says. "They just maybe would've been happier if they'd lived in separate houses. Or separate states." She laughs.

I've heard all this before, but I smile anyway. It's hard to imagine my sweet Memee and Poppy ever screaming at each other the way my mother describes. They belonged together like an antique set of ceramic salt and pepper shakers.

"Your *dad's* parents were really bad. His father would physically abuse him growing up. I think that's why he's a little…distant sometimes."

Her eyes unfocus for a moment, and I feel a painful squeeze in my chest.

Mom shakes her head and gives me a faint smile. "You met his mother, your grandma, when you were a baby, but your dad cut them out of our lives after a big argument when you were around two. He can be…overly hard on people."

She tells me that giving Dad time and space to allow him to slowly grow vulnerable is very similar to the way adding water to a watercolor painting makes it "open back up."

"You and he can be so much alike at times," she says. "Quick to make decisions and then stubborn about changing your mind." Mom can't keep the sadness from her voice, and I look away until she laughs. "But of course, Rory, everyone knows you're more like me."

Yes. I'm just like her.

When I was younger, I loved hearing how much I was like my dad, as if being headstrong and inflexible were good things. Then, Mom helped me embrace art, and it made me softer and more open-minded.

I don't have her level of talent, but her influence can be seen in my work. Like the way two people who are related can have similar handwriting or mannerisms.

As if reading my thoughts, Mom makes a gesture, pointing her first two fingers at me like a sideways finger pistol. It's a common way we both emphasize our words, and I point the same way back at her and laugh.

The warmth I feel toward our connection lingers a moment before I allow my hand to drop.

Mom goes on to talk about my dad and his conversion from hoodlum-who-just-never-got-caught to police academy graduate while I methodically shred a napkin into ghostly strips.

I knew Dad had broken the law on a few occasions by swimming in a neighbor's pool while they were away and stealing a few street signs, but he never got busted, and right now, Mom's description of him as a "rascally little bugger" is maddening.

Obviously, I didn't get *all* my artistic ability from my mom because my dad is a major *con artist*.

I want to shove a whole hand towel into my mouth when she starts telling the story about Dad asking her to marry him.

It was the happiest day of her life—next to the day she found out she was going to have an exhibit at the Sean Kelly Gallery in New York City. Oh, and of course there was the day I was born. "I guess I've had a few happiest days," she says, laughing, and I feel that warm connection again.

My mother describes herself sitting beside Dad in their favorite restaurant while she unwrapped smaller and smaller packages-within-packages, and I curse the fact that tonight of all nights, my conversation with Mom has veered into her history with Dad. *What was I thinking?*

"My hands were shaking by the time I got to the smallest

package," she says with joy. "A small, red leather ring box with a little gold snap on top."

I picture the small red box, lying quietly in the back of my top drawer.

"I undid the snap and the box fell open. When I looked back up, that rascally father of yours was down on one knee, looking up at me with so much love I could've wept." She has tears in her eyes and I wonder if she ever imagined things could get so fucked up between them.

Also, he's not a rascal; he's a heap of human feces.

Before I get so upset my head explodes, I say good night and make my way up to bed. I'm still wide-awake when I hear Dad's car pull into the driveway an hour later.

The timing is right for him to have just finished his shift, but I wonder what else he's been up to.

Mom has always been way too trusting of him. And so have I.

When I hear him come up the stairs, I turn to face the wall. His footsteps stop outside my door a moment, but he doesn't come inside.

He has no idea that I know now. All this time I've been trying to keep him from my secrets, not realizing he has even bigger bombshells than I do.

I listen as he moves down the hallway to his bedroom. Maybe I'm more like him than anyone can see.

"Well, aren't you just a regular ray of sunshine in the morning?"

We're at the Water Street Market parking lot, and Hayes has a travel mug in each hand as he approaches my hatchback.

Fortunately, Stony Kill Falls is actually worth getting up for at this ungodly hour.

It's a waterfall that only the locals know how to find, despite a number of photos of it posted online. Its long, lacy gush is ethereally beautiful and we've done a fairly decent job of keeping its location a local secret.

Hayes grins at me now and holds out a silver travel mug that has the Starbucks logo stamped boldly on the side. Points go to him for using a travel mug rather than a disposable cup. But *major* points get subtracted for the evil corporate logo on the side.

"Sorry," I say, "but I'm committed to supporting our local coffee houses, not Starbucks."

He grins. "It's cool. I made the coffee at home."

"I'm still not drinking from a mug with that arrogant symbol on the side. If I'm going to help promote a coffee shop, it's going to be the Mud Puddle."

He shrugs and takes a sip from the tumbler he was trying to hand me. "More for me, I guess."

"Yes, because you need even more caffeinating." I motion for him to get into the passenger seat of my car.

Driving up the mountain, I open the window and blast the radio while Hayes sings along to the music. Loudly. Also, so out of tune I let out a small chuckle against my will.

He sings even louder, and I shake my head in feigned annoyance.

Just as he's drawing out a long, screeching note, I reach over and flip the volume way down.

Without the loud music backing him up, his horrible howl lingers in the car for a moment before he realizes and bursts into laughter.

"Nice alley cat impression," I say. "You must be channeling your spirit animal."

"Go ahead, mock my lion obsession. You're the one who's been painting giant cats all over town."

"Let me guess. You saw *The Lion King* too many times as a kid." I dismiss him with a wave.

He reaches over, and I think he's going to crank the tunes back up, but instead he turns them the rest of the way down. "My dad read me the first Chronicles of Narnia book aloud when I was seven and it just…got inside me."

He repositions himself to a comfortable lounge, and I want to pull over and kick him out of my passenger seat for shifting to such an intimate tone of voice without warning.

He asks, "You've heard of *The Lion, the Witch and the Wardrobe*?"

I shrug noncommittally. "I saw the movie a long time ago."

"Yeah, they did a nice job on that, but the book is just remarkable. Think about it: you walk into a closet and disappear to this other world. It sounded great to me."

I keep my expression neutral. "I thought you didn't really have anything to escape?"

"I still had boredom." He laughs. "Besides, it wasn't just about getting away. Narnia was all about entering this amazing world. These kids got to join in the huge battle and they kicked ass. I've never loved a book that much, before or since."

There is a pure brightness radiating from him that I want to pinch with my fingers. I thought this guy was supposed to be some troubled alcoholic. I take the switchback extra hard, but he just leans into it, unfazed.

I say, "So, this dad who used to read you kiddie stories, he kicked you out after your DWI?"

"*Second* DWI, and kicking me out would've been better than what he did do. Instead, he got this sad look in his eyes anytime I was around. I hadn't realized how proud he'd always been of me until he wasn't anymore."

I swallow. "And what about your mom?"

"She just stopped trusting me." He rubs the center of his forehead with his thumb. "I have two younger sisters who I used to help out with all the time, and she stopped letting me even babysit them." He looks at the cup he's holding. "I seriously miss those two."

I don't ask their names as I make a left onto an unpaved road. Hayes sits up and leans toward the windshield. "I never would've even noticed this turnoff."

"I feel like I'm betraying my whole town," I say, "showing some spoiled brat from *Lawng Eyeland* how to get to our private waterfall."

He glances at me. "What makes you think I'm a spoiled brat?"

I aim pistol fingers at him. "No jail time?"

"I lost my license for a year and I'm on probation for three. I started going to AA because the court mandated it, but I'm working my program and trying to turn things around here. Nobody is doing the work for me." He takes a deep breath. "Besides, I was never actually convicted for the second DWI."

"Right, because your rich parents hired a big-time lawyer—"

"No," he interrupts. "Because I drove home in a black-out and had sobered up by the time we called the cops the next morning."

My hands tighten on the wheel as the road gets rough. "Why did you even notify the cops then?"

"Because," he says, "when my mother went to take out the recyclables the next morning, she noticed blood smeared on the front grill of my car. We had to call in and report it."

"So you *killed* someone and got away with it?"

"No! It wasn't like that!" His temper flares hot for a moment before he sinks back down into the passenger seat, glaring at the dashboard in front of his face. Finally, he says calmly, "It was a really scary morning. I made a promise to myself that I would never drink again and thankfully everything turned out okay. It was just, I mean…the thing that I hit…it was just a dog."

"Oh, well, if it was *just* a dog then." A court might not have convicted him, but I just did.

He's quiet while I drive down increasingly haggard dirt roads until I reach a dead end and pull over to one side. I turn off the car and open my door, but he grabs my arm before I can climb out.

"Listen, I know that there's a lot you already don't like about me," he says. "But when I first rolled into town, I saw one of your lions and it was like a sign that I'm on the right path. That I can *do* this." I don't answer him and he adds, "I swear I could hear that thing roar."

I look at him unblinkingly for what feels like a long time. "Yeah, well, good luck with the giant cat voices in your head," I finally say. "Now clear out of my car before the scent of your cologne is permanently imbedded in my seats."

I try to outpace Hayes as we head across the field toward the woods where the waterfall is hidden. He's my height, but like with most guys, his legs aren't quite as long as mine. Still, he has no problem keeping up while he marvels out loud at the huge, fenced-in area we're passing.

"What is this?" he asks. "Some sort of Area 51 secret location?"

"Yeah, this is where we keep all the east coast aliens. Now that you've discovered our secret, you must report to the town square for a public anal probing."

He points to the overgrown patch of cement with a giant yellow circle painted on it. "A helipad? Seriously? This is definitely some kind of top-secret shite."

"You've clearly read too much science fiction. This was an old power facility. The helipad was for emergencies in case the power ever went out."

His face clouds for a moment before he breaks out a fresh smile. "*Or* is that just the story the government *wants* everyone to believe in order to cover up the truth?"

"Ha-ha. Come on, Mr. Conspiracy Theory. The falls are this way."

As we reach the far end of the field and enter the woods, the distant hiss of rushing water grows louder.

"I hear it," Hayes says as if we're approaching a mythological beast.

The sound rises as we close in on the stream and start following it uphill, toward the roaring falls.

Picking my way through the trees, I ignore Hayes's gasp when the tall, vertical pillar of fast-moving water stumbles into view far above us.

"This is amazing," he says as we reach the steep rock scramble that leads to the bottom of the falls. "Do you hear that?"

"Waterfalls speak to you now too?"

"Of course. This one is calling us to come inside and play." He grins and launches over a big boulder ahead of me, like a kid who wants to be the first one to the top of the jungle gym. Hayes's enthusiasm tries to catch me, but I hold back a moment before calmly climbing after him.

I notice he chooses the most challenging route up the rocks. In a moment, he's effortlessly pulling himself onto the enormous flat stone that serves as a small beach for the deep pool of water at the bottom of the falls.

He's not even breathing heavy, and the tiniest notch of an idea clicks into place. A dangerous idea.

Hayes stands tall beside the waterfall with his face full of open wonder as he takes in our surroundings. I realize there may be a reason he's inserted himself into my life after all.

So he can help me break the law.

Stripping off his shoes and shirt, Hayes looks like he goes for regularly scheduled manscaping appointments in between his obvious trips to the gym.

Ugh. So very not my type.

He actually gives a few cheesy flexing poses like he's in on the joke. As a response, I pretend to heave into the scrub bushes beside me.

Laughing, he does a cannonball into the clear pool of water. When he resurfaces, he waves for me to join him.

The woods are warm even in the early morning shade, and I'm wearing a bikini underneath my clothes, but I still don't jump in. Instead, I lie down face up on the rock, watching the tree branches and trying to figure out how I can lure this "enlightened" muscle head into helping me. His being on probation may be a deterrent.

"There's a rainbow in the mist!" he calls out.

I don't lift my head. "You sure that's not a *double rainbow*, dude?"

"It's *sooo* beautiful!" he says miming a stoner, and I smile in spite of myself. Finally, I can't take it anymore and scoot across the rock to the water's edge.

I pull off both of my sandals at once and have to hold back a groan of pleasure as I drop my feet into the icy water. It's so clear there's no visible line between where the air ends and the water begins.

Hayes is making his way toward the falls, and I use his distracted state as an opportunity to study him.

He's definitely been hitting the gym, but maybe not too hard after all. Maybe just hard enough.

I'm pretty sure Hayes is not an artist of any kind. *But what if he is?*

He's reached the falls and steps directly underneath the stream, letting the water run over his shoulders like he's in some sort of shower ad for men's bodywash. A supersexy shower ad.

I watch as he angles his face into the water and slowly slides his hands back through his hair. He opens his mouth slightly, and I wonder if he's literally putting on a show for me right now.

As if in response, he looks directly at me and raises one eyebrow. *Damn.* I physically feel that. I look away.

His total obsession with my lions is more than a little disturbing. I can find another apprentice. Maybe my buddy Kat from the art shop. Though, she may not have Hayes's athleticism. In fact, just coaxing her up that long water tower ladder will be a giant challenge, but as her piercings and bloodred hair attest, she's not a big fan of rule following. Plus, she's artsy and talented as hell.

It was actually Kat's long-winded rant about the Sparkle Soda people "raping our landscape" and "invading our right to ad-free space" that got me started on the whole idea of painting the water tower in the first place.

I start putting my shoes back on while Hayes continues his sensual performance underneath the waterfall. I want to join him so badly, I actually need to scrape my palm against the grainy surface of the rock I'm sitting on as a distraction.

I don't care if this guy happens to have some form of artistic talent. He's clearly too dangerous.

If I want to be the one in control, my only move here is to walk away.

Hayes scrubs at his still-damp hair with his T-shirt as I drive us back into town. With all the styling product washed out, he looks completely different.

Plus, now I can't stop imagining what he looks like in the shower.

"I'm heading to my shift at Danny's," I say. "Do you want me to drop you back off at Water Street Market on my way?"

"Danny's is the art shop in town, right? I'll come along, thanks."

I glance at the way his arm muscles dance as he continues riffling the side of his hair. I say, "No problem."

"You picking up painting supplies?" he asks suggestively.

He drops his arms just in time to catch me watching

him, and I glimpse the hint of a smirk as I snap my gaze to the windshield straight ahead.

"It's my other part-time job," I say. "I mostly do it for the employee discount."

I don't say that it's also my spray paint hook-up, since my purchases would raise a red flag with Dad if I had deliveries sent to the house. I get everything though the shop, then drive the boxes straight to my cabin. In fact, I'm placing a big special order for my project during my shift today.

But Hayes already knows enough of my secrets.

He is still distractingly shirtless and I turn up the air-conditioning, hoping he'll be inspired to clothe himself.

Instead, he leans back and raises his arms as if the icy blast is a new way to get high.

He keeps his eyes closed as he says, "I think I've figured out why we've been put into each other's lives."

"Excuse me? We are not *in each other's lives*. You have tried to insert yourself into mine, but this is where our paths officially part ways."

I'm already at the switchback heading down the mountain, and I take the turn fast enough to force Hayes to clutch the armrest.

He says, "You have to admit it's strange that I've been so drawn to your lions and then caught you painting one."

I shrug. "Weird coincidence."

"Fine, call it a coincidence. But you *need* me to keep your secret. I *need* an extended tour of New Paltz. It's a win-win."

"I can't *believe* you want to keep blackmailing me."

"Firstly, I'm not blackmailing you. I'm just using some information to my advantage until I win you over."

"What makes you think you can win me over?" The cornfields of the Walkill Farm zip past us on our right, the broad, green promise of a delicious corn-on-the-cob season ahead.

"We're connected, Rory. I knew it the first second I saw you." When I glance over, his eyes grab at me. "You can fight this thing, but you can't deny it."

I laugh hysterically for nearly a full minute, but he just grins and drums his hands on the armrest. When my laughter and his drumming gradually stop, the silence pulls at my throat.

I turn up the radio to blast level in order to stop myself from asking him whether or not he's an artist.

Hayes follows me around Danny's as I straighten up the shelves. "I'm thinking the ice caves should be our next adventure. They sound amazing," he says.

"The ice caves *are* amazing. They're right in Ellenville. You can use google maps to guide you, and I hope you have a very lovely hike."

Taking off the wide elastic tie I always wear around my wrist, I use it to pull my dreadlocks back before bending down to straighten some writing pads.

Hayes picks a red sketchbook from the stack. "Oh yeah,

I'm about ready for a new one of these. And where do you keep the colored pencils?"

I turn my face away so he can't see me close my eyes. I swallow to make my voice sound natural. "You're an artist?"

"No, not really."

I exhale.

"I'm actually a writer, but I've been teaching myself to draw. I'm almost finished with a dragon novel for middle schoolers and I thought it would be cool if I could sketch a few illustrations. Or at least give some idea what the dragon looks like in my mind."

I stand up and scan him up and down. "You plan on writing *kids'* books?"

"Yup. Better than writing for boring adults who think they have everything figured out."

"So you basically plan to remain at middle-school maturity level."

"C. S. Lewis said that eventually we grow mature enough to turn back to fantastic stories."

"I'm a little embarrassed for you. Do you wear superhero underwear as well?"

"As a matter of fact, I've got Spider-Man boxers on right now. Of course they're still damp." He reaches around as if he's about to show me his underwear and I stiffen. "Sorry," he says. "I didn't mean to embarrass you."

"I'm not embarrassed."

"You look flushed."

"I'm...annoyed. Come on. The colored pencils are over here."

As I lead him through the store toward the writing utensils, I curse myself for letting him get in my head. Everything with Hayes feels backward and out of control. I don't like feeling out of control.

And now I can't stop wondering if children's authors count as artists or not.

"*There's* that chick who's really cool to hang out with." Before I know what's happening, Lego Bong Guy, a.k.a. Mr. Finance Frat Boy, has scooped an arm around my waist as he leans in for a kiss.

His lips land on my cheek and I pull away, slapping at his arm. He won't let go and forces his affection on me until it gets to be too much. I'm trying not to overreact, but I still regret our hookup and I need him to let go of me, *now*.

Finally, I'm forced to use the hold break my dad taught me way back before I could even talk in full sentences.

With a quick twist and a chop, I'm free.

"Wow, someone's ticklish." His knowing grin is beyond irksome.

"Excuse me. I'm working." My voice is dead as I push past him, not looking to see Hayes's reaction.

"What time you get off, sweet thing?" He follows too close.

"My shift just started, and I'm with a *customer*." We've reached the aisle with colored pencils, and I thrust a thumb toward them, turning just as Hayes catches up.

Hayes looks at my recent shame with utter amusement, but Frat Boy stays focused on me. "What gives? Are you mad I didn't call?"

"What? I never even gave you my number. When I left, I *literally* told you it was a one-time thing." I look back and forth between the two of them. "What is *with* the boys in this town, anyway?"

"I *knew* I should've tried reaching you sooner." Frat Boy cringes. "I didn't think to call you here at the store."

Nobody has ever mistaken me for pouting over a neglected phone call.

I say, "If I wanted to see you again, I would've gotten in touch with you." I point a finger at Hayes. "And the same goes for you."

The two of them look at each other for a beat before Hayes's face breaks into one of his easy, lopsided smiles. "Name's Hayes." He puts a hand out and Frat Boy shakes it with a look of confusion. "Recently moved into town and I'm Rory's new friend."

"You are not my—"

Hayes interrupts me. "I take it you two are, er, *were* together?"

Frat Boy runs a hand through his curls, looking confused.

"No," I say. "Nobody here is together. There are no new friendships blooming. I just need to get back to work."

I leave the two of them looking bewildered while I move behind the counter.

Kat has been straightening up a rack of temporary tattoos

beside the register while pretending she's not listening. I can see she's trying not to snicker.

"Seriously, what is happening with the world?" I say to her. "Could either of those two guys be any *less* my type?"

She looks over to where Hayes is talking to Frat Boy and pretends she's noticing them for the first time. "I don't know. The guy with the wet hair is pretty hot."

"He's not—" I give a small growl. "He doesn't usually look like that."

Kat raises a pierced eyebrow. "*Usually?* As in, you've hung out with him on numerous occasions?"

"No. *Usually*, as in, I just gave him a ride up to Stony Falls and he went for a swim. That guy is *usually* coated in cologne and hair gel."

"He still gets my vote."

I don't respond as we both watch Hayes lean down to study the colored pencils. Frat Boy is walking in our direction.

"Looks like they've come to some sort of agreement," Kat says. "Perhaps they're planning to share you?"

"Ha. Like I'm some rubber, girl-shaped chew toy. Dumb dogs."

Kat looks toward Hayes and says under her breath, "Still, woof, *woof*." She moves to the other side of the counter as Frat Boy approaches.

He says, "So, your friend over there explained the situation."

I put my hands on my hips and tilt my head up at him. "Oh yeah? And what *situation* is that?"

"That the two of you just started seeing each other and would I kindly mind stepping aside since things between you could get serious and I'm clearly just in it for a fun time anyway."

I laugh and look over at Hayes, who's busy trying to open a small tin of colored pencils.

"I told him you're a big girl who seems capable of making her own decisions."

"Thank you. You are absolutely right."

He grins the way he did that first time we met. "Well, then, what time do you get off work?"

"Easy there. I've *decided* you and I are never happening again. I wasn't playing hard to get. I'm just genuinely not interested in another go. Sorry to be so forward, but let's not waste any more time, shall we?"

His smile hangs on for a moment before slipping off his face. "But I don't—"

"Thanks for the Lego bong hits. But bye now." I give him a cheerful wave.

Kat moves to stand beside me and her bright-pink lips draw into a phony smile. We wave in sync like a couple of animatronic dummies at Disney until Frat Boy finally gives a nod and backs away.

At the door, he turns back to the two of us as we continue waving mechanically. "Well, if you change your mind…"

But I keep my phony smile aimed a foot above his head, and he finally, *finally* gets the point and leaves.

Kat and I dissolve into giggles as the bell chimes on the closing door.

"I had no idea how to picture your friends, but I'm not surprised." Hayes slides a box of quality colored pencils and a Moleskine notebook onto the counter.

My laughter cuts off. "Kat, you want to take care of this one?"

"Hello, Kat. I'm Hayes, Rory's new friend."

I give an annoyed growl, and Kat bites her lower lip. "So, what about my appearance doesn't surprise you?" she asks.

He smiles at us. "It's not your appearance. It's your attitude. Exactly what I expected—your position so far above it all that you judge everything. Everything is a joke to you."

I snap, "Not everything is a joke to us."

Hayes nods his head toward the doorway. "That guy was. He was honestly under the impression that you liked him."

Kat moves in front of the register and starts ringing him up.

"How do you know I *don't* like him?"

"You don't seem the type to play hard to get." He has no idea how true this is. "Besides, if you liked him, I would've been able to tell."

"Oh, so we just met and now you think you can read my mind or something?"

"Not your mind, your body language."

"You *did* just use a self-defense move on the guy," Kat chimes in as if that's being at all helpful.

I cross my arms in front of my chest. "Well, then, *Hayes*, what is my body language telling you right now?"

He looks me up and down with a sultriness and confidence that I find utterly maddening. "It's saying that you don't trust yourself around me."

"That'll be...twenty-four thirty-seven," Kat whispers as if she doesn't really want to interrupt us.

Hayes keeps his eyes trained on me as he pulls a square of folded bills out of his back pocket and peels off two twenties. He slides them across the counter to Kat.

"These are wet," she says, but he doesn't break eye contact with me.

Laying the bills side by side on the counter to dry, Kat counts out his change and puts it in his outstretched hand.

I pull my crossed arms tighter against my chest as his gaze softens with amusement. "Until next time," he says to me, and before I can respond the bell on the door is ringing and he is gone.

"*Holy shit* that was a lot of heat," Kat says as soon as he's out of earshot. "Did you hook up with him?" She picks up the two wet bills and waves them back and forth to air dry.

"No. I told you, he's not my type." I start rifling through the tattoos she's already straightened.

"Yeah. Right," she says. "If *that* boy is not your type, then you don't have a type. Or eyes. Or a pulse. Or a—"

"All right, all right. You've made your point." I elbow her jokingly.

"When are you seeing him again?"

I shrug and realize I was just wondering the same exact thing.

"Judging by the way he was looking at you, my guess is soon."

I hate the fact that I hope she's right.

CHAPTER FIVE

"Heartbreak. Now there's one that I wish I could spare you."
Mom's brow furrows and she looks down at her hands as they
rub together. "I still think of the time when you were little and
we were walking along the road together. You were holding on
to your stroller and walking beside it, instead of riding, and we
were moving so slowly. When we came across a dead squirrel,
you asked me why he was lying so still."

I laugh. "Without hesitating you told me, 'He's sleeping.'"

"I thought the concept of death was too sad for a toddler,"
Mom says. "But when I told you he was sleeping, your response
was, 'That's funny. He looks *dead.*'"

She laughs and goes on to talk about the way my matter-
of-fact approach will serve me well in life. "Death is real,"
she says, but I can't help thinking she's always had me figured
wrong. Calling her out on her denial of the obviously squished
squirrel was just my way of trying to get her to tell the truth, to
admit she'd fibbed.

Parents should never lie to their children.

Now she says, "No matter how hard our hearts are, they are all broken eventually by someone."

I don't react. I am a rock, sitting completely still. Rory stone.

I barely blink as she segues smoothly from heartbreak to the topic of sex. "It's important that you ask yourself if you're really ready. You should never feel pressured into it. Sex is best when it is experienced with someone you truly love and you only have one first time. Spend it wisely. It should be with someone *really* special who treats you well." She repeats, "You only have one first time."

After a pause, she confesses that Dad wasn't her first, and I feel a wave of satisfaction at that. When a tear rolls down her cheek, I reach out but stop myself before touching her smooth face. She smiles and wipes the tear herself while shaking her head. "I was crazy about him."

As Mom describes her first wild love affair, I try to imagine what she was like when she was young. Before she was my mother.

I have a picture of her when she was about my age in a frame on my dresser, and it shows her sitting on a bench in Central Park with a sunbeam illuminating her smile. She's a beautiful stranger in that photo. Someone who looks a lot like me. Somebody I can never know. A young woman glowing with a freedom and happiness that, for some reason, makes me immensely sad every time I look at that photo.

I've never seen my mother smile that purely in real life.

I need to figure out a way to protect some part of that glowing girl who's long gone.

Dad needs to be confronted head-on. He's still out, so I end the conversation with Mom early and sneak into his office, which is technically just a computer table in a corner of our den. I need to figure out when he's meeting his mistress. This all has to end now.

Since dad always uses RoryGrrl1 as his password, it's a snap to jump onto his calendar. Technically, what I'm doing can't even be considered hacking, since he knows that I know the password to all his stuff.

Still, I'd rather avoid a confrontation at this point. Better to save the real screaming for *after* I have hard-core proof of his philandering ways.

A quick scan of his past few months reveals nothing other than the fact that, here and there, he's apparently been attending church. I'm upset by this for some reason.

Not that I'd jump at an invitation to church, but Dad never even mentioned he was going, and it takes me a moment to shake off feeling excluded.

I take a closer look at this month's calendar. There's nothing obviously out of place at first glance.

Then I notice the semicolons scattered here and there, sometimes as many as three in one week.

I think of the way I create events that contain only a period to track my monthly cycle and know immediately that I've broken his code.

Sure enough, there's a mark in the time slot from when

he butt-dialed me while on his *date*. I cringe at that remembered half conversation and scan for more clues to bust him.

Unfortunately, he must write down where he's meeting his mistress in a different, secret calendar. Either that or he just keeps it stored in his head. He's extremely "trust averse," so that's probably his method.

I'm so frustrated, I want to fling the computer against the wall. I want to run into the other room and scream for Mom to see what's happening right now, but I can't even come up with actual evidence to catch the bastard.

I should've thought to hit Record on that message.

The next semicolon is just a few days away, but unless I manage to follow him without his knowing, an utter impossibility due to his stupid intuition, Dad is going to continue getting away with this.

When he comes home, he's carrying a big sack of Chinese takeout as some sort of bribe or peace offering or way of sucking me back in.

I tell him I already ate and that I have to get started on my summer assignments. I do *have* summer assignments; I'm just not really doing anything about them.

Grabbing a bag of chips from the pantry, I storm upstairs, telling myself that I just need to have patience. Because if there's one thing I trust absolutely, it's that the truth will always come out eventually.

It's overcast and so the beach is empty as Scott and I sit on our lifeguard bench exchanging hiking stories.

I'm rubbing on a layer of sunblock, since I got sunburned the last time it was overcast, and he's telling me about the bear he saw when he first started working here at the park.

"I couldn't believe it," he says. "When I came around the bend, there was this huge, black, furry thing. It took me a minute to realize it wasn't a giant dog."

"What did you do?"

"I was actually reaching for my phone to take a picture, and the bear stopped walking, turned, and looked directly at me."

"Did you get a picture?"

Scott's eyes follow my hands as I rub lotion onto my leg. "Hell no. I got busy trying to scope out a tree that would be easy for me to climb."

"Wait," I say. "Climbing trees is how you escape grizzlies. Black bears are really *good* tree climbers." We only have black bears here in the Northeast.

"Yes, I know. But I was totally new to the woods, and my mind just went blank with terror. I knew enough to look around for cubs, but couldn't remember if I was supposed to run or stand my ground or hold my arms up to look bigger."

"Please tell me you didn't start running." I slide both hands up and down my thigh, partially to avoid streaks, but mostly just to mess with him.

He watches me openly for a moment before shaking his head and looking out toward the lake. "No, I instinctively backed away real slow, and he lost interest and walked off into the woods."

"Yeah, they usually don't mess with humans."

"I know that now, but wow was I ever amped-up for the rest of that day."

"Now do you wear a bell when you check the trails?" One of Scott's jobs is to hike the trails to make sure there aren't any fallen trees blocking the various paths.

"Nah." Scott dismisses me with a wave. "Rattlesnakes are the bigger danger out there."

"That's true." I put the lid on my lotion and shove it back into my bag.

He says, "But I do carry bear spray."

I roll my eyes. "Because being armed is somehow better than trying to avoid conflict in the first place. I'm getting you a bell. You'll never have to worry again."

"Oh, hey," Scott says. "I've been meaning to ask how things turned out with the sarge?" At my confused look, he goes on. "The other day? When he butt-dialed you?"

"Oh, yeah. That situation is all shades of fucked up." I jump down from the bench, pick up a handful of stones, and pull out the flattest ones I can find.

"Are you okay?" he asks from above me.

"I've been checking his calendar"—*Toss.* Skip-skip-splash!—"trying to catch him in the act." *Toss.* Skip-skip-skip-splash! "I figured out how he marks the times he meets his mistress"—*Toss.* Skip-skip-splash!—"but

I have no idea how to track down a location." *Toss.*
Skip-skip-skip-skip-splash!

"Have you considered shadowing him?" Scott asks.

"I really don't want to resort to that. He has this weird
sixth sense and would definitely bust me."

"Hey!" A familiar voice rings out, and with an
involuntary startle, I throw in the rest of my rocks.
Splash-splash-splash-splash-splash!

I spin around and see Hayes strolling across the rocky beach
toward me. "No need to shadow me, Rory. I'm right here."

"Because *of course* you are." I wipe my hands on the
butt of my suit and leap back up to the lifeguard bench
beside Scott.

Hayes stands directly in front of us and reaches a hand up
toward Scott. "Name's Hayes. Friend of Rory's."

Scott looks Hayes up and down as if he's just been
challenged to a pissing contest but leans down and gives his
hand a quick shake.

"You do realize that telling everyone that doesn't make it
true." I turn to Scott. "We're not really friends."

"See, now, that's just hurtful." Hayes looks at Scott. "Is
she always so hurtful?"

Scott twirls his whistle, winding the string up his two
fingers. "Yeah, she's a real heartbreaker, all right." He squints
out over the lake and hunches down in his seat.

"Just ignore him." I pretend to scan the smooth water.

Hayes says, "Why? He seems like a perfectly nice guy."

"Not *him*," I spit. "You. *We're* ignoring *you*. Trying to work here."

Hayes turns and looks around. "You're guarding an empty lake?"

Scott looks down, but I elbow him and nod for him to continue looking off into the middle distance.

I'm half-messing with Hayes and half-avoiding that growing zing of desire that makes me feel out of control whenever I'm around him.

Zero eye contact with Hayes means zero zinging.

The three of us stay like that in silence for a time until I hear the distinct sound of a fly unzipping. "Hey, you can't—"

Hayes draws his shorts down seductively.

"Oh," I say when I see he's wearing colorful swim trunks underneath. Okay, so maybe eye contact isn't really necessary for me to feel the zing.

"Disappointed?" He grins up at me.

"I'm sure you're used to girls being disappointed when you unzip your shorts." I laugh at my own joke but swallow when he puts his hands on his hips and raises an eyebrow.

He looks more amused than flustered. "Good one," he mocks, looking fully confident, and there's that zinging sensation again. *What the hell is it about this guy?*

I look away, refusing to give Hayes any of my attention. As he goes from clearing his throat to waving his arms and pretending to do a barefoot tap dance, it gets harder to ignore him.

Finally, he starts humming the opening theme song to an

old Disney TV show that everyone in our age bracket watched ad nauseam when we were kids. Hayes gets louder and louder until he's singing at the top of his lungs.

After a few minutes of this nonsense, Scott starts humming along.

I thrust an elbow into his ribs.

"Ouch." Scott stops humming and lets his whistle fall and dangle from his hand.

I go back to ignoring Hayes, finally digging out my phone and scrolling through some pictures Kat sent me from the store this morning. Apparently, things are a little slow at Danny's, and she's kept herself busy by taking selfies while wearing a series of rainbow mustaches from our toy and novelty section.

I'm responding that the purple porn 'stache is my favorite when I hear footsteps thundering along the floating metal dock that juts out into the lake. I immediately drop my phone just in time to see Hayes do a perfect somersault off the deep end of the dock.

SPLASH! I'd be impressed by his form if diving off the dock wasn't against the rules.

"No flips off the dock," Scott calls at him the second Hayes surfaces.

In response, Hayes waves his arms, splashing wildly.

I look at Scott and roll my eyes, but we both stand as Hayes ducks underneath the floating ropes.

When he pops up just outside the designated swim area, Scott blasts his whistle. "Inside the ropes, buddy!" he calls.

Hayes dives down, kicking his feet and swimming deep enough for Scott and I to shift from annoyed to alert. I grab the orange life buoy from where it hangs on the back of the chair and glance at Scott just as Hayes finally resurfaces.

He's holding up a handful of black pebbles from the bottom of the lake. He lets them roll through his fingers as he continues treading water just outside the ropes.

"Come on, Hayes," I call. "Stop being a dick."

Out in the water, he spreads his arms wide, leans back, and begins to float on his back with his eyes closed.

"I know you can hear me." With a surge of rage, I hop down and throw the long strap of the orange life buoy across one shoulder as I rocket down the dock.

"Rory," Scott calls after me, "what are you doing? Obviously the guy can swim."

Hayes's head snaps up from the water, and when he sees me sprinting toward him, a welcoming smile spreads across his face.

I make a perfect dive off the dock into the deep section, letting the buoy drop behind me into the water like it's my floating orange puppy on a leash.

I swim the breaststroke over to Hayes with the buoy chasing me the whole way.

When I get close enough, Hayes reaches for me, and I grab his wrist, expertly swinging him around so his arm is tucked behind his back. It's a rescue technique we learned in training, for when drowning victims panic and try to pull us underwater.

With a laugh, Hayes tries to wiggle free. "Whoa, easy there," he says, but I reach around with my other arm and gather his neck neatly into the bend of my elbow.

With a pull on my buoy leash, I call my puppy to me and position the orange flotation device underneath my free arm.

With Hayes in a secure headlock, I use my hip to push his body toward the surface as I begin towing him to shore. The water is cold from the rain we had overnight, and his body is pure heat against mine. His warm hands wrap around my arms and I tighten my grip.

"Okay, Rory. I'm really sorry." He tries to wiggle free. "I'm good now."

I've done plenty of training exercises for this exact scenario, and so I know just how to hang on to him. Then again, I suspect he might not be trying all *that* hard to get free.

Eventually, he just goes completely limp. "This is sort of nice," he says as I pull his heavy body into the shallow water.

Half carrying him on my back, I drag him from the lake.

Once we hit dry land, I thrust him off my shoulder, shoving him roughly to the pebbled beach. He falls back on his elbows, lying face up and aiming his bent grin in my direction. "Amazing."

"Stay out of the water if you can't listen to instructions." I squeeze my dreadlocks out onto his chest and fling the excess water in his face with both hands.

He laughs, and when he reaches up to wipe the water from his face, my eyes fall to his shirtless chest.

I pull my gaze away before he can bust me.

Bending over with my hands on my knees, I work on catching my breath. I'm seriously winded, *mostly* due to the rescue exercise.

"Excuse me, *lifeguard*?" Hayes lies back down. "I think I could use a little mouth-to-mouth resuscitation." He taps a finger to his lower lip.

Pausing a beat, I allow an evil grin to spread across my face and drop to my knees beside him. He looks up at me with a joking smile, but as he watches my face draw closer, his expression turns serious.

I ignore Scott clearing his throat from the lifeguard chair behind me. My breath is still heavy as I lean over and whisper, "You need a little *air*, Hayes?"

He nods while looking at my lips. His jaw juts forward, and I ignore the zing I feel as he wraps his hands around my back and—

"Psyche!" I whip away from him, slapping him with my thick, wet hair. I stand and take a few steps backward, leaving him lying like a turtle on its back.

In one smooth motion, I turn and pull myself up to the lifeguard bench where Scott is waiting to give me a tidy high five.

Hayes is still lying on the beach as Scott stands up on the lifeguard bench and calls, "*That's* the way we handle rule breakers around here."

"Speaking of *rule breakers*…" Hayes gives me a knowing wink and I look back and forth between him and Scott.

I widen my eyes and mouth the word *no* to Hayes. The last thing I need is to have two guys blackmailing me.

Besides, knowing Scott, if he found out I'm the graffiti artist right now, he'd probably run directly to tell my dad.

He'd say it was because he was worried about me, but really he'd be looking for an in with the DEC. Working with the Department of Environmental Conservation is Scott's dream, and unfortunately, getting on my dad's good side would have to mean throwing me under the bus.

Scott and I are friendly, but we're not exactly friends.

"So, Rory." Hayes mouths a roar and mimes clawing the air like a big cat. "What time are you done saving lives?"

Scott crosses his arms. "Take a hike, buddy. Rory's not interested."

Hayes raises his eyebrows at me, and I flash him two fingers against my arm. Scott can't see me mouth, *Two o'clock.*

I nod my head toward the path that leads away from the lake, and Hayes does a fantastic job of playing it cool. Scott has no idea.

Hayes picks up his shirt and uses it to wipe his face before tucking it behind his head and lying back down. Closing his eyes, Hayes acts as if the sun is shining on his bare skin, despite the overcast day and his obvious goose bumps.

I'm working to forget the warmth of that body against mine as I "rescued" him.

His expression is peaceful until his gaze jumps suddenly and he catches me watching him.

Zing. *Damn!*

With a satisfied grin, he makes his biceps flex as he lays his head back down.

I stop violating him with my mind as I hear a group of people speaking over each other in Chinese approaching. We get a ton of international visitors here at the park, which is one of the many things I love about this place.

As the multigenerational group quickly moves onto the beach, Hayes stands up and makes his way to where his backpack is parked by the edge of the trees.

After spending an inordinate amount of time combing back his hair, he pulls out his new sketchbook and pencils and starts to draw. I'm practically clawing the wooden lifeguard bench wanting to see his work.

But a glance at Scott tells me he's already suspicious.

I need to play this ultrasmooth.

Problem is, I'm getting sick of playing. What the hell am I so afraid of, anyway? Hayes is just another guy. And he's not even from around here.

A hookup with him would have zero consequences.

I need to make sure I stay in control, but that doesn't mean I can't risk making a move.

I come to a clear decision.

As soon as I get Hayes alone, I'm following that *zing* to see where it leads.

The hours fly by as the lake fills up with groups of swimmers and empties twice. I'm focused on the people in the water and purposely not checking on what Hayes is doing, letting my anticipation build.

But the water is basically empty right now, with only a middle-aged couple talking as they stand beside each other in the shallow end. I glance back and catch Hayes tearing a page from his sketchbook and handing it to a little girl. I can't see what he's drawn for her, only the delight on her face as she runs to show her mother.

He glances over and smiles when he catches me watching him. I don't smile back, but I don't look away either. His smile fades, and the look of intensity that replaces it makes my stomach dip.

He can feel it, I'm sure. The craving. I bite my lip and turn back around as the waiting grows into exquisite agony.

When my shift is finally over, I greet the older male lifeguards replacing Scott and me and tell Scott to enjoy his days off.

He asks if I'd like to "hang out or something" tomorrow, and I can't stop my eyes from skipping to Hayes.

Scott says, "Oh, I mean, unless you have plans," and I wonder what made him decide to ask me out now. It's probably because I've been half-smiling all day, instead of sporting my usual resting bitch face.

I've been picturing myself getting blissfully physical with Hayes, and I can already tell things will be good between us.

"You know I don't mix work and pleasure, Scott."

This is, of course, a lie. Pleasure goes just fine with every-thing, including work. I am *all about* pleasure, but there's no need to make Scott feel rejected just because I'm in the process of rejecting him.

I make my way up the path to the row of rustic bathrooms, pull open one of the heavy doors, and use the warped mirror to check my flushed face as I rifle in my bag for my freshen-up kit.

I brush my teeth and take a quick sink shower, drawing out the suspense. When I emerge, Hayes is waiting for me with his backpack on his shoulder and a sly grin on his face.

"How was work, dear?" he says.

In response, I turn and wordlessly lead the way down the long, twisted path toward my cabin.

There's no need to engage in playful banter now. The time for verbal foreplay is over, and the long hike is infused with an eagerness that I know he feels too.

Anticipation continues to build, and I widen my stride as we get closer and closer. By the time we reach my cabin's door, I'm practically jogging, but Hayes is still right at my heels.

As soon as we're inside, with the door closed, I turn and draw both of my hands through either side of his dark, slicked-back hair. His waves have dried by now, but they're surprisingly soft with the gel washed out.

His look of wonder only lasts a moment. Narrowing his gaze, he tips his head forward, pushes a dreadlock away from my ear, and whispers, "Told you I'd win you over."

I smile. "Pure games, Hayes. I'm the one in control here."

"Oh, we'll just see about that."

I hesitate a moment. *I want this too much.* I should wait for him to make the first move.

I pull back and look into his eyes, showing how much willpower I have. Just because his eyes go so deep they're giving me vertigo doesn't mean I can't control myself.

I am in control.

He gives me a knowing grin without breaking his gaze. We are in a standoff.

I have absolute and complete control.

He licks his lips and…

I lose control.

Rising onto my toes so we're the same height, I tilt my chin upward and use my fingertips to guide his face toward mine. I pause for one delicious beat before brushing my lips ever so gently against his.

He responds immediately, pressing against me, drawing me up and into a kiss with the perfect amount of pressure. We are both really good kissers.

I stop thinking about control and allow myself to drop into a puddle of sensations. I'm aware of every muscle shift, each breath.

As our kiss grows deeper, the *zing* is expanding inside me, growing wider and moving further.

I want it to keep going.

I can't tell who's guiding who as we expertly make our

way across the room to the art table standing against the far wall. We don't break our kiss, and my fingers reach out for the flat surface covered in layers of dried paint.

We bump against it, and there's a moment of awkward struggle as I attempt to bend him back over the table. He stays upright, trying to keep the top position.

I've never brought a boy back to my cabin before, and now this boy is trying to take charge.

Finally, I relent, and he turns us and lowers me slowly down onto the table. It's vaguely thrilling, and I try to hide how heavy my breath is getting.

Enjoying our encounter is one thing, but it's dangerous to get this excited. This isn't an escape right now. I'm fully present and with Hayes, and my blood is flowing too fast, and my head won't let me go anyplace else right now. I can't disappear.

My lions aren't going to sleep. They are here, and I am being torn open with all that I'm feeling. I'm too vulnerable and exposed.

With a panicked grunt, I place both palms on Hayes's chest as we continue kissing. After a pause, I give a light shove and he leaps off me.

As he backs away, I see he's flushed and breathing just as hard as I am.

"Holy hell." His voice is rough. "You have some *serious* self-control."

"Told you I was in charge," I say breathlessly, even as I

resist the urge to grab him around the neck and drag him back on top of me.

"Well, I'm glad you keep a level head." He takes a half step back, puts his hands on both knees, and leans over, like he's catching his breath after a sprint. "My sponsor says I can't get into a relationship right now."

Now *this* is good news. The stakes just dropped down a notch.

I point my foot and run it seductively up his leg. "Who said anything about a relationship?"

He laughs and shifts out of my toes' range. "Listen. I'm serious. We can't take things to the next level until I've worked through some issues. Otherwise, my recovery could be stunted by our relationship."

"You keep using this word: *relationship*," I tease. "I'm unfamiliar with this word."

"I'm trying to take my sobriety seriously." He drags a hand through his hair, trying to slick down the edges I've messed up. "I told my sponsor, Roger, about hanging out with you, and he already said it was *inadvisable*. At least until after I finish my ninth step."

I sit up straight. "Did you tell him about my lions?"

Hayes shakes his head. "Of course not. He'd never let me see you if he knew you were a criminal."

"I'm not a…*total* criminal. And, anyway, who is this Roger guy, and why does he get to have a say in what we do together?"

"He's my sponsor." Hayes moves to sit next to me on

the table, our thighs touching, so now that's where all my focus is aimed. "Kind of like a sobriety guru." He laughs at my eye roll. "He's a guy who has been through the steps himself and who wants to help me get my life in order."

"Including your sex life." I fling my leg seductively over his.

"Especially stuff like sex since that's one of the things that would send me down a path to trouble in the past." Hayes subtly strokes my leg, driving me wild as he goes on. "Conflicting expectations. Different opinions on what physical intimacy signifies. Basically just a lot of trouble I'm better off without right now."

I smile and run a finger lightly down his neck. "Well, I won't be *any* trouble at all, trust me."

"Trust *me*. You already *are* trouble." With a gentle touch, he lifts my chin so I'm looking directly at him. "I don't think I've ever seen eyes that shade of gray before," he says. "It's as if your irises are in black and white and the rest of you is in color."

I look down at my hands. "I have my mother's eyes."

"Well, they're amazing, but they're really sad too. That's the other reason we can't get involved. I feel like you have some things you need to work through yourself." He forces me to look at him again. "Rory, why do you paint such angry lions? I really want to understand whatever you're going through."

"I'm great. You're the one here who's not even allowed

to hook up without a permission note from some alcoholic voodoo man."

"Maybe I'm not looking to just *hook up*."

"Yeah, well maybe you should've stopped *stalking* me sooner then. If you're not interested in us hooking up, why are you even here?"

He looks around the small cabin for the first time. "What is this place, anyway? Your painting studio?"

I move to a corner and pull a tarp over a crowd of spray paint cans dripping with assorted colors. My adrenaline is all jammed up from the implied promise of physical release, and it's making me cranky. I want Hayes to go now.

"Wait a minute." His eyes grow wide and he looks around with fresh wonder. "This is your *lair*, isn't it? This is where you plan all your new graffiti hits?"

Drat. Before I can stop him, he's reached down and picked up a giant cardboard piece of stencil. It's a portion of the left haunch of my larger-than-life water tower lion.

"What is this thing for?" His eyes snap to mine with understanding.

I look away. "It's just a little something I've been working on."

He picks up another section, and I can see him trying to piece together just how big the finished lion will be. "Where the *hell* is this thing going?" His brow creases. "Are you planning on spray-painting the side of the moon?"

I shrug.

"Rory?"

"Just the water tower. I want to cover up that awful Sparkle Soda ad. This lion is a way to reclaim our public space."

"Wha—? Okay. So *that's* ambitious. Clearly, this is a cry for attention."

"It's not about getting attention. I'm not planning on getting caught, so nobody will ever even know it's me."

"Well, then, who the hell is helping you?"

"Well, that's sort of the thing…"

He drops the stencil he's holding and it floats smoothly to the ground.

"So, you, what? Brought me here to seduce me into being your accomplice?"

"No. That's not it at all." My mind races. "It's insulting that you'd even think that." *And why didn't I think of that?*

"So then who's helping you? You said I'm the only one who even knows you're the artist."

"I haven't worked out every little detail, but I'm sure things will come together." I move over to the pile of stencils on the floor and begin straightening up the stack.

Hayes puts his hands on his hips as he watches me. "You are aware that spray-painting is a crime, right?"

"Don't worry about it. This doesn't involve you."

"What would make you even attempt something this crazy?"

I won't look at him. "You wouldn't understand."

With a sigh, he leans down and helps me straighten up the rest of the stencils.

After we've finished, we find ourselves sitting on the floor, facing each other.

My emotions are a soupy mixture of wanting to kiss him again and wanting him to leave so I can be alone.

He's watching me so closely I feel heat working its way up my neck. I am not the type to overheat. It's as if he's even controlling my temperature gauge.

I break eye contact, pretending to study my paint supplies.

"I don't like ignoring my sponsor's advice, you know," Hayes finally says. "Roger has some solid wisdom, and he's helped me in a lot of areas. Without even asking him, I'm *positive* he would be against me helping you."

"I told you to forget it. And you should probably forget all about this cabin and me too." I stand up. "Let's both do the right thing here."

Hayes smirks and shakes his head. "How is it that you make doing the right thing sound so damn horrible?"

I give a small smile as I reach down and pull him to his feet.

We stand looking at each other and I wonder if he's feeling an ounce of the physical pull that I feel right now.

Finally, he says, "You really are trouble, aren't you?"

This statement would normally make me laugh and possibly give the guy a tackle hug, but Hayes isn't just any guy.

"Don't worry." I lean forward. "I'm only trouble if you cross me."

He takes a step closer. "And I'm only trouble when I'm drinking or getting high. But then I'm *really big* trouble."

"I suppose the lines are drawn, then. I'm not looking to get you drunk, and you can be my own private secret keeper."

"Go get a diary to keep your secrets." He smiles. "What you need is a partner in crime."

I stare at him. "Are you really considering maybe helping me? I *promise* you I'll take the fall if anything goes down."

His eyes sweep around the cabin and land back on me. With a glance up and down my height, Hayes roughs up the front of his hair. He's given up on it staying slicked back.

"I'm going to need to think about it," he says. "Can I finally get your cell number?"

I raise an eyebrow. "Won't that take all the fun out of stalking me?"

He gives me a face that says, *Come on*, and I relent. Grabbing a Sharpie from a messy pile of supplies on the floor, I gesture for him to give me his hand.

Thrusting out his upturned fist, he squeezes it so tightly all his arm muscles are flexed. I pull his wrist toward me and write my number along his forearm, ending with a quick sketch of a lion that makes him smile.

"I could've just put you in my phone."

"I'd rather be on your arm." I try to keep the flirtatious lilt out of my voice, but it's there.

He gives a ragged sigh. "I'd better go call my sponsor." He grabs his bag and pauses in front of me. With a deep breath, he leans down and gives me the briefest kiss at the very outermost corner of my lips.

Before I can even decide whether or not to turn my head and kiss him back, he tells me bye, and he's out the door.

I stand nailed to the spot where he left me and absently touch my fingertips to my raw lips as I ask myself, *What the hell just happened?*

CHAPTER SIX

By the time I get home, Dad has dinner from Taco Shack spread out on the table. I thank him and gather up the white wax paper holding my burrito to carry it up to my room.

Dad puts a hand on my shoulder, stopping me. "Come on, Ror. I never see you anymore."

"You sure you don't want me to pee in a cup first?" I widen my eyes and lean in close. "Want to check my pupils?"

He looks away, and I almost feel bad. Then I remember him being a damn cheater and want to hurt him even more.

He says, "I got you your favorite: a Chili Davis Burrito."

"I can enjoy it just fine up in my room."

His expression hardens. "Kelly?" he calls to the dog, who is, of course, parked right at his feet. She looks up at him, tail wagging. He asks her, "Would you like Rory's burrito for your dinner?"

"Come *on*, man." The burritos smell delicious. "You wouldn't really do that."

"Try me," Dad says. "That dog's ass can blow spicy gas into next week for all I care."

With a growl, I pull out my chair, fall into it, and bow my head slightly as Dad blesses the food.

Trying to ignore Dad's disgusting mention of dog farts, I attack my enormous Chili Davis. It's a perfect blend of cheese and meat and beans and fiery goodness, and a small groan escapes as I chew because the thing is just that good.

Of course, giving in to eating with Dad has a cost. Pretending to be nonchalant about it, he starts to interrogate me about my summer.

"Overcast today," he says. "Many people up at the lake?"

"Some." I shrug.

"You've been putting in some serious hours lately. How do you like it?"

"Okay." I hide any trace of enthusiasm.

His seemingly benign questions continue, and I answer with growing hostility that gets hotter and hotter until I finally snap, "Want to know what shade of brown my shit was this morning too, Dad? How about the scent of *my* farts." I half stand and wave my hand behind me as if offering him a waft from my butt.

I sit back down hard, and his ears turn red, but he finally quits talking to me. We both chew our food in silence.

It is completely his fault that we hate each other. He wasn't quite this awful before things went bad with Mom and he turned into a total dick.

He claims that he had to ban me from making art because I need to learn that relationships are more important, but he has no idea how to even have a relationship with me.

I know he's capable of being a decent father because he used to be. But that was before he stopped trusting me. And long before that day he busted me carrying pot, the kill shot on our relationship.

The fact that he turned our family pet into my snitch was only one of the many messed-up things about the whole incident.

I'd come home and flung my backpack on the stairs as I grabbed a snack from the kitchen. I was only gone a moment. When I crossed back through the living room, Dad was blocking my way to the steps.

"I have a few questions, young lady," he said, holding up the condemning sandwich baggie filled with herb.

Kelly, the traitor, stood beside him as if she had a few questions of her own.

I'll admit, my response of, "It's just a little weed, Dad," was a pretty poor opener, but it was only a dime bag I was holding for a friend, and I wasn't expecting him to treat me like I was some sort of depraved drug addict who'd just come in off the street.

Of course, he refused to believe the weed wasn't mine. Cops always want to think the worst about a person, even when that person is their own daughter.

That weekend, he actually made me sit through some stupid Scared Straight program at the nearby Ossining prison.

It's basically this thing where a bunch of inmates take turns yelling at bad kids in an attempt to freak us out and turn us into good kids.

The inmates with their spittle-filled screams had some compelling arguments for staying out of jail.

Of course, instead of finding myself scared straight, I made friends with a cute stoner from High Falls who's about five inches shorter than me who got busted dealing chronic.

The two of us couldn't stop laughing the whole time and we hooked up after our big "release from prison."

I'm sure word got back to my dad that I didn't take the exercise all that seriously.

After that, it was clear that he saw me as a completely different person—like I wasn't even related to him.

Finally, he resorted to banning me from my artwork and tried to put me into some dumb therapy group for teens who are unhappy. It was total bullshit.

Dad will never understand art, and I only pretended to go to his stupid group until he finally caught on that I was ditching and gave up.

If anyone in this household needs therapy, it's him. I still can't believe he's been having a freaking affair.

And now I've lost my appetite.

Wrapping the paper around what's left of my burrito, I stand. "Gotta go." I head for the kitchen with my leftovers.

"Rory, wait, please. Can we talk?"

"Sorry, Dad. I have to cover a closing shift at Danny's tonight."

I walk out of the room and into the kitchen. I'm putting my rewrapped burrito in the fridge when I hear what is most likely his fist pounding hard against the dining room table.

I glance over to the counter, thinking of Mom. I can't help but smile at his rage.

Got 'em, I think, and head upstairs to put on a pair of jean shorts and get the hell away from this house.

Okay, so, I'm not *technically* on the schedule to work at the art store tonight, but I enjoy Kat's company way more than my dad's.

After I get dressed, I head straight over to Danny's since I wouldn't put it past my dad to check up on me. I doubt he'd push things by showing up here at work after our disastrous dinner, but it's probably best I stick close to where I'm supposed to be.

As usual, once I'm hanging around Danny's, I can't help but pitch in anyway. I genuinely love this art store.

Tonight, I'm using Sharpie pens to make a colorful sign that calls attention to our vast selection of Sharpie pens.

Kat is leaning against the counter, watching me. "You do know that Ken will take credit for this, right?" Ken is the store manager, and he loves to let the owner think every new display idea came out of his prematurely balding head.

"I don't mind." I tilt back to inspect my handwriting on the bright sign. Grabbing a fresh marker, I start adding thick shadows to my letters.

"Well, obviously *you* don't mind. Heck, you're not even

getting paid to be here right now, but it really grates my cheese. If it wasn't for you and me, this place would have absolutely zero character."

"So, Ken gets to be the manager. Who needs that level of responsibility?"

Kat spikes up her short, red hair with her fingers. Tonight, her lipstick matches the shade perfectly. "Did you know he and I got hired the same week? We trained together."

"You've mentioned."

"It's just so annoying that my clear lack of a nut sack is what cost me that promotion."

I turn and look at her. "You've got lady balls to spare, my friend. Ken just knows how to schmooze with the customers better."

To emphasize my point, I nod toward the two young women who have been studying the knitting section for the past ten minutes.

Kat rolls her eyes. "I know, I know." She grudgingly moves out from behind the counter and makes her way over to the yarn girls.

My phone buzzes just as I hear Kat give an artificially cheerful greeting and ask if she can help them find anything. I smile while I check my phone.

When I read the text, my smile drops and my blood pressure soars. It's from Hayes.

I have a proposition for you.

I stand, staring at the phone for a moment. I've

experienced my share of booty calls from boys. Usually, I know just how to respond based on an intuitive algorithm that factors in my opinion of the guy who sent it multiplied by my handful of daddy issues and divided by how lonely I'm feeling at that moment.

But I don't know how to respond to this.

And right now, I hate the way my heart is drumming to a rhythm I've never heard before.

"Hey, Kat," I call. The knitters are talking to her animatedly, but she abandons them to see what just made my voice go all weird.

Leaning over my shoulder, she reads the text. "Who's it from?"

"That guy, Hayes, who was in the other day." She looks at me blankly. "The guy with the wet hair who you said was *everyone-with-a-pulse's type*."

"Ah, yes, Mr. Hotness. I thought you weren't interested."

"Yeah, well, he can be quite convincing."

"So you've been seeing him?"

"I *have seen* him. That's all I'm willing to say."

Kat looks at me. "Yeah. The look on your face right now says all it needs to. What's the problem?"

"Things have gotten…weird and complex. He might be more intense than I can handle."

"Intense can be good." She arches a pierced eyebrow.

"I'm freaking out over a simple text from the guy right now," I say. "This is not good."

"Okay, okay. Just ask yourself: Is a proposition from this guy something you feel interested in?"

I roll my eyes. "You met him. Of course I'm interested in messing around. But I'm *not* interested in a relationship and he seems to think that's, I don't know…part of it."

"So, he wants a relationship and you don't?"

"Actually, he's not looking for a relationship either. At least not until he does some sort of AA homework. Like I said, it's weird and complex."

"Maybe he just wants to hook up."

I smile. "Yes. Maybe it's just a hookup." I type back: **What sort of proposition?**

He writes back right away: **Two words. Ice. Caves.**

Kat reads his text out loud and says, "Nice and kinky, but not very convenient. Does he know the ice caves are open to the general public? There could be children present."

I shake my head. "He doesn't want sex. He wants me to take him on an actual tour of the ice caves."

"Oh. Are you sure? I mean, this exchange could be interpreted in several ways."

"No, I'm sure." I wonder if he's agreeing to help me with my project and this is the cost, or if he's simply continuing to blackmail me as his own personal tour guide for the whole Hudson Valley area.

I type: **What are you offering in return?** I hope his response isn't something like "secret keeping," but he quickly writes back.

All that lies beyond the wardrobe.

Of course it's a nerdy Narnia reference. Kat wrinkles her nose and says, "Beyond the wardrobe? Is this him promising to take you clothes shopping, or is he saying he wants you naked?"

"I don't know. It's weird and com—"

"Yeah, yeah. It's complex. I get it." She heads back to sort out the yarn girls who are now pawing through a rainbow of wool. Over her shoulder, Kat calls to me, "Just be careful the two of you don't get caught." She turns and walks backward a few steps so she can admonish, "And try not to *melt* all that *ice*."

I laugh as I text Hayes, letting him know I'm free to take him to the caves tomorrow. It seems like putting ourselves on ice is the best thing the two of us can do right now.

Mom is giving me a pep talk about the importance of staying dedicated to my art no matter what, and she has me feeling like a total slacker. While listening to her, I'm sitting at the kitchen counter, doodling lions in my sketchbook.

"You need to trust the little voice inside your head that tells you that you can do better, that prodding to try harder. It's the harsh, cruel taunting that will push you to make great art, not that gentle whisper that looks at your work and says, 'Hey, that's pretty good.'"

I tear out my page of doodles and crumple it into a ball.

Beginning with a clean sheet, I bear down on my pencil

and draw more deliberately now. *Must focus. Envision each stroke magnified, that water tower lion coming to life.*

"If you are not willing to sacrifice everything for your art, you have no right calling yourself an artist." Mom's voice rises. "Art costs. Always. The greater the art, the greater the cost. Sometimes, the cost seems more than you can imagine. More than you feel you can bear to give. But if you don't flinch or falter, you might one day create something great."

She smiles to herself and I'm mesmerized for a moment by how beautiful she is. Her features are much more delicate than mine, but I'm glad I at least have her eyes.

Her brow collapses. "Of course, when you do create something truly great, the masses will rise up to label you a phony or a hack or, worst of all, *unoriginal.*"

I flinch at that last word. The word that crushed her.

I was about seven years old when Mom finally felt ready to share her artwork with the world. I still remember how she agonized over which galleries to submit to, carefully writing the perfect artist's statement and cover letter, putting her heart on the line. She got rejected again and again, and each time she would be devastated for days. Anyone reading through her rejections could see that she was so, so close but she took each one so hard.

It was clear all she needed was more time to really break through. But an artist can stay stuck at *so, so close* for many, many years. It can become a scorching desert of hopeless wandering.

Finally, after almost seven years of rejections, a small gallery in New York City agreed to host her exhibit. When she got the phone call with the good news, it was a euphoric day for all of us—the happiest I'd ever seen her by far. Almost as happy as she looks in that old photograph on my dresser.

Mom worked night and day for weeks on her installation. When it was finally time for the opening reception, she bought a new dress, and we all went into the city, and she announced that everything was finally beginning.

Dad and I hung back in a corner, watching her blossom before our eyes. She wasn't ours anymore.

Everyone raved over what she had created. A guy came from some big prestigious art magazine and took pictures. Everything was great, and even though the article was shorter than we'd hoped and the exhibit eventually had to make way for the next new, exciting *breakout artist*, Mom was walking around like a brighter, shinier version of herself.

If only she'd never googled her name.

"That guy had nothing to lose," I say quietly. "He wasn't even using his real name; it was easy for him to be careless and cruel."

She knows who I'm talking about. An anonymous poster on a popular online discussion forum about local artists who pointed out some minor shortcomings in Mom's big exhibit. I mean, minor, *perceived* shortcomings in his humble, fucked-up opinion.

He had the nerve to call Mom's work unoriginal.

She couldn't get out of bed for a week after reading his comments.

"I don't know if anyone can appreciate how hard it is for an artist to put their work out there." I can see Mom's eyes are welling up with tears now, and my throat clenches as she goes on. "Why continue creating when someone can just come along and, metaphorically yet very *publically*, shit all over you and your work?"

I know she's given so much for her art, and with a tug, my mind turns to all *I've* sacrificed for her art. All the small neglects. The losses that can never be regained, time she spent locked away from me where I wasn't allowed, while her art kept her distracted and made her whole.

My mom's art is amazing and moving, and I know that it is genuinely great, but it has been a selfish sibling to grow up with.

Not all my sacrifices have been small.

Just then, I hear Dad's car pull into the driveway. The engine cuts off, and I scamper quickly upstairs.

As his footsteps move into the kitchen, I can hear Mom's voice getting high with sorrow. "Art is all that matters. Art is my breath. It's my life. If I can't make art, I am nothing."

Before I hear Dad's response, I close my door quietly. And when he comes upstairs to check on me, I pretend to be asleep.

I hear him shuffle to his bedroom, probably getting to bed early, so he's fresh for the semicolon that's set in his calendar for tomorrow morning.

That blasphemous punctuation means he's obviously meeting that woman again; I just wish I knew where. I need to put an end to this. He wouldn't meet her anyplace local, and I haven't figured out a way to track him down and confront him.

Our electronic devices are connected through an app that lets us find each other on the map, but using the app makes the device that's being traced beep loudly. It's not exactly a stealthy way to track a person down.

I'm actually pretty grateful for that loud beeping feature, since without it, Dad would be able to find me anytime he wanted. I'd hate my life even more if I had to worry about my father tracking me all around New Paltz by my phone without my knowledge. I pull the covers tight against my neck at the thought.

I should really get up and brush my teeth, but it's been such a long day, I don't want to move. I let the tiredness wash over me a moment, then force myself to go quietly to the bathroom and get ready for bed.

While flossing, I think back to what Mom was saying about art and sacrifice. I've gotten soft lately, reaching for satisfaction outside of my creating, seeking comfort when I know that the life of an artist is not meant to be comfortable.

I need to get moving on painting my giant lion. If Hayes isn't the right person to help me, I'll find someone else, but if I don't continue moving forward, making better art, I'm doomed to stay stuck forever.

Dad might never understand, but Mom and I are so connected, we're like the same person. I know that she gets it. Absolutely.

CHAPTER SEVEN

I agree to pick Hayes up at his aunt's house the next morning, since she's working and he still can't drive legally. She lives just outside of town in a very snazzy A-frame log cabin that has huge windows with mountain views.

"This place is awesome," I say as I walk into the combination living room/kitchen with wood beam ceilings that rise cathedral high. A long tabby immediately weaves herself around my legs. I bend down to give her a pat. "What does your aunt do?"

He points out the window toward the Shawangunk Ridge. "She's a massage therapist up at Mohonk."

"Nice." I look out to the tower, visible on top of the mountain from where we're standing. "I know someone who used to work in the kitchen up there. Would you believe that the light at the top of that tower is just a regular sixty-watt bulb?"

Hayes bends down to catch the cat who hasn't stopped

tracing an endless infinity symbol around my legs. "That's nuts," he says. "It looks so bright every night from here."

"He took me up there and showed me himself. It's just a regular lightbulb, like one you'd put in a lamp." I mask my memory of making out with the guy up on top of that tower.

If Hayes suspects, he doesn't show it. Dropping the cat so it lands on all fours, he moves over to the center island, picks up a purple tumbler, and hands it to me. "Organic blend. Light and sweet."

I smile and point to the Mud Puddle's logo on the side of the tumbler. "Did you lose your Starbucks club card or something?"

The cat has already made her way back to me and resumes making her obsessive-compulsive figure eights.

"Go ahead. Try it," he says. "I promise I'm not trying to roofie you."

"See, I didn't *think* you were trying to roofie me until you just now said that."

"Sorry. Very bad joke."

"Not that you'd do anything to me anyway," I say.

"I don't know. Watching you sleep sounds—"

"Creepy as hell?"

He laughs. "Yeah, I guess it kinda does. Better to leave the hallucinogens out of our discussion."

"So *no* narcotics whatsoever?"

He gives me a look that says the two of us will never be getting stoned together. "Just try your drink," he says. "I made it special for you."

"Thanks." I take a sip. This coffee is about the most delicious thing I've ever tasted. I feel my pupils widen. "I mean, *thanks!*"

"Caffeine is my one remaining drug, so I'm a little particular about my coffee. I use a French press and grind the beans myself."

"You seriously need help." I greedily take another sip. "But this is fantastic."

Hayes is eager to get going to the ice caves, but I need to see what type of sweetener (cane sugar with a dollop of honey) and cream (fresh whole milk from the farmer's market) he used. With some pressing, he also admits to adding a pinch of cinnamon to the grounds. By the time we head out, I'm already halfway through my delicious beverage and am completely covered in cat hair.

As we climb into my car, he pauses a moment and looks out toward the tower. "That's pretty amazing, you know."

"What?" I take another sip from the tumbler.

"That something as ordinary as a household lightbulb can be seen from this far away." He turns his eyes on me. "It shines so brightly in the night sky."

Gazing at the tower that juts up from the ridge, I say, "Well, it doesn't do shit right now. It's actually turned on during the day, but you can't tell even up close."

He laughs. "So much for getting all philosophical with you."

"Nice try." I roll my eyes and slide what's left of my coffee into my car's drink holder. He buckles himself into the passenger side as I start the engine.

Without meaning to, I kick up gravel with my tires pulling out and the two of us laugh. Hayes hums the theme song to an old TV show that featured at least three car chases per episode.

The windows are down, and I make the music loud, and I'm not sure if it's a premonition or if it's just all the caffeine I've recently ingested, but it feels like it's going to be a really good day.

The two of us don't talk as I take the back way out of town, toward Ellenville and the ice caves. The road is long and winding and lined with thick forest on either side.

A hawk swings by overhead, searching for small animals to devour, but they are all too busy scurrying for food to care about the danger.

A good song comes on, and Hayes is using every available surface inside the car to play percussion.

He's busy mimicking the beat of the tune on his chest when I look over at him scornfully. His thumping slows, and he drops his hands into his lap. "Sorry," he says sheepishly.

The chorus starts up, and I snatch my coffee tumbler out of the drink holder, hold it up, and belt into it like it's a microphone.

He laughs and the two of us shout out the lyrics together, passing the "mic" back and forth.

When the song ends he tells me, "We killed it!" and I have to smile in agreement.

I don't want to ask because it feels like revealing that I need him too much, but I've bitten my tongue for as long as I can. I slow down and lower the radio.

"Have you thought more about helping me paint over the ad on the water tower?"

He makes me wait for his answer, continuing to tap a hand on his knee as he looks out the window.

Finally, he shifts in his seat to face me. "I talked it over with Roger."

I swerve slightly. "Are you freaking crazy?"

"Not specific details or anything, just the basics. The fact that there could be legal consequences."

"I *swear* I won't get you in trouble. If anything goes down, I'll take the fall. Honestly."

My dad may hate me, but I grew up knowing most of the other officers, and I feel sure I could protect Hayes from a parole violation even if we did get caught. Plus, we won't get caught.

"Listen, Rory, I really want to help you. And I can see just how much that water tower needs one of your lions on it. Roaring down over the town. Just like, *roar!*" He holds up his hands like claws.

I laugh and breathe a sigh of relief. *He's actually going to help me.* I say, "That thing is going to wake everybody up."

He holds up a hand as if to stop my big grin. "What my sponsor helped me decide is that I honestly want to help you, but I need to know why."

"Why what? Why the lion? You just said it: that water tower *needs* this." I wrinkle my nose and imitate his roar, but a glance at his face says he's not buying it. I drop my hand that's making "claws."

"I know what the lion would represent for me," he says. "I could look up and always see Aslan from Narnia watching over us and reminding me that I have a higher power who is kind yet absolutely fierce. It would be an uneasy image, but one with deep meaning."

"That's perfect," I say. "Let's go with your Narnia thing. This lion will be, like, up there, roaring at all of us, warning everyone to shape up and act right."

"That's not at all what Aslan's about. You clearly need to go back and rewatch the movie or, better yet, *read the book*."

I nod enthusiastically, keeping my eyes on the road. I'll read whatever he wants if he'll just help me paint.

He says, "But what I really need to know is what these lions mean to *you*. Besides the name thing, what drove you to make the first one?"

My mind tries to land on memories, but each one is too sharp.

"I guess you could say I've been going through some stuff this past year or so." I shrug casually, but my knuckles are white as I grip the steering wheel with both hands.

"I'm sorry." Hayes puts a palm on my shoulder and I stop at the T in the road.

I flick on my left turn signal and look out the window. "Yeah, well. Shit happens."

"You mean shit happens *for a reason*," he says, but I don't respond because something has just caught my eye.

In the parking lot of the German restaurant on the corner,

a police cruiser is parked with all the other cars. Like a goose hanging out in a crowd of ducks, thinking it will just blend in. But it *does not* blend in.

I'm vaguely aware of Hayes watching me, but I can't unfreeze my stare as I slowly remove my sunglasses.

The cruiser is one of the D.A.R.E. ones, complete with a picture of the condescending cartoon dog in uniform on the side. Just like the police car my dad drives. The puzzle pieces fall into place.

That semicolon marking this morning in his calendar.

The unpopular restaurant. The perfect distance outside of town.

He's here. *With her.* I'm certain of it.

Of course, I don't remember my dad ever eating German food before, let alone for breakfast. I'm probably wrong about all of this.

Except that I *know* that I'm not.

Impulsively, I pull into the parking lot. There are plenty of spaces open, but I drive directly up to the front door and park diagonally on the painted yellow *X*'s marking the entryway.

Hayes's exclamations of, "What's happening?" and, "Rory, are you okay?" are faint background noise behind the long and steady high note playing in my head.

I am not in control of my actions as I jump out of the car and rip open the heavy front door and charge into the space beyond. I'm plunged into dark-wood-paneled politeness, and I freeze for a moment, allowing my pupils to adjust.

It takes long enough that Hayes moves in behind me and puts a hand on each of my shoulders. "You left the car running. Is everything okay?"

I shake him off as I spot them.

Over by the window. A private little table for two. *How romantic.*

Without a plan, I march directly to where they sit. A handsome middle-aged woman with a dreamy smile on her face.

And across from her: my dad.

I shout, "*What the actual fuck?*"

Dad looks surprised for a moment, and then covers his forehead with one hand. To the woman, he says, "I'm so sorry, Linda."

"So, that's her name? Huh?" I stick my face directly in front of hers. "Hello, *Linda*. Who the hell do you think you are?"

She stammers at me while twisting the cloth napkin on her lap with both hands. Looking back and forth between my dad and me, she seems about to cry. But that's not my fault. It's his.

I swing around on him. "I knew it too. You called me by accident last week, and I could hear you out on a date with this, this, this…*hobag.*"

"Rory!" My dad's face is red as he rises and the little-kid part of my brain is saying *holy shit* because he hardly ever loses it and it's scary when he does, but I don't back down.

The two of us stand nose to nose, and my teeth are clenched so tight I can feel my heart beating in my jaw. Hayes gently touches my arm and I realize I have my right hand balled into a fist. I release it.

"Hey, there, Hayes," I say sarcastically over my shoulder. "This is my dad, the cheating cheater who *cheats* on my mom." My voice rises with each word, drawing stares from around the sparsely filled room.

Dad glances to Hayes for a moment before fixing his eyes back on me. "You know that's *not true*, Rory."

"Are you seriously going to tell me this *isn't* a date?" I laugh and gesture to the cozy table for two in front of us. "What *is* this, Dad?"

His face is still flushed, but his voice is controlled. "This is breakfast between two people who met at their grief counseling group. Two widowed adults who are trying to move on with their lives. Linda here lost her husband two years ago."

Linda is still sitting, and her voice is weak as she tells me, "I'm so sorry about your mom."

I swing my hand all the way back and before Dad or Hayes can stop me, I slap the plate of eggs off the table in front of her. She folds up like a flower, ducking down in her seat as the plate bounces off the paneled wall, sending eggs and home fries flying.

"Now we're *both* sorry," I say and turn on my heel.

"Rory!" my dad yells as Hayes bends down to pick the plate up off the ground.

I stride back through the restaurant, pausing at the neat little hostess stand and shoving the glass bowl of mints onto the floor. The dish makes a satisfying crash against the tile floor as the mints scatter in a panic.

When I get outside, the brightness is blinding. I jump into the driver's seat, grab my sunglasses from the dashboard, and…

There's no key in the ignition.

Hayes flies out through the restaurant's front door with a look of dread on his face. His expression relaxes when he sees me sitting in my car.

"Come on." He gestures for me to get out of the car.

"No way am I going back in there. Where are my keys?"

He dangles the keys in front of me. "I'll drive."

"You don't even have a license."

"So I'll be careful."

I sit, staring out the front window for what feels like forever as my mind chants, *I hate him. I hate him. I hate him.*

Finally, my dad opens the door of the restaurant and bellows, "RORY!"

I give him the finger as I slide over to the passenger seat.

Hayes turns to look at him, and I scream, "Let's go!"

He tells my dad, "I'll take care of her," with such calm assurance it pisses me off to no end. But at least he climbs into the car, puts the key in the ignition, and starts it.

Dad comes over to the window, looking more deflated than angry now. "Rory, we need to deal with this. You practically assaulted my girlfriend and that is not okay. I'm tempted to arrest you right now."

"Oh, so now she's your *girlfriend*?" I am seething with rage.

"Yes. Your mom has been gone for over a year now. I still miss her, but I need to have a life. You can't just continue this fantasy that she's still with us and nothing happened."

I command Hayes, "Hit the gas, right now."

Hayes looks sheepishly at my dad. "I'm terribly sorry, sir. I think it's best if she maybe cools off before you two try sorting this out."

Dad holds his hands up in the air in surrender as Hayes slowly lets the car roll forward.

"This is not what I call hitting the gas." I press down on Hayes's right knee with both my hands, trying to force him to go faster. But after an initial jump forward, we continue crawling slowly.

I can still see Dad framed in the driver's side window. "I should go check on Linda anyway." To me he snaps, "You scared the hell out of her."

"Good!" I say, and Hayes finally pulls away.

I watch as Dad drags the door to the restaurant open. With one last look in our direction, he heads back inside.

"Which way?" Hayes asks once we reach the parking lot exit.

"Left, I guess." My arms are crossed, and my foot is tapping, and I feel like I'm bouncing around the inside of the car like a bouncy ball. "Although the ice caves don't sound like such a hot idea anymore."

"They sound like a perfect place for you to cool off."

"I really need to paint."

He looks over at me. "No need to explain *why* anymore."

Hayes drives in silence for a time. His voice is so low it's nearly a whisper when he says, "I'm so sorry about your mom."

I slump farther down in my seat and fold my arms even tighter. Then cover my face with my hands.

"How did she die?" he croaks.

"I don't want to talk about it," I say and turn the radio up before the thoughts can get their claws into my mind.

"I'm not going to help you rest in denial." Hayes turns the radio back down and looks over at me. "Would you prefer I take you back to your dad right now?"

I sit up. "No, don't. Just…give me a few minutes." I never want to see my dad again. "We're almost there. Make the next right and I'll tell you everything as we hike to the caves."

Hayes nods and turns the music back up. I'm glad he's driving slowly because I'm not looking forward to answering his questions.

Or to finding out how he'll treat me after he knows my whole story.

We're silent as we walk up the path toward the reservoir and the caves beyond. Finally, Hayes tries to open a dialogue by asking about what appear to be outhouses poking from the overgrown blueberry bushes at random intervals.

I know that they were single-room huts built for migrant

berry pickers nearly a century ago, but I just shrug in response. *This isn't some fifth-grade informative-ass field trip.*

The pickers used to start fires to encourage bigger harvests and the blueberries still grow abundantly here, but it's too early in the season to eat them now.

This does not stop Hayes from picking a small handful and popping them into his mouth. He immediately spits the sour berries out onto the ground and pulls a face that makes me smile in spite of everything.

"Maybe I should've warned you they're still tart this time of year."

He wipes his tongue with his palm and gives a muffled, "D'ya think?"

"Well, the greenish hue should've maybe been a tip-off."

"Oh, is that right?" He pinches another premature berry off the bush and tosses it at me. It glances off my shoulder. But instead of engaging in a berry battle, I turn back to stone.

"Nice try." I continue along the path, and he follows in silence until we eventually emerge into the clearing that surrounds the reservoir.

The still water reflects the sky, and the scene is so beautiful, if it were a landscape oil painting, it would be cheesy as hell. I want to wreck it. Grabbing a handful of smooth stones, I pick out a flat one and skip it expertly across the water.

It skips four times before sinking below the surface.

"Not bad." Hayes moves beside me as I select another skipping rock and let it fly.

Six skips this time and a low whistle from Hayes.

Leaning over, he carefully scans the ground and selects a rock. He blows it off, winds up, and lets it loose with a huge *kerplunk*.

"If you were trying to make the *biggest* splash, you win." I release another stone, and it skims perfectly across the surface.

"I live closer to the ocean than any lakes," he says. "There's no way to skip rocks into the ocean's waves. They never stop."

With a sigh, I pick up a perfect, flat skipping stone and put it in Hayes's hand. Guiding his fingers around it so that his pointer finger is hooked along the thin edge, I turn his wrist on its side and position his arm so he's ready to throw.

I stand behind him to guide his throwing hand, and he jokes, "You're not putting me into another headlock, are you?"

I don't smile, but when he twists and looks down into my face, our closeness forms a hairline crack inside me.

"Keep your forearm level with the ground and snap your wrist," I say. "Aim for just above the water. You want the flat part of the rock to skim across the surface."

We wind up in sync, and with my hand guiding him, he manages to toss his stone evenly across the lake.

Skip-skip-skip-splash!

"Three skips!" He's as excited as a little kid. "That was awesome."

He puts a hand on each of my shoulders and kisses me quickly on the lips.

Judging by the look on his face, he's as startled as I am by his burst of affection.

I tell him, "You could still use some practice."

His mouth falls open and his face goes red.

I cover my laugh with my hand. "With the *skipping*. Not the kissing." Under my breath I add, "Your kissing just about kills me."

He turns away, searching for more flat rocks, and I can't tell if he heard that last part or not.

Hayes doesn't ask me to explain the scene in the restaurant with my dad until we nearly reach the caves.

Rather than tiptoe around it with prodding questions and the dance of never-ending sympathies, he simply asks his same question from the car, "How did your mom die?"

We walk silently side by side for a time, but he doesn't repeat the question again.

Finally, I stop walking and turn to him. "Remember that story I told you about me getting lost at the zoo as a little kid and ending up at the Lion House?"

"Yes." He says it quietly, as if he doesn't want to spook me from opening up.

"At the time, I thought L-I-O-N was how you spelled *lying*, like it was the lyin' house and that's where I would find my mom. She'd always do things like tell me, 'One more minute,' and emerge hours later, wild-eyed from working, to find I'd made dinner for myself. She'd constantly tell half truths out of convenience or lie for no apparent reason at all."

I angle my body sideways, and after a few painful breaths, I go on. "My mother always had her secrets. I knew it before I knew how to spell *lying* the right way." I feel each word as I say it. "And fifteen months ago, she came up with an elaborate plan to kill herself."

Under his breath, Hayes says, "Shit."

I start walking again, and when I reach the thick, wooden ladder that leads to the ice caves below, I grasp the sides and start climbing down. When I get to the bottom, I look up for the first time.

Hayes is still standing at the top with his hands on his hips and his head bowed as he watches me.

"Don't you dare give me that look," I call up.

He nods and clears his expression before starting down the ladder after me. I hate this. The fact that he knows now changes everything.

Now a mindless fling can never happen between us.

And I could really use a mindless fling with a warm body right about now.

Hayes follows me along the rock scramble toward the caves.

He's silent, but I can feel him wanting to reach out and fix me, and it's starting to piss me off.

It's always like this after people find out what happened.

They start thinking of me as some sort of broken doll in need of repair.

I haul myself quickly over the rocks, trying to prove to Hayes that I'm not fragile.

I'm working to outpace him, using my knowledge of the route to my advantage, but he stays close behind.

When we reach the first wall of rock that's covered in ice crystals, Hayes runs his hand across it. "This is amazing," he says. "It must be eighty-five degrees today, but this wall is completely frozen."

I point to the small pile of frost in a corner. "There's your Narnia. Always winter here."

I step closer, and he instinctively puts a hand on my back, forgetting that it's still freezing cold from the wall. I squeal in surprise.

"You *didn't* just do that." I place both palms flat against the smooth sheet of ice and hold them there as he backs away, his hands raised in surrender.

"No, no, no," he says. "That was honestly an accident."

"Yeah? Well, so is *this*." I lunge for him, grabbing his shoulder with one hand and wrapping the other around the back of his neck. I expect him to flinch and wiggle free, but instead, he takes his punishment and relaxes, pressing his neck into my palm.

His hands slide around my waist, and I can see that despite our horsing around, he's still thinking of my dead mom.

His gaze holds more caring concern and less lust now.

With a grunt I pull away and continue on the path beside

the ice walls, moving more slowly now, like the power of gravity has just doubled.

After a moment, Hayes follows. "This place really is like Narnia."

I don't respond as I walk, trailing a finger along the wall's icy surface.

"It feels like we've entered a place that is 'other.'" His voice is strained, and when I turn back, he's not looking at the icicles hanging above our heads. He's looking directly at me.

The air is cool as I suck in my breath.

He crosses his arms and leans against the wall without breaking eye contact. He flinches at the cold but then continues leaning and watching me.

Finally, he says, "Rory, I really want to be here for you."

I roll my eyes. "What does that even mean?"

He laughs. "I don't know. I just... I've never hung out with a girl while totally present and sober."

"So am I making you want to drink now?" There's a tease in my voice, but I can sense that if the answer is yes, he's done hanging out with me. Like he's a carnival ride with a warning sign: "You may only be *this* fucked up to hang out with the cute boy who's in AA."

"Everything makes me want to drink, Rory. I'm an alcoholic." He stands upright and briskly rubs his shoulder. "Brrr. Frosty." He hugs himself, calling way too much attention to his biceps.

I slide my hands around myself so we're both essentially wearing invisible straitjackets as we face each other.

I ask, "Are you afraid I'm bad for you? For your sobriety? Because I think I might be."

He gives a sad smile. "I'm more afraid *for* you."

"I hate when people worry about me."

"Makes sense. That's why you pretend everything's normal."

"Everything *is* normal."

"Normal is just a setting on the dryer."

"That sounds like something abnormal people say to feel better about being abnormal."

"That haunting thing I could see in your lions? I know what it is now. It's grief. You've buried your feelings so you can stay in denial about your mom's...suicide."

That fucking *word*. I uncross my arms and make a half turn away from him. "You don't know anything about it."

"I know that your dad is willing to risk loving again, and that's not a terrible thing. Going out with Linda is like saying that despite all the pain it caused him, loving your mother was worth it."

"Or maybe it just means he didn't love my mom at all and was happy to move on after she was finally gone." I cross my arms again.

Hayes rubs his chin. "I guess that's possible too. I never knew your mom. But either way, your job isn't to judge your dad for how *he* grieves." I look at my feet and he adds, "And you can't accuse a man of cheating when he's a widow."

Just then, a family with two tween girls comes around the bend and files past us. The younger girl looks up at Hayes and me and gives a giggle as she turns to watch her sister's reaction to noticing us.

I hold up a hand in greeting. I want to tell her this is not what it looks like at all because she obviously thinks we're a sweet couple with zero problems who are out on a hike and also deeply in love.

She has no way of seeing how wrong and broken and weird and complex and freaking abnormal everything is with us.

When the family is gone, Hayes says, "I get that you hate pity, Rory, but how can I help if you won't open up?"

"I want to… I don't know." I want a tranquilizer gun to make all the lions behave, but when I look at Hayes, the dark ache inside begins to churn.

He knows about her now, and he wants to know more. I long for a can of spray paint in my hand to control what I'm feeling.

Instead, the truth leaps from my mouth. "I'm afraid I'm exactly like her. I'm afraid I'll turn into my mother."

The confession is like an explosive *pssshttt* that surprises me with its forceful release.

"Exactly like her in what way?"

"My dad is terrified of me turning into her. It's the reason why he's banned me from making art." I pick up a stick and start tracing the grooves of the rock face, trying to ignore the way my pulse is racing right now.

"Is that why you secretly paint your graffiti lions?"

"The lions are just what comes out when I paint. They're how my art expresses itself."

"As repressed rage?"

"Yes, I like that—repressed rage. But that rage can't technically be considered repressed if I'm putting it out there for everyone to see, can it?" My stick breaks, but I continue tracing with the piece that's left.

"But you're not actually connected to your lions."

I laugh. "I'm more connected to them than you can know." I drop my stick. "Besides, this is better. I avoid the pitfall of negative feedback. You see, my mom's a perfectionist. She can't deal with criticism…"

He tilts his head. "Pretending she's alive isn't healthy, Rory. You can't heal while living in denial."

I cross my arms. "This from a guy who can't handle drinking a single beer."

"You're right. I can't handle drinking. Even one beer can set me off. That's why I'm getting help. There's no shame in admitting you're powerless. The first step in AA is admitting we're powerless over drinking."

"I'm not powerless over anything." I start walking away.

Hayes follows me. "Aren't there five stages of grief? I think anger is pretty early on, no? Isn't it the very first stage?"

I don't look back as I growl at him, "No. The first stage is denial."

CHAPTER EIGHT

As we make our way through the rocky labyrinth, Hayes asks me what my mom was like.

I answer just to prove to him that I can think of her in the past tense. "My mom wasn't just a regular mom person, you know. She was an amazing artist. Super talented."

"So that's where you get it, obviously."

"No. I mean, I do fine, but she could've been one of the greats. Actually, I think she could still become one of the greats."

Hayes's expression falls. "Rory, you know—"

"Yes, of course I know she's *dead*." I pause a moment and draw a deep breath. "I mean, lots of artists break through posthumously. Have you ever heard of the Sean Kelly Gallery?"

"No. Not exactly."

"Well, it's an important gallery down in Hell's Kitchen, and my mom was a featured artist there once." I lean against a wall of rock that is cool but not frozen.

"Wow, that's impressive." Hayes pulls a Nalgene bottle from his pack and unscrews the top. "When was this?"

I shake my head when he offers me a sip of his water. "Around two years ago." I wait for him to take a short drink and add, "It was a really big deal that she got her own exhibit at such a selective gallery. They're known for discovering new artists."

"Wow. Good for her." He screws the top back onto his bottle and slides it in his bag. "But that must've been a little rough on you. I know when I was little and my mom got absorbed with work, it was easy for me to feel neglected." He puts a hand on my arm. "And my mom just sells real estate part-time."

A little too quickly, I shoot, "I loved having an artist for a mom."

The truth is, my relationship with my mother was more complicated before she died. Before she made the videos I've been watching on repeat at the kitchen counter every night. Pretending she's not only alive, but that she now also has time to sit and talk to me endlessly.

When she was alive for real, I loved Mom's bouts of spontaneity. We had so much fun going on discovery hikes and scavenging for art supplies, but her moods were wildly unpredictable. One day, the two of us found ourselves at the dump gathering a discarded flock of plastic flamingos for her to melt down and form into pink furniture for my Barbies, and the next week, she was camped in her bed, unable or unwilling to do anything at all with me.

Dad was always working, making a big reputation for himself on the force, and so it was my job to get her up and moving when she had her "low energy" days. Thinking about it now makes me exhausted.

I say, "My mom was always big on achieving creative flow. You know, getting to that place where time just seems to stop and the world falls away? She lived for that. Do you ever feel it while writing?"

"This sounds like an attempt to change the subject, but yes, I have gotten into flow while working on my dragon books."

"Getting high is not the same thing as achieving flow." I step over a jutting stone in the path.

"I'm aware." Hayes follows me. "Although, before I got sober, I noticed that giving a drink to my inner critic seemed to shut her up. Now it can be harder to push past that harsh negative voice that says my work is crap."

I turn and squint at him. "And the critical voice in your head is a female because *of course*."

"It's not like that. My mom is great and encourages me all the time, but interior scolding will always sound like her voice to me."

I turn and walk faster. I love listening to Mom's tapes, but I can't allow her voice to really enter my head. If I do, I'm afraid it will take root and won't stop harping on me to make art until I'm crazy too.

That unintentional *too* hits my collarbone like an ice pick. Before I even think the words, I say them out loud. "My mom was broken."

"I'm sorry." I can feel Hayes's now-warm palm press into my upper arm, but I pull away.

"I mean, she was isolated but brilliant. It was part of her becoming a great artist." I step out into the open air, letting the breeze steal the rest of my words before they form. *And I'm destined to be like her.*

Hayes moves close behind me but doesn't try to touch my arm again. "Tell me more about her."

I stand, looking off through the trees for a full minute, but he doesn't move. His silent patience pulls a good memory of Mom forward and I sigh. "Her installment for the Sean Kelly Gallery was amazing. It was even featured on their website for a few months."

"What did she do for her exhibit?" Hayes asks.

"She blew up photographs of all these unique people, so that they were each life-size; then she mounted them on pressboard and cut around their silhouettes. She turned each person into a sort of door that gallery visitors would pull open to find an indent in the exact shape and size of the person."

"Cool." Hayes is watching me, and I look away as I keep talking.

"Written inside the indent behind each person's head were words that represented what that person was thinking."

He squints in confusion, so I go on.

"For instance, there was a woman standing with a screaming child and inside her head she's thinking, 'Please, everyone stop judging me. I want my kid to shut the fuck up too.' And one bald guy wearing a suit had the whole top half of his body filled with run-on sentences about what a bitch his wife was and how he was going to get even with her and win."

"Sounds like a cool concept. That must've been intense."

"There was one of me," I say. "I felt like a superstar. My picture was the one they featured on the front page of their website."

"What did it say inside your head?"

I shrug.

Hayes leans forward and looks at me in a way that says, *Spill your guts*, and I know he won't let this go.

If he really searched, he could probably still find the picture and quotes someplace online anyway. I draw in a breath.

I make him wait another beat, still wondering why I'm opening up to Hayes so easily when I say, "I was about fourteen in the picture and looking into a small hand mirror. Pulling my picture door open on its hinges revealed a series of questions inside my head."

"Asking?" he prods.

I sigh. "They asked things like, 'What is happening to me?' and 'Will I ever get to be beautiful?'"

He wrinkles his nose. "What did you look like when you were fourteen?"

I laugh. "Aaaaaaaa-awk-ward." I point to my teeth. "Braces." Hold up a dreadlock. "Ungodly mass of frizz." I frame a section of my chin with my fingers. "Stress acne. I was a mess."

He smiles and leans closer. "It couldn't have been that bad. And at least one of your questions got answered."

I look at him, confused.

"You're beautiful now." He says it in a way that's clearly designed to make me swoon, but I am not so easily swooned.

"Or something corny like that," I say and turn away.

He follows me along the worn path that leads back up toward the lake. "Well, was she right? Were those the things you were thinking about?"

"No." I keep walking. "I never really cared much about how I looked. I was wondering if I would ever be a true artist like she was."

"Did you tell her that?"

"She said the piece was meant to represent adolescent girls in general, not just me specifically. She thought that most girls consider beauty more important than having talent."

"If that's true, that's really sad." He's still directly behind me even though my strides have been picking up speed.

"The whole installment was pretty sad. They even referred to parts of it as my mom's 'suicide note' in the article after she…"

Hayes tries to take my hand, but I keep it limp until he gives up. We're silent as we climb back up and around to the pond.

We skip only one stone apiece when we reach the water, each of our throws making three hops before sinking below the surface.

I'm not sure if it's pity over all the stuff about my mom or if Hayes is honestly worried about me, but when we get back to the car, he stops me.

"Rory? I'm going to help you." He nods decisively. "I'll be your painting assistant."

I'm afraid to say anything because I don't know how I feel about him doing this for me. It makes me feel grateful but guilty, and I finally look down at the dirt and give a quiet, "Thank you."

We climb into the car and I pull out of the lot, taking a different route toward town. I'm sure my dad's date is over by now, but I'd rather not even pass that restaurant again.

It just so happens this road leads us right by the water tower, and I point at it and wink at him as we drive past.

"I seriously need to avoid getting arrested," Hayes says. "My parents will *kill* me if I violate probation."

I bite down on my lip, promising myself I won't allow anything bad to happen to him because of me.

"I can't wait to start your graffiti lessons," I say. "Are you free tomorrow?"

"I certainly am, *beautiful girl*."

"Oh my God. Stop that."

"Now that I know calling you beautiful gets you flustered, get ready to hear it *constantly*."

"I'm not flustered. I just know we're not each other's type." I gesture to his slicked-back hair. "That whole metrosexual thing you've got happening is fine, but it's basically the opposite of my European approach to grooming."

141

"Rory, I know I've been saying we can't be in a relationship," he says. "But that's for the sake of my sobriety, not because I don't think you are beautiful as hell."

"I was just jok—"

He cuts me off. "Didn't you even wonder about that first day we met? How big of a coincidence that was?"

"When we saw each other in the woods and I fell into the bushes?" I laugh at the image of my arms flailing.

His voice stays serious. "In the woods. On the lake. By the cliff where you were painting. You didn't think it was strange I kept running into you?"

I can feel my eyes widen as I grip the wheel. "Are you saying you actually *were* stalking me?"

"Well, no. I wouldn't say I was *stalking* you. I mean, that first encounter really was an accident."

"You followed me to the lake and then later to the swim hole? *That's* how you caught me?" I should've realized that wasn't an accident. I *never* get caught.

"I was going to confess that day you brought me back to your cabin, but then, we didn't exactly get around to talking right away."

I envision the two of us making out on my art table, and when I glance over, I can sense Hayes is picturing the same thing.

I say, "Please remind me again why we haven't gotten around to, er…" My words speed up and run together. "*That thing we were doing instead of talking that day.*"

He laughs. "I have to at least get through my ninth step. Losing myself in that sort of thing will only hurt my recovery."

"And what is step nine?"

"Making a list of people we've harmed and then telling them we're sorry."

"Yikes."

"Yeah, I know." He rubs his arms. "At least I'm young; the list of people I've hurt is pretty short."

"Well, are you planning to step up those steps? We won't be young forever." I shove him playfully, and he catches my hand.

"I'm working on it." He traces a finger along my open palm. "But I need you to make me a promise."

I pull my hand away. "I don't make promises."

"I just need you to tackle your own issues. Maybe consider the effects of your grief over your mom and the problems you have with your dad."

"She's dead; he's a dick. What's to consider?"

"I'm serious, Rory. A healthy relationship requires two healthy people."

"Who said anything about a healthy relationship? Sounds boring."

He sighs loudly and I relent.

"Listen, Hayes. My lions have been a way of dealing with...everything." I feel like my insides are being exposed. "If you'll just help me with the big one, I really think he's the key to finding acceptance with...what my mother did."

"I've never heard of trespassing and vandalism as a pathway to spiritual wholeness."

I laugh. "It's art. It's all about making art. Art is the best form of healing, and art knows no laws."

He nods and lets it go, but all I can think is how much that just sounded like something my mom might say.

CHAPTER NINE

I can't go home.

Instead, after dropping Hayes off, I head to my cabin and work on the water tower design. Now that he's agreed to help me, I feel a renewed sense of purpose. Like my fantasy project has more heft all of a sudden.

I grind away in creative flow as my lions roll in the grass and bat at butterflies until it gets so dark I need to turn my big lantern on. Then I continue working until the giant battery in my big lantern decides it's had about enough.

The light gives two brief warning flickers before I'm plunged into sudden darkness. Ripped from the intense focus on my work, I feel utterly and completely alone.

My eyes adjust slowly, but the thin reed of moonlight coming through the small, high window of the cabin is almost nonexistent.

I wish I had the laptop with the videos of my mom with me now. The videos are safe. They're all the happy version of Mom, the version of herself she showed the outside world, and the version she wanted everyone to remember forever.

I'm pretty sure she expected me to share them in one final posthumous art exhibit. Her grand masterpiece.

Over the final months of her life, she made the recordings while I was at school and Dad was at work. One by one, she covered topic after topic and hid the laptop on the top shelf of her closet.

If at any point during those months Dad or I had thought to check her closet, we would've seen what she was up to. But as it was, nothing made us curious. Nothing seemed suspicious.

When she stopped making art, we didn't wonder what she did all day while she was home alone.

We were fatally uncurious.

If anything, we were relieved at how much happier she seemed overall those last months, more able to balance real life and the art life inside her—the side of her that so often made me feel invisible.

Suddenly, Mom was paying attention when I talked, like she wanted to get to know me better. My mother truly mothered me. And I loved it.

I know now she was only gathering information for the next day's recording, but at the time, I took her attention at face value. I thought I deserved it.

I was the one who found the note.

Standing in the kitchen, with my school bag at my feet, my heart pounding with growing understanding. My feet pounding even louder up the stairs, racing against time—two hours too late for anything I did to matter.

I saw her body first.

Of course, my mother chose the most dramatic version of suicide.

Hanging would be too quick and prim for her, unless perhaps she could've done it in the center of a huge open space. Preferably a round room with sunlight dramatically spotlighting her swaying body. But our ceilings are not grand enough.

And pills would only look like she was sleeping peacefully. Gunshot to the head? Too damn unpredictable. Splatter is such a difficult medium, with its varying shape and size and projection.

No, Mom staged the scene of her suicide as if it were a piece of performance art.

After making her final recording, which was the day she made video number forty-seven, she wrote the brief note with a flourish and headed upstairs to the bathroom.

I wonder sometimes if her plan began the day she decided to renovate that bathroom and make everything pure white. Or perhaps she found her inspiration in the perfection of the shining, white floor tiles after they were laid.

Twisting a long string of cheap, plastic pearls around her neck, she applied her darkest red lipstick and removed her dress. Folded it neatly and laid it on the closed toilet.

She even tidied the bathroom, hiding the half-used bottles with glops of conditioner dripping down the sides, staging her set.

Naked, aside from the pearls and lipstick, she climbed into our deep, claw-foot tub. Let the water fill partway but twisted the knob to off while it was still too shallow to hide her body. Much too shallow.

Old-fashioned straight razor that she got God knows where in her hand.

Like two swift brushstrokes, she drew that razor that Dad and I had never seen across each wrist. Just a couple dramatic drops of blood for display on those pure-white floor tiles. Accents of red placed just so.

Hands resting on naked thighs, she reclined in the pool of shallow water and watched it transition from clear to ribboned to red.

Waited for the world to go dark and for her daughter to find her and grab her and pull her out, hugging her cold, wet mother with sightless, staring eyes and getting blood everywhere. Ruining the carefully staged scene with desperate, tearful flailing.

Stop it, Rory! I command.

I need to get out of my head right now. I bang on the lantern until its weak beam flickers back awake.

I pick up my blade and find the handle has gone cold.

I make a quick swipe at the piece of stencil I've been working on. My cut is impulsive and too fast, and now I'll probably need to redo that section. *Damn.*

I wish I'd brought Hayes back here with me. I could be losing myself in slow, delicious moves. The two of us fitting together so beautifully…

Then I remember he knows. Everything is ruined. Even though he's agreed to help me paint my masterpiece, I need to stop thinking about him in that way.

Checking my phone, I realize it's nearly midnight, which explains why I'm feeling so drained. In addition to the numerous call alerts from my dad, I see Hayes sent me a text a few hours ago asking how I'm doing.

I ignore all that and try to figure out where I should sleep tonight. No way am I going home and dealing with Dad.

I can either try to make myself comfortable inside my small cabin, or I can curl up in my car. I'm thinking there's a blanket in the back…

My phone vibrates violently in my hand while emitting an alarming beeping sound. One look at the screen tells me my electronic device isn't just having a stroke; Dad is tracking my phone right now.

He's had enough of me ignoring his calls. This is the first time he's resorted to using my phone's finder to hunt me down this way. It's an admission of weakness and desperation. In a way, it means I've won, but he absolutely cannot find my cabin. So right now, he wins.

I rush to the door, trying to concoct a story of how I was driving through the woods, cooling off before coming home for the night. I decided to stop for an innocent little hike.

Sure, it's the middle of the night, but it's the only lie I can come up with, and I need to get the hell home and sell it before Dad comes here looking for me.

I shine the flickering lantern around my tiny cabin as I open the door and shudder at the damning evidence strewn about. One glance would tell my dad exactly what I've been up to.

Who I am.

And he won't hesitate to arrest me for vandalism, of that I am certain. The chance to send me away to some reformatory school for delinquent girls would be like a dream come true for him.

If I stop to hide everything, it'll just give him more time to track me here, and if I turn my phone off now it will just lock him onto this location.

All I can do is keep moving and pull the signal along with me and hope he buys my weak excuse.

My phone sounds off every few minutes as my dad continues tracking my progress home. The beep that sounds over the roar of my car engine makes me flinch each time.

When I finally pull into the driveway, the silhouette of him standing with his arms crossed is waiting for me in the middle of the front lawn.

"What were you doing out in those woods?" he demands as soon as I open my car door.

My anger blocks the lie I planned, and instead I shoot back, "Wouldn't you like to know?"

I try pushing past him, but he grabs my arm and stops me.

"Ouch!" I'm overreacting to his grip, but this is the roughest he's ever handled me in my life.

"Give me a break, Rory. You are *not* that delicate."

Kelly starts barking from inside the house.

"So, what're you going to do? Beat the shit out of me here on the front lawn in front of all the neighbors?" I don't need to see Mrs. Delprete looking out her bedroom window to know she's watching us. She's always watching us.

Dad flings my arm back at me. "You know what? If I thought it would do any good, I'd be tempted to try it. But I just don't even know how to reach you anymore, Rory."

I smirk. "Giving up? So easily?"

He points a finger in my face. "I will never give up on you. Not *ever*. Do you understand me? You might think you've shut everyone out, but I know who you are, and this person standing in front of me is not the girl I raised."

My fury hits like a gunshot. "I'm not your little girl anymore!" The words fire out of me. "Do you have *any* idea how fucked up I am? How much I'm like her? Or are you just so happy she's dead you want to forget about Mom *forever*."

Dad looks like he might really hit me. Which would be fantastic. But he just clenches his fist and hisses, "Your mother killed herself as part of some psychotic art installment because she didn't see any value in reality. Or in being married to me. Or in being a mother to you."

"She was an amazing artist!" I'm practically screaming. "You couldn't stand her success and did everything you could to undermine her talent."

"I supported her every step of the way, and you know that. She was depressed, and she refused to go on antidepressants."

"She couldn't create on those drugs. You wanted her to stop being an artist and just be some stupid, boring housewife."

"I *wanted* her to take the medication the doctor prescribed so she wouldn't try to kill herself." He grabs my shoulders hard. "I cared more about *her* than I did about her damn artwork."

"She *was* her art."

"I don't even understand that."

"See, and that's why you could never understand her. You never really knew her and now you don't know me." I lean forward and growl at him. "It's the reason why you and I hate each other."

He grips my shoulders. "I have *never* hated you, Rory." He lets go and actually tries to hug me.

I fight him off. "Just stop it, Dad."

Kelly is going wild inside the house, and Dad's eyes slide to the lights that just flipped on in Mrs. Delprete's upstairs window.

"Come on, Rory. We'll go inside and you'll tell me what you've *really* been up to."

"Why?" I step back and yell, "Is screaming on the front lawn not acceptable behavior for a sergeant's daughter?" I start putting on a big show now, distracting him from asking about where I've been.

He wipes his face with his palm in frustration. "This isn't you."

I egg him on. "You can't say this isn't me, *Sarge*." I raise my voice even higher. "I decide who I am, not you."

The porch light goes on next door, and through clenched teeth, Dad says, "Let's continue this *inside*, Rory."

"You can't lock me up in some tower, you know. I'm not the one who's supposed to be mourning my dead wife. I'm allowed to be young and go out and have fun." I fling my arms out dramatically. "I'm free to *fuck around* with whoever I want."

Oh shit. Did I really just yell that?

In the beam from the Delprete's porch light, I can see that this declaration has finally made Dad's eye start twitching.

With a grunt, he spins around and heads for the front door of our house.

"Everything okay out here?" Mrs. Delprete calls through her screen door.

All the fight drains out of me at the sound of her voice. She's used to dramatic scenes playing out on our front lawn—vulgar performance art—but it's been years since the last show.

And this is the first time I've been cast in the starring role of raving lunatic, instead of my mother.

I'm turning out exactly like her. The thought sends me following Dad into the house.

We're both so angry we slam drawers and doors as we each get ready for bed, and then neither one of us says good night.

Most nights, my dad's snores are deafening, but I'm still awake when the first morning birds start singing, and there hasn't been a sound from his room.

The next thing I know, sunlight is slicing through my

blinds, trying to pry my eyelids open. I must've drifted off for the last few hours of darkness.

Pulling the covers over my head, I roll toward the wall and listen to Dad getting ready for work.

When my door creaks open, I force my breathing to go slow and deep even though my heart is beating in my ears. I even manage to add a slight nose whistle—that little something extra to prove I'm really sleeping peacefully.

Dad quietly closes the door, but I keep pretending I'm asleep until I hear his car leave for work.

CHAPTER TEN

Striding through the woods toward my cabin a few hours later, I text Hayes to come and meet me as soon as he can. It's time to get to work.

The place is trashed from my late-night interruption from flow. I straighten up quickly and get busy reworking the stencil piece I ruined at the end.

In broad daylight, it's harder to push away the sense of impending doom that, even with two people, this project is actually impossible.

I'd hate to attempt this and fail. A half-finished Sparkle-ad-and-lion mash-up looking over the town as my legacy? *No thank you.*

I hear heavy footsteps approaching, and for a moment, I'm afraid my dad has actually traced my location from the original hit he got on my phone last night. I hold my breath.

Two quick knuckle raps make me relax. Dad would've barged right in.

I call, "Come on in, Hayes."

The door swings open, and Hayes strides in with a pack on his back and his hair still wet from his morning shower.

"Good morning," he says, interrupting my brief daydream of picturing him in his morning shower.

"Morning. Glad you could make it." I stand up and the tingles in my legs make me realize I've been working so long they've begun to fall asleep.

"Came as fast as I could." He grins and drops his pack by the door. "Ready for my vandalism lessons."

I give him a wry smile. "Welcome to the dark side."

"It's a colorful side, anyway." His eyes slide over me and land on the spray cans I've lined up in order. A job this big requires meticulous organization.

"Color is the one element you don't need to worry about," I say. "That's my department." I guide him over to the cabin wall that I've prepped with a blue-gray paint, close to the shade of the water tower. "Today's lesson is all about technique."

He raises one eyebrow at me. "I like the sound of that."

"No flirting now. Just painting."

"I love it when you take charge."

I stop and glare at him with my hands on my hips.

He holds up his palms. "I wasn't being flirty. Just…okay, teach me everything I need to know."

I lean over, aiming my back assets seductively in his direction as I pick up a can of spray paint.

He blushes. "Hey, come on now."

I turn around, slapping the can into his right hand. "Keep your mind out of the gutter, Hayes. You've got a lot to learn."

He takes the can from me and switches it to his left hand. With a few strong shakes, he makes the bearings clink loudly, considers the blank wall for just a moment, and then looks me in the eye with a knowing smirk.

My face is a giant question mark because he's clearly hiding something.

He turns and rushes the wall with the can of red paint.

I'm shocked into silence as he works quickly and smoothly. It's obvious this guy has spray-painted graffiti before.

In fact, he's moving like a pro.

I stand, mutely watching as he fills in the letters he's thrown up on my wall, a large, 3-D outline that reads *HMM* with an ellipsis at the end.

When he's finished, he tosses the can into the air, allowing it to whirl around before catching it with one hand. I look back and forth from him to his tag and he shrugs. "Just my initials."

I shove him so hard he has to step back to keep his balance. "I can't *believe* you kept this from me. *How* long have you been doing graffiti?"

He laughs and rubs his shoulder where I hit him. "I'm not a real artist like you or anything. I'd just mess around sometimes, go out tagging with my friends in Brooklyn. It's the other reason why I was so drawn to your lions."

I cross my arms and consider his design. "Hmm…" I read. "What's your full name?"

157

"Hayes Michael Mcallaster." He looks uncomfortable when he asks, "What's yours?"

"Rory Capers. No middle name." I'm still studying his initials. "Do you do any effects?"

He picks up a can of gray and goes to work. As he paints, he tells me a story about him and his friends getting chased by a gang one night and almost getting caught.

"We didn't realize we'd shown disrespect by painting over this one guy's tag," he says as he switches spray cans. "Let me tell you, things got *real*. We thought we were so tough going out, painting our graffiti, but that was the night we realized we were actually just a group of soft rich kids from the suburbs who had no business wandering outside our neighborhood after dark. I never ran so fast in my life."

He steps back to show off the letters, which now look like they've been cast in cement with cracks running through them. One corner of the letter *H* looks like it's crumbling into rubble.

He's just brought an urban edge to my little cabin here in the woods. Moving closer, I inspect his work. "This isn't bad. I can give you a few pointers, but actually, I need to see what angle you used for this." I point to a section of the rock crumble.

With a smile, he shows me, and for the next few hours, the two of us take turns working on the big wall, teaching each other spray techniques and effects.

Hayes is a natural with a spray can, and he picks up new tricks quickly.

He even shows me how to use a razor blade to create a cap stencil, which is way more of a turn-on than that may sound.

Each time our hands touch, a current of attraction runs so strong I'm surprised it doesn't manifest in an actual glowing spark between us.

For the rest of the morning, we have some serious sitcom-worthy, will-they-or-won't-they, romantic tension happening between us.

I prime over our practice area with a layer of white and say, "Go ahead. Forget the initials and the spray techniques. Let me see you paint something original. Anything you'd like."

He looks at the blank wall in front of him, tilting his head from side to side, considering. This moment of watching him draws out long, and the anticipation inside me builds. But there is no way I'm ever making the first move with Hayes again.

On impulse, I grab the closest paint marker, and with a few quick flicks, I draw a purple doodle of a cup of coffee on his bicep. He laughs as I add a goofy face smiling over the rim of the cup. I pick up a can of silver spray paint and quickly complete the piece with a small swirl of steam flowing up his shoulder.

"Thought you could use a little caffeine boost," I say.

"Thanks." He holds up his arm to consider my work. "It's perfect."

Turning his attention back to the wall, he runs the fingers of his right hand along the surface. Nodding to himself, he begins.

Keeping the nozzle close to the wall so his lines are ultra thin, he moves the can fast and smooth. His broad strokes begin to connect, forming the image of a detailed cartoon lion wearing a gangster-looking suit. I laugh as he adds a top hat and a red rose in the lion's lapel. Finally, he gives his lion a spiffy cane and labels his drawing across the top: "A Dandy Lion."

"Okay, so that's adorable. And not bad for your first freestyle lion." I point to a few drips running down from the red flower in the giant cat's lapel. "But it looks like someone shot him. You want to be sure to check the pressure anytime you switch cans."

Hayes laughs. "Yeah, I should've realized the pressure was way too high."

I look at him, and his eyes shift to serious for a beat. It's as if we can read each other's minds in that instant. *Of course he feels this too.*

I break the tension by looking back at the wall. "So, the more we practice, the more precise we'll be up there on the tower, and the faster we'll finish."

"I want to be ready, Ro, but can we maybe take a little break? We've been at this for hours and I could use an *actual* caffeine hit."

I sigh. "Fine. We should eat something too. I have protein bars around here somewhere. Want one?" I move toward the bin that holds my emergency provisions in small, airtight containers. "Most all of them involve some form of peanuts or peanut butter, so I hope you're not allergic."

"That's okay. I actually brought a little lunch for the both of us."

I've wrenched the lid off one of the bins, and I'm holding a shoebox container filled with prepackaged bars out toward him.

He pulls a largish cooler bag from his backpack and pats it invitingly.

"I'm good with a bar," I say. "But thanks anyway."

Fishing one of the whey protein bars out of my box, I rip the foil wrapper open with my teeth and shove the container back inside the plastic bin it came from.

When I turn around, Hayes is stepping out of the cabin's door with the cooler bag in his hand and a tablecloth folded under his arm.

I follow him outside as I bite into my bar. The texture inspires me to check the expiration date printed on the wrapper.

Hayes glances back at me as he spreads the small tablecloth on a nearby rock and I resist the urge to spit the dry bite of protein bar out onto the ground. Instead, I swallow the crumbly mass and head back inside for my water bottle.

I stop when Hayes asks, "Can I interest you in a refreshing beverage?"

"Did you bring water?"

"I have *infused* water."

I squint at him. "Infused with what? Anything fun?"

He smiles. "Just cucumber. But I also made you an iced coffee, if you like."

I feel my face light up. "Gimme."

Perching on a nearby log, I hug my cold tumbler of deliciousness as I watch Hayes unpack baggies filled with sandwiches, pita chips, two apples, and a plastic container of strawberries.

"You're really going to eat all that?" I'm suddenly ravenous.

He gestures to the opposite side of the rock. "I told you, this is for both of us. Come sit."

I move closer as he holds out a wrapped sandwich. "Thanks, but I'm a little fussy. I can't stand mustard or pickles or—"

"Good ole PB&J." He smiles as he shakes the sandwich enticingly.

I take the bait. "My favorite. Thanks."

"That does not surprise me."

"What kind are you having?"

He holds it up. "It's called a Cubano. Roast pork, ham, and Swiss, with extra mustard and pickles all toasted on a panini press."

I aim my nose in the air and make a face that makes him laugh.

We unwrap our sandwiches and bite into them. The bread on mine is whole wheat but the soft kind, which I consider one of the most important features of a proper PB&J. I take a sip from my tumbler.

I say, "You need to teach me how to make amazing coffee like this before you go back home to Lawng Eyeland."

"Trying to get rid of me already?" He raises an eyebrow.

"No, it's just…" How do I say this without making it sound like I'm only lowering my guard and letting him into my life because he's leaving at the end of the summer? "You eventually do need to go home, right?"

He takes a swig from a glass bottle with cucumber wedges floating at the bottom. "I don't know. There's a chance I might decide to stay here."

I shove the rest of my PB&J half into my mouth to hide my expression. "You graduated already?" The question is muffled by sandwich.

"One year to go. I can finish up here at New Paltz High School."

"Ugh. That sadistic hellhole."

"The place can't be *that* terrible."

Actually, school wasn't so bad before everyone turned phony over my mom dying and I had to go full-on antisocial, but I'm not telling Hayes this. I shrug. "I'm sure you'd do just fine—jump into sports, join a bunch of clubs, and make heaps of friends."

"Will *you* be my friend?" He bats his eyes at me playfully.

I shake my head. "Nope. I don't do friendship."

"Of course you do." He gestures to the picnic lunch in front of us. "You're doing it right now."

"This is… I don't know what this is, but it's temporary."

"*Unless* I stay here."

"Did you really leave that big of a mess for yourself back home?"

"No. But I did leave a lot of unhealthy 'brother' bonds based on episodes of binge drinking that I'm better off letting go of. Even going out to run around and paint graffiti usually meant getting bombed first, which was just stupid and the reason we got into trouble with that gang."

"You'd get bombed to go bomb?" I joke.

His expression stays serious. "There's no good reason to risk my sobriety when I'm going to college in another year anyway."

"So you're being real right now? You might actually move here?" My spark of happiness at this thought disturbs me, and I stamp it out like an old campfire.

"Well, if I do, will you be my friend?"

"Let's not get carried away defining things, okay?"

He laughs. "Okay. We'll just go with the clichéd 'it's complicated,' and leave it at that."

"That's exactly what I was trying to explain to my friend Kat the other day—oh shit. *Kat.*"

I grab my phone and hit the little icon with her face on it. Including Kat, there are only three Favorites on my phone, and one of those is Dad, who I'm not speaking to. The third one is Hayes, you know, for convenience, but he doesn't need to know this.

Kat picks up on the first ring. "Hey, girl, talk to me."

"Did today's shipment come in yet?" Hayes is watching my face as I try to keep my voice calm and casual.

"What?"

"Um, the supply shipment? I forgot it was being delivered today, and I need you to do me a favor."

"The supplies came in, sure. Ken's in the back unpacking the boxes right now. Of course, he's *taking his time*—"

"Listen to me, Kat. I put in a special order." I stand up and start pacing. "I have the cash all set to make the purchase when I come in, but nobody can know what's in those extra boxes."

"How am I supposed to stop him? If I volunteer to inventory the shipment myself, you know he'll be suspicious."

"That could... I mean, you can at least... No, you're right. He'll immediately know something's up if you volunteer to do extra work." I wrap one arm over my head. "I am so screwed."

There's a pause, and then Kat says, "Leave it to me, sweets. I've got your back."

"Seriously?"

"Yeah, I have an idea. Which supply company?"

"*OhmyGod*, thank you! There will be a decent-size box that will say it's from Scrap Yard and two big, heavy boxes from Krylon. Are you sure about this?"

"Leave it to me. I'll see you for your shift in a few hours."

"You are a giant cherry lifesaver, Kat. Good luck and I owe you big."

"You have *no idea* how big you are about to owe me, but you'll get me back."

"Yes. I will. I promise to get you back."

I thank her once more before hanging up. She didn't even ask what the supplies were for, but I'm pretty sure she'll guess if she looks up Scrap Yard. It's a graffiti supply store in the city that I once took the Trailways bus to visit by myself. It was smaller than I'd expected, but of course it was packed with pure awesomeness.

Even if Kat doesn't google it or check inside the boxes, I'm pretty sure Krylon is universally known for selling spray paint.

I tell Hayes, "Kat is probably about to figure out my secret identity."

"*No.* I liked being the only one who knew you as Graffiti Girl."

I give a superhero pose, with my fists on my waist and my head held high. "Picture me with a cape," I say as I use one arm to mime a flow of fabric blowing behind me. "Graffiti Girl, to the rescue!"

Hayes says, "To be honest though, I don't think this is such a terrible thing. I've been thinking maybe Graffiti Girl needs to come clean. If you open up to your dad about your lions, it could be the first step to help you two start healing your relationship."

"What? No!" My arms drop to my sides. "Why the hell would I tell my dad? Kat will keep my secret. She's already covering for me with our boss."

"Listen, Rory." He's eating strawberries with a metal fork, which seems a bit formal for a picnic. "I go to a lot of AA meetings at all different times during the day. I get to hear a *lot* of people's stories. Each of us is there because we lost something due to our drinking. Some lost their jobs, some their cars…" He rolls his eyes and raises his hand. "Some lost their whole identities. But the thing that people regret losing the most? The trust of their loved ones. Those relationships are what truly matter, and once they're gone, they'll never be the same again."

The adrenaline from my frenzied call to Kat settles into my nerve endings, and I turn on him. "Are you freaking kidding me? My dad has a secret relationship with some woman, and you think *I'm* the one who needs to risk everything and confess to him about my graffiti?"

Hayes stands to look me in the eye. "The way you acted in that restaurant was wrong, Rory. There's no other way of seeing it. I completely understand *why* you flipped out, but you're the one who should be apologizing."

"This isn't any of your business."

"It is because I care about you. If your dad finds out what you've been up to, it will change things between you two forever."

"Good! I want things changed. You have no idea what it's been like, living under his thumb all this time."

"I get that you feel like he's trying to control you, but he can't be all bad."

I can feel the pressure building as Hayes continues to undermine my frustration. "I've always *hated* my dad." Even as I say it, I can feel it isn't the truth, but I double down on my lie. "I can't *wait* to never see him again."

"You don't mean that."

"Says the guy who wants to move ninety miles north of

all his problems. Are you seriously going to lecture me, Mr. *It's Complicated*? I'll bet that could describe all your relationships, huh?"

"Rory, come on. You know I want us to be together. I just need to finish my step work."

"Oh. My. God!" I try to control my volume because I'm afraid someone will hear us from three miles away if I release my full rage.

First, he completely disregards how impossible my dad is, and now he assumes I'm just pining away for some big, fat, fairy-tale happy ending with him.

"You think you're some sort of prince who rode in on his rainbow-shitting unicorn to rescue me? I do *not* want a relationship with you, Hayes. I wanted a simple hookup and then you got all in my business and now you won't stop trying to get into my head."

"Rory, wait, I didn't—"

But my wild lions are roaring and they refuse to be tamed. I practically shout, "I'm in control here, and I say *this* is no longer complicated or complex. This is very simple. *Good-bye.*"

I storm back into the cabin, and as soon as I see the wall Hayes and I have been working on together, I collapse in tears. I don't even know what just happened. His "dandy lion" stands there, mocking me politely.

There's a knock at the door. "Rory, you okay?"

I try to make my voice sound as normal as possible. "Go away."

"Rory? I'm coming in."

My sobs are getting worse, and I can't pull myself together enough to respond. My feelings are rising up faster than I can shove them down, like some game of emotional whack-a-mole.

Dad has a girlfriend. *Whack.*

Hayes is taking Dad's side. *Whack.*

Kat is taking risks for me that could wreck our friendship. *Whack.*

My mom is gone. My mom is gone. My mom is gone. *Whack-whack-whack.*

The door starts to swing open, and I slide backward so I'm blocking it. "Go away, Hayes. Go back to Long Island or wherever you want. I don't care. Just leave me alone."

"Rory, I can hear you crying in there. You can't expect me to—"

I stand up and grab his backpack, quickly swing the door open, and fling it directly at his head. I close the door before I can see whether or not I hit him. "Go. Away."

Too much caffeine is obviously bad for me anyway.

CHAPTER ELEVEN

Anger has eclipsed whatever motivated that tearful outburst moment, and I get busy organizing my cans. It's too bad I can't quite picture Kat up there on top of the water tower with me because I feel certain she would never betray my trust.

Or suggest my asshole father is somehow right about keeping his girlfriend a secret from me.

Dad texted me earlier to ask if we can please talk. When I didn't respond, he said he's putting away the laptop with Mom's videos. He thinks taking a break from listening to her will help my healing process.

It's a good thing I've already copied them onto a jump drive that I keep in the back of my top drawer, right near all Mom's jewelry.

I can envision the exhibit she described in her suicide note: Monitors lined up in a row with her videos playing in a loop. Photographs of the crime scene blown up and arranged on the ground for visitors to either walk over or around as they choose. It would be a powerful installation.

Mom had no way of knowing I'd wreck her suicide scene before it got captured on film.

When I open the door and step out of my cabin an hour later to head to my shift at Danny's, I'm surprised to find Hayes still sitting there on that giant rock. His backpack rests neatly at his feet while he reads a book. The same pose I saw him in the first day we met.

"Are you kidding me?"

"I couldn't just leave you when you were that upset, Rory." He nods toward the cabin. "Sounds like you took out some of your anger on those cans."

I think of how I've been slamming things around. I hadn't realized he was still out here listening. Most people leave after you scream at them to go away and fling their stuff in their faces.

I push past him and head toward my car. "Well, I didn't off myself, if that's what you were worried about. You're free to go now."

"I wasn't worried about that. I just… Come on, Ro. I want to help."

Looking him up and down, I give a small laugh. "You found out how screwed up I am and how messy things are with my dad, and now you want to fix me. No thank you. Go worry about fixing yourself."

"Listen, I get how life can change in an instant and it can

be scary to realize that everything is already different—all you can do is accept it."

"Yeah, well, accept *this*," I say, flipping him double birdies and walking down the path to my car.

I jump in the driver's seat, and with a crank and a shift, my tires are blowing pine needles while I pull away.

I try not to look in my rearview mirror, but I can't resist one quick glance.

Hayes has followed me to the clearing, and now he slides his pack onto his back with his head hung low as he watches me go.

I notice his stupid bicep with the goofy coffee-cup face, still grinning at me.

A vague sense of self-loathing creeps from my car's air vents. *What the hell is wrong with me?* This guy just spent the whole morning trying to be nice. He even packed a damn fine picnic.

I stop the car and slide it into reverse. Hayes straightens as I slowly back up and pull alongside him. I roll down the passenger-side window and he leans through it.

"Get in," I say. "I'll give you a ride home."

"I don't mind walking, really," he tells me. But he's opening the car door and climbing inside as he says it. He twists to slide his pack onto the backseat and pulls on his seat belt.

We don't talk or play the radio as I drive him to his aunt's A-frame, but when I pull up the driveway and stop the car, he turns to me.

"Listen, I'm sorry I asked you to talk to your dad. I didn't bring it up to upset you. It's just that I can see where things are headed between you two, and I want to try and spare you a lot of heartache."

"Well, go get a hobby. Or better yet, a *job*. I've dealt with my dad my whole life. I don't need your help now."

"From what I see, the two of you are two sides to the same coin. It can be hard to even see each other when you're so much alike."

"I am *nothing* like him. Get out of my car. I need to get to work." I press the button to unbuckle his belt and start shoving him toward the door.

"Easy there." Without standing, he reaches into the backseat to grab his knapsack.

Pulling it onto his lap, he pauses a moment to look at me.

Annoyed, I gesture to the door.

A small smile plays in his eyes, and without provocation, he leans in quickly and gives me a peck on the cheek. Before I can react, he whispers, "I *like* you," and scurries out of the car just as my fist lands on his empty seat.

I shout after him, "If you ever kiss me again, Hayes Michael Mcallaster, you had better *mean* it!"

Of course, I didn't notice the thin woman wearing all black, standing on the side deck and watching us through her bangs. She's obviously Hayes's aunt and *completely* within earshot.

Hayes takes long strides to where she's standing, hangs an arm around her shoulders, and gives me a big, cheesy smile as he waves good-bye. He leans over to whisper something to his aunt, and she smiles and joins him in waving to me as I pull away.

I cannot believe how frustrating, yet occasionally irresistible, one human being can be. The fact that he would even suggest I tell my dad everything just proves Hayes doesn't get me. Or my dad.

All I can hope is that Kat managed to distract Ken from my delivery because, otherwise, there might be a squad car waiting for me at Danny's. And if Dad is the officer on the scene, I can count on getting arrested today.

Because inmates, unlike daughters, can be controlled. And if there's one way I'm even a little bit like my father, it's that we both need to feel in control.

"Hey there, girlie girl," Kat greets me when I walk in.

I rush up to the counter where she's standing. "How did things go?"

She widens her eyes and nods her head toward the novelty section. Her voice is totally fake as she says, "Great. Everything here is just *great*."

I lean back and see Ken on his hands and knees, rooting through a box beside the display. He pulls out a set of blue fairy wings, and after giving them a few test flaps, he hangs them on a hook with the others.

When he catches me watching him, he smiles. "Hey there, Rory. Glad to see you here on time."

I turn to Kat, lean close, and whisper, "What the hell did you do? Get him stoned or something?" Because this is not the way Ken greets any of his employees *ever*. "Why is he acting so nice?"

Kat blushes and looks down at her black fingernails. "No. Nothing. I didn't… I mean, what?" She squints at me.

"Are you okay?" I squint back at her, and she nods but goes right back to examining her fingernails.

"Okay," I say in a fake-slash-loud voice. "Well, I'm just going to go start straightening things up back in the stockroom."

I walk casually past Ken and through the swinging doors to the back room.

As soon as the doors close behind me, I make a mad dash to the tall metal shelves that line two of the stockroom walls and begin rooting for my boxes. I check from back to front, hoping Kat was discreet when she tucked them away.

But I can't find them anywhere.

I'm just starting to panic over the missing boxes when a text comes through from Kat. It says: **Don't worry. Your boxes are secure. Hidden in plain sight.**

What the hell does that mean?

I'm about to write her back and ask when Ken comes strolling through the swinging stockroom door, his button-down shirt so loose it billows behind him.

My phone buzzes, and I glance down to see another text from Kat: **Alert! Ken's coming back there.**

Gee. Thanks, girlfriend.

"Mind if we have a word?" Ken asks as he sits down on a box by the door. He pats the one on the ground beside him. Of course it's much lower than the one he's sitting on.

"What's up?" I don't sit down.

He leans back and crosses his arms, considering a moment, then asks, "Does Kat have any particular interests or hobbies that you know of? Anything specific that comes to mind?"

Oh crap. What the heck did she do to get him away from my order?

My eyes move to the box I just refused to sit on, and they grow wide. The shipping label on top clearly reads SCRAP YARD.

I scramble to cover it with my butt.

Once I'm sitting, I look over and spot the KRYLON logo peeking out from the space between Ken's legs. *Because, of course.*

"Rory?" He's watching me closely. "You okay? You'd better not be stoned right now."

I try to look like I'm insulted by this accusation. "I'd never come to work stoned. Just wondering why all these questions about Kat. Is she in any sort of trouble?"

"Nope." He scratches the side of his nose with one hooked finger. "I'm just working on employee evaluations. Thought it might be good to get a coworker's perspective."

He throws an ankle over a knee and crosses his arms, and I realize the "dress shoes" he's been wearing actually have "Crocs" written across the sole. It kind of wrecks the image I've had of him as an uptight douche bag. Apparently, he's more of a laid-back douche bag.

"Oh, Kat's great," I say. "Just great. I love working with her. Very responsible. *Great* with customers."

"I understand the two of you are friends. I'm trying to get a real sense of her as a person. Do the two of you ever hang out outside of work?"

"Um, nope. But as you know, I do have another job. And she's got her own artwork keeping her busy."

"Tell me about Kat's art." Ken leans forward.

I glance down at the damning KRYLON logo that may as well be a neon light, waiting to bust me. I suddenly wonder if Ken suspects Kat is the one who ordered the graffiti supplies. Which would actually explain all these questions. I have to throw him off the trail.

"She's interested solely in the textile arts," I say. At Ken's confused look, I add, "Like screen printing? She makes these amazing patterns and T-shirts. Haven't you ever noticed the drawings of punked-out cat cartoons on her bags and clothes?"

"The shirts that say 'Crazy Katz' on the back shoulder?" Ken smiles a little. "I had no idea she made those. Did she ever ask Danny about selling her designs here at the store?"

"I don't think so. She sells them online and does a booth over at the fairgrounds for the Arts Festival every year. I helped out last summer and she made a killing." Ken sits, nodding his head for a long while before I finally ask, "Was there anything else? I should really get to work."

"Right. Sorry." He stands up, and I will him to not look at the box he was just sitting on. He takes a step back and I slide my knees over to one side in an attempt to cover the logo with my legs.

He swings back around so quickly I actually flinch.

"Has she ever said anything about me being named store manager?" He looks at me with wide eyes.

"Um…" My mind whirls with all the things Kat has said about his promotion. All of them are pretty terrible.

"No." Ken shakes his head and waves his hands as if erasing the question. "Never mind. I shouldn't have asked that. You two just seem to share a real bond."

I think about this a minute. In the time since my mother died, I've pretty much cut all my old friends out of my life. Kat was the only person who (a) knew about "the tragedy" and yet (b) treated me just the same as ever. Like I was still me.

Ever since I was a little kid, I've been coming to Danny's with my mother. When Kat got a job stacking shelves as a teen, the two of us would talk while Mom shopped for supplies. I avoided the place for months after she died.

When I finally ventured back into the store, I braced myself for the same annoying pity looks and condolences I'd been getting endlessly at school, but Kat was working the counter alone.

After one simple, "You okay?" she accepted my answer of "Yes," and dropped the subject. Showed me some new supplies they'd started carrying and went right back to talking about art as if nothing had changed.

I say to Ken, "Kat is the reason I'm working here. I have

only good things to tell you about her, so if you're looking for some sort of dirt to pin on her, you can just keep on looking." I pause a moment and add, "Or pin it on me."

His brow creases. "I wasn't asking because…" His head drops. "Never mind. It was stupid."

What the hell did Kat do? Ken seems to be studying the boxes I'm trying to hide and I lean over even more to cover as much of the KRYLON label as I can with my elbow.

Between the obvious discomfort emanating from Ken's pores and my bizarro sitting/leaning pose, the awkwardness in the stockroom is thickening fast.

I give him a painful smile. "Welp, lots of work to do today."

"Yes. Good point." He gestures to the set of our strange exchange. "Sorry about all this." He heads for the door but stops and turns back. "Oh, and Kat mentioned you're the one who helped out with that special order you're sitting on there. Mind giving them a call at some point during your shift to follow up?"

"What, these?" I look down at the boxes with false surprise. "Um, yeah, okay, sure. I'll get on it."

Whew.

Kat and I are straightening up behind the counter when Ken finally leaves out the front door. The bell's chime is still ringing when I grab her wrist.

"Thank you so much for covering for me. Did you

hypnotize Ken or something? He totally bought whatever it was you sold him."

Kat looks uncomfortable for a second and continues straightening up with the hand I'm not holding. "Sure, no problem, Rory. Anytime. Glad to do it."

I narrow my eyes at her and release her wrist. "What did you tell him anyway? He seemed fine with the fact that I was handling that big special order on my own."

"Yeah, well, I told him you'd been showing more initiative lately and he seemed really impressed." She still hasn't looked me in the eye.

"Kat." I wait for her to finally look at me. "What is happening right now? Did you...?" She glances down at the counter and blushes. "Oh. My. God. Kat!"

She starts talking very quickly. "It was an accident really it didn't mean anything stop looking at me that way so okay fine I kissed Ken you happy?"

"Wait, what? Did you just say you kissed Ken? Why? Oh my gosh, I'm so sorry. Was distracting him really that hard? You must want to kill me!"

Her face is pink and growing pinker. "It wasn't a big deal, really."

"That's *nuts*. I owe you so big. I had no idea."

"I said it's fine. It wasn't so bad." She has reached maximum facial pinkness.

"Hold on a minute." I'm scrutinizing her and she closes her eyes.

"Yes. I'll admit it. It actually got kind of…hot?" She runs a hand through her freshly dyed magenta hair. "It started off with me just trying to distract him, and well, it sort of went on from there."

I stand unmoving, looking at her with my mouth hanging open. Finally, she reaches under my chin with the tips of her fingers and closes it for me.

I ask, "Are you planning on kissing him again?"

"*God* no. I mean. I don't know. Like I said, it got pretty hot. He's obviously inexperienced, but *wow* did he get onboard quick. Like he'd been thinking about it all along or something. Anyway, *no*. That was a one-time favor, and now you owe me one."

"I'll do anything, really."

"I will be holding you to that. But also, enough with *you* interrogating *me*. What the *h-e*-double toothpicks are you planning to do with all those fucking supplies? Do you really think I don't recognize the materials for making graffiti art, *Rory*?"

I wanted to keep the number of people who knew my secret to an absolute minimum. But Kat just made a huge and arguably disgusting sacrifice for my sake. She deserves to be let in on the truth.

I look around, checking that the store is completely empty.

"Okay, so you know those graffiti lions that have been showing up over the past year?" I take a deep breath. "Well—"

"OhmyGod, you're the artist!" Kat finishes my sentence for me.

I nod slowly, bracing myself.

"I should've *guessed*. Holy cow, it's so obviously your *style*. Those lions are badass! And how did I miss the whole Rory connection? And the timing on when they started showing up…"

She's clearly a fan of me defacing public property.

She wants to know why I ordered all the extra paint and when I describe the water tower project to her, she *freaks*. The news that I'm planning to turn the eyesore of a corporate soda ad into a bold work of art gets her grinning from triple-pierced ear to quadruple-pierced ear.

"I want in," she announces. "You can't do it yourself."

"Hayes is already helping me. Well, I mean he *was*, anyway."

"Did the two of you finally hook up?"

"Not exactly. There's a definite attraction, but things are still really…weird and complex. He pissed me off today, and I don't think he can handle getting in trouble, but I could really use his help."

"Hmmm."

"What? Don't look at me like that."

"Oh, nothing. Just that I agree you need that boy, but for more than holding your purse up there while you paint that water tower."

"I don't carry a purse."

"I know. I'm just… Fine, I'm saying you need him for more than just holding your *ladder* then."

"The tower has a bunch of built-in pegs that I can climb. I don't need anybody really."

"Yeah, except you're wrong. We *all* need someone." She

drops a hand on my shoulder and forces me to look at her. "Rory, you and I have known each other for a long time. There are things the two of us don't talk about, and that's the way this friendship works."

"I really need to get those boxes loaded into my car."

"We've never discussed the ways that shitty thing with your mom changed you, but here is something you need to hear." I roll my eyes from the ceiling to her as she squeezes both of my shoulders. "You've been different this past little while, since you started hanging out with Hayes. I'm not going to get all sappy and talk about a light that went out of your eyes a year and a half ago, but I do feel the need to point out that you're finally laughing more. When you walk into the store, I don't get that heart-clench feeling of sadness for you as much."

I just look at her for a long time. Kat doesn't talk this way ever. It's one of the reasons we're friends. "You've been secretly pitying me all this time?"

"No." She gives me a small shove. "Not pity. *Empathy.* That was a fucked-up thing that happened to you, and I am capable of empathy, you know."

"I didn't realize our whole friendship was based on you feeling sorry for me over losing my mom."

"Nice try. You know that's total bullshit. Now, I've said my piece. Give Hayes another chance. Let's go get those boxes."

She helps me move them into my car and rings me up, insisting that she honor my employee discount. I hand her the rolls of cash I've saved up lifeguarding, and she still has to chip in twelve dollars from her own colorful Blue Q bag.

"Thanks," I say. "Tax was more than I realized. I'll pay you back."

"My contribution to the anti-advertisement arts. Way to reclaim our public space." There's a pause, and I wonder if she's about to pressure me more about Hayes. "So, this water tower project," she says. "You have a date in the calendar yet?"

I tell her I've been watching the sunsets get earlier every night, and once they hit around seven o'clock, it should give me enough time. Then, I need to get as close as possible to a half moon to balance light for working with darkness for hiding.

"I should be good to go within a couple weeks," I say.

"Okay, now show me what you've got planned."

With a grin, I pull a fresh sheet of paper from the open ream underneath the counter and start sketching a rough image of the ad I'll be covering up. Next, I sketch the lines that will transform the ad into my lion, and Kat is practically salivating over my makeover plans.

She points out a way I can use one of the existing curves of the ad to save some time, and the two of us get so absorbed, I actually give a jump-squeal when the bell rings over the front door.

I laugh at myself as I thrust the page we've been working on underneath the counter.

"What are you two up to?" The familiar voice is gruff, and when I hear it, I give another jump-squeal and want to throw up.

In her most innocent voice, Kat says, "We're not up to a single thing, Officer. Just planning signs for Danny's big end-of-summer sale coming up. Is there anything I can help you find today?"

I'd probably laugh at her fake enthusiasm if I didn't feel so sick. "Relax, Kat. This is my dad."

"Oh, wow. Good to meet you, Mr...er, Officer...oh, wait I mean, *Sergeant*. Sergeant Capers it must be." Kat scurries around from behind the counter to grab my dad's hand. She pumps it up and down with both of hers. "Let me tell you, Rory is a *wonderful* employee. You must be very proud."

"It's okay, Kat." I glare at my dad as he gives my one true friend a once-over. "He's just here to hand me my ass."

Dad growls, "What is that supposed to mean, Rory?"

"It means whatever you think it means, Dad."

He asks Kat if he can talk to me alone, and after looking back and forth between us a few times, she nods toward the stockroom. "You're due for a break anyway," she says, which isn't true, but whatever. There are reasons she's not the manager.

Leading my dad into the back room, I'm grateful that we moved the boxes of spray cans to my car already. My dad is a much better detective than Ken will ever be.

"We haven't had a chance to talk," Dad says, "but I wanted to apologize to you."

I cross my arms and wait for the punch line as we stand facing each other. We both watch my toe dig into the cement stockroom floor for a long moment as the smell of dusty cardboard closes in around us.

Finally, Dad says, "I should've been more honest with you about Linda. I guess I was just feeling lonely, and it was nice having someone to talk to." He stands there watching me like I'm supposed to absolve him or something.

I uncross my arms. "I'm pretty sure you know where you can stick your shitty apology."

"This is *not* a shitty apology." He smiles. "This is actually a not-half-bad apology." Dad is trying to joke me out of being mad at him.

It's not going to work. I know I acted like a jerk in the restaurant and when I lost it on the front lawn, but I'm not ready to just pretend Dad didn't hurt me when he moved on with his life and shut me out of it.

I say, "Listen, I've got a lot of stuff to do here before my shift ends, so if you're about finished…" I gesture toward the door.

"Rory, we need to talk about this. I need to know what you've been up to. Things are getting worse, not better. *You're* getting worse."

"Maybe if you let me spend some time back in the art studio—"

Dad cuts me off. "You know why I can't do that. Not yet anyway. You need to learn that art will never love you back."

"Says the man who is incapable of showing love at all," I say with a grunt.

"That's not fair." Dad crosses his arms. "Rory, we need to find a way of moving forward. Of being a *family*."

"We are *not* a family anymore."

"It's been just you and me for a long time, kiddo. Now we can stop pretending is all. You've been watching your mom's videos on the laptop in the kitchen, but your mother hardly ever went into that kitchen. She had no idea how to mother you. Most of that footage is bullshit and you know it."

"You're just trying to control me and ruin my memories of her."

"I loved your mother, Rory, but I remember the bad parts too. Trying to take her insane advice isn't going to help you heal."

"No, but it will help me become an artist like her."

Dad covers both eyes with one palm. "Her obsession with being an artist drove her crazy."

"How do you know art wasn't the one thing that was keeping her sane?" I turn toward the metal shelving and angrily place both palms against a large box. With a grunt, I slide it farther back on its shelf. I continue shifting boxes around as Dad silently watches me.

My thoughts rock violently back and forth as I work. *Mom went crazy. I'm just like her, so I'm probably going crazy too. Is this what crazy feels like? Does wondering if you're crazy mean you can't be? Or that you already are?*

Finally, Dad asks if I need any help. It's unclear if he means help with the boxes right now or if he means some form of help in the greater sense.

I don't know how to answer, so I ignore his question, and he goes back to watching me in silence.

After it grows obvious I'm just moving the boxes back and forth with no purpose, Dad gives a deep sigh. He tells me he has a late shift but he'll see me at home after.

I'm careful to keep my back to him as he leaves, so he can't see the tears that have sprung in my eyes.

It must be the stupid dust I stirred up from moving all these damn boxes.

CHAPTER TWELVE

"Are you sure this is safe?"

Hayes and I are standing at the top of a cliff, looking down at a wide pool of water forty feet below.

"I texted you promising a true New Paltzian adventure." The sunshine warms my belly as I reach up to retie my bikini top. "This is what you've been begging me for. You coming or not?"

I run a finger seductively across the manscaped hair on his bare chest and his lips form a crooked smirk. "You really are trouble, aren't you?" His eyes sparkle in a way that implies he likes the sort of trouble I am.

Without pausing, I turn and step over the edge. My hair lifts gently from my face, and my arms hang delicately in the air over my head as I drop. The water neatly envelops me in its murky coolness, and I keep my arrow form until I hit the bottom. Coiled in a crouch on the deep, slick rocks, I smile at Hayes's muffled shouting from far above.

I'm waiting. Waiting. Waiting…

He's silent for a moment before the water suddenly rumbles directly overhead. He's leapt after me, invading my underwater lair, and I push off the bottom—springing upward. The water presses roughly against my shoulder as I rise and he sinks, blowing past each other by less than a foot.

A short breath after I burst out of the water, he surfaces beside me and I shove his chest. "Are you trying to kill me?"

He splashes me back, hard. "Are you trying to scare the shit out of me? I thought the drop was too much and you were drowning. Why would you stay under the water so long?"

I blink at him. "You thought the fall was too much, so you jumped in after me?"

He's breathing heavy. "It wasn't a decision. It was an impulse."

Treading water, we watch each other as our breath gradually slows to normal. When it does, Hayes turns and swims away from me.

His arms flex as he pulls himself out of the water, and he shakes his hair like a dog. My adrenaline is pumping, and I want to wrap myself around him right now, but he's somber when he turns back to me.

I pull myself from the water after him and recline on a rock that's been warming in the sunshine.

I'm killing it in this bikini with my cleavage and strong legs, but he doesn't look at me as he asks, "Remember when I told you about hitting that dog while driving home in a blackout?"

"Yeah, you said there was blood on your car and it freaked you out. It's the reason you're taking a break from drinking."

He closes his eyes. "I'm not just taking a break, Rory. I am an alcoholic and I can never drink again." He rubs the water off his face with both hands and mumbles, "One day at a time. With God's grace."

"Sorry. I didn't mean—"

"I lied to you, okay?" He looks directly at me now. "I didn't want you to judge me before you got to know me."

I gesture to the air around us. "Hey, this is a zero-judgment zone."

Hayes watches his hands as they massage each other. "It wasn't a dog that I hit. It was a man."

Holy shit. I keep my reaction tucked tight in my chest, but it isn't easy. I don't know what to say, and the silence draws out awkwardly. It feels as if I should know what to say, but *damn*, what do you say to something like that?

Hayes murdered someone with his car?

Finally he breaks the silence. "There was a whole investigation. I wasn't supposed to be driving because of my first DWI, but they had no way of knowing I'd been drinking that second night. I'd left the scene while I was in the blackout. And then I got really lucky. It wasn't technically a crime."

"H-how did…?" The image of a team of high-priced lawyers marches through my mind, and I imagine my dad complaining about rich criminals paying to get away with murder.

I remind myself about the "zero-judgment zone" and nod for Hayes to go on.

"The autopsy showed that the guy had a .32 blood alcohol level, and the blunt-force trauma from getting hit by my car happened postmortem. He technically died of alcohol poisoning while he was passed out on the road."

"Wow" is all I can say.

"Yeah."

He kicks the yellow dirt with his bare toes before stepping onto the rock I'm sitting on. He stands over me and says, "An hour sooner and I'd probably be in jail for vehicular manslaughter right now, no matter how much money my family has." He openly takes in my bikini a moment before crouching down beside me. "Rory, I am trying not to act impulsively anymore. I'm *trying* to think of consequences." He traces my wet cheek with his thumb. "Being around you is making this so much harder."

I don't move, but I instinctively lick my lips.

He leans closer and hovers for a moment. My whole body is humming with anticipation.

Finally, he dips his head forward, whispers in my ear, "You are too dangerous," and springs up to make a running dive into the deep water.

The splash hits me with a light spray, and I lie back on the warm rock, stunned.

"I'm sorry," Hayes calls from the center of the pool of water. "I just can't. I need to work through these steps and focus on my sobriety. It's the only shot I've got."

I roll onto my stomach and watch him treading water. At least Hayes makes a little more sense now. Thinking for days that he'd killed a man must've really messed with his head. No wonder he ended up feeling so drawn to me.

I ask, "So the guy was just lying there, dead in the street?"

"His wife had kicked him out of the house. His life was a complete mess. It was like a snapshot of what I could turn into after many more years of heavy drinking. I feel so sorry for the guy on one hand but am grateful to him too."

I sit up, brushing the wet dirt from my stomach. I have the fleeting thought that it should be Hayes's hands on my bare body right now.

Moving to the edge of the rock, I drop my feet into the cool pool. Cupping my fingers, I draw handfuls of water and dump them onto my chest to clean the mud.

When I look up, I realize Hayes is watching me with open longing. "You are killing me, Rory. Really killing me."

I lean back on my arms. "You know, I don't mind messing around a little bit on this hot August afternoon. No strings attached."

He slowly sinks underwater and releases a big cloud of bubbles. When he resurfaces, he's smiling. "I'll just stay here in the nice, cold water, thanks."

"Fine, I'll join you." I slide into the murky coolness and we swim toward each other. "But I'm keeping my distance," I say. "If staying platonic is helping you cope, I'm good with that."

"Thank you," he says and assumes a brooding expression.

After a few minutes of silently floating on opposite sides of the swimming hole, he adds, "You know, I don't usually tell that story, and when I do, I absolutely stick with the dog version."

"Well, I appreciate you opening up to me."

He nods, but I don't feel like he understands just how much I appreciate his trust. I want him to know how much his brutal honesty means to me.

I blurt out, "I lost my virginity in a stranger's car the day after we buried my mom." My mind spins back to the feeling as I left my body and endured the sweaty encounter.

The guy was older and had expertly produced a condom and taken charge. I was in my numb bubble of shock and grief and was desperate to feel anything. What I did finally feel amid muffled grunting and clumsy groping was a sharp, stabbing pain in my lady parts and a flow of blood to rival my heaviest period to date. The guy freaked out over my flair for bleeding all over the passenger seat of his car, and I resolved to forget the encounter ever happened.

I rewrote everything. I did not lose my virginity to some creep in his car. I was never a virgin at all.

And yet, here I am, treading water in a swimming hole in the middle of the woods as I reveal the whole truth to Hayes.

"I'm so sorry that happened to you," he says. After a pause, he asks if it was consensual.

I nod but can't help thinking of the time that it wasn't. The next time.

"So, what happened? Did you ever see the guy again?"

I swim away from him, deciding how I'm going to respond to that. Finally, I say, "Unfortunately, yes." I glare at him. "I can feel you judging me right now."

"Hey, zero-judgment zone. You're the one who called it."

I look up to the trees. "He was sorry for his reaction. And it was a *really* nice car."

"So you kept on seeing him?"

"We went out again." I cringe at the memory, but then remember that Hayes has just shared that he hit someone with his car. I can trust him with this. The words rush out of me. "But when we started making out, I changed my mind midway and told him I wanted to stop."

Hayes is just watching me. Waiting for me to go on.

"He...laughed," I say. "At the time I didn't feel like I really had the right to stop him that late in the game. So I pretended to fall asleep. I figured that would get my point across, but he just kept on going. Eventually I opened my eyes and lay there, rigid, while he...finished."

I plunge my head underwater like my confession needs a baptism of some sort.

When I come back up, Hayes looks away and says, "What an epic asshole."

"I tried to tell myself it was no big deal," I say, "but I hate that he thought that was okay."

Hayes turns his eyes to me. "That was *not* okay."

I dip my chin underwater. "We were both high. Shit happens. Not always for a reason."

"What did you do?" he asks.

I think about all the times I dreamed of getting revenge on the guy. "I didn't really do anything. Just left and never saw him again. I know it isn't right, but it's not like I could let my dad know what happened. My mom's death had put us all in shock."

The rage and regret wash over me afresh, and I try to hush the lions back down, but they're awake now and can't be easily lulled back to sleep. This is why I've kept this tucked away. Now they want to hunt.

Hayes has a look in his eyes I've never seen before. I recognize for a moment the lion inside him, and it's vaguely thrilling. He asks, "Do you know where this guy lives?"

"It's over. I've let it go."

Hayes moves closer and looks directly into my face. "You did not deserve to have that happen. I wish you could see yourself more clearly." Frustrated, he tells me, "You are a precious daughter of Eve."

"Daughter of Eve?"

"It's from the Narnia books. I thought you said you saw the movie."

"It was a long time ago, but that sounds familiar." I swim to the side and pull myself out of the pool. Avoiding eye contact, I squeeze the extra water out of my dreadlocks and lie back.

Hayes follows me out onto the rock and stands with his hands on his hips, dripping all over me.

"Do you mind, *son of Adam*?" I ask, acting more annoyed than I am.

"Why? Am I dripping my boy cooties all over you?" He gives a juvenile grin as he moves to sit next to me.

I sit up and stare at him, and his grin turns to a look of horror.

"Holy shit, I'm sorry." He covers his face with both hands. "I wasn't even thinking…and here you just told me about getting—"

"Don't say it." I put my hand on his arm, but he continues covering his face with his hands. "I'm fine. Really. And I've always used protection, so I have almost no fear of boy cooties."

"Good." He moves his hands from his face, and as we look at each other, he gets an impish sparkle in his eyes. "Then take this!" He shakes himself off like a dog, making me squeal as I try covering myself in defense.

"What are you? In middle school?" I ask, wiping his invisible boy cooties off my arms.

"No, but actually, the book I'm working on is for kids that age."

I've known plenty of people who talk about writing books who never get around to doing the actual work of writing books.

Even my dad has always talked about his idea for a murder mystery based on a local historic case. My mom loved the thought of him getting published, and he would sit and tinker on his laptop sometimes. But I think he did it more for her than for himself. He hasn't written at all since she died.

"Anyone can say that they're writing a book," I tell Hayes. "I'm impressed by people who actually finish them."

"That's cool. I look forward to impressing you."

"Yeah, I'm not easily impressed."

"Oh, really?" He raises an eyebrow in a flirty way, and I reach back into the water and use my cupped hand to splash him.

"Yes, really," I say. "Come on. Now that you realize we're not jumping to certain death, let's give it another go."

It's a long, steep hike back up, around the backside of the cliff, but as we climb higher, the two of us begin speeding up more and more. Within moments, we're engaged in an undeclared race to the top.

I grab his forearm and pull back hard as he laughs. With a burst of speed, he blows by me, braking when he reaches the top. He steps up to the edge, allowing his toes to poke out into bare air as he waits for me to catch up.

When I reach him, he leans forward, winding his arms as if he's losing his balance. I can tell he's joking, but I stretch out and wrap both hands around his bicep, dragging him backward, away from the edge.

"Pay attention," I tell him. "The jump is safe but not *entirely* safe." I point to the rocks jutting around the edges of the water.

He peers down and his face turns somber. "*Shit.* See that? Being around you is seriously bad for my impulse control."

"That's not fair. *I'm* the one who told you to watch out."

He looks at me. "I was still showing off, trying to impress you."

I squint at him. "You do know that telling someone you're trying to impress them sort of negates the effort, right?"

He runs a hand through his hair, peering down at the water below. "I was clowning around. Wasn't even thinking." He looks at my hand, which is still holding on to his bicep, then looks back up at me.

He jerks his arm forward, pulling me along with it, and neatly catches me around the waist. He pauses only a moment before his lips are on mine.

The perfect balance of pressure and softness combine to make my head light and my body heavy.

Someplace in the back of my mind, I remind myself that Hayes and I falling for each other is something that should be avoided, but his excellent kissing is not helping me remember why right now.

We pull apart, look at each other, and then both dive back in for more kissing.

I rise up on my tiptoes, so I'm his height, and he picks me up, so I'm even higher above him. Leaning down to kiss his upturned face, I feel a vibration run through me and realize he's humming. His hum morphs into an openmouthed groan, and I smile against his parted lips.

"Oh, so you like that?"

"Not bad." I look down at him and think, *I like you.* Which terrifies me more than jumping off the cliff.

I wiggle free and move back to the edge. "Come on," I say, and he moves in beside me. "It's safe if we jump together."

"You know I can't full-on metaphorically *jump* jump with you until I finish my ninth step, right?"

"Well, what the hell are you waiting for, then?"

He reaches over and takes my hand. "I've been asking myself the same thing."

"The least you can do is *literally* jump with me."

"Just not figuratively," he laughs.

"Counting down from step nine, then."

We smile at each other and together count off, "Nine… eight…seven…"

We're still holding hands when we call out, "One!" and I step over the edge a split-moment before him.

Flying through space and time, we don't let go until we're blasted by the cool water below.

CHAPTER THIRTEEN

Driving home, I ask Hayes, "You free later?" It's time to admit I like hanging out with him. I'm even driving along the scenic route that I almost never take back from the cliff dive just so we can be together longer.

"Actually, I'm starting my first shift at Starbucks at four o'clock today." He grins at me as if this is great news.

I growl. "You *would* embrace the one big corporation that the town sold out to." Kat and I have many strong feelings about the superiority of the independent local businesses of New Paltz.

He shrugs. "I really like their coffee, and the Mud Puddle wasn't hiring. I can't spend all my time stalking you, sorry."

I sigh. "How about tomorrow, then?"

"I still have a lot of recovery work to do." He rubs his hand back and forth over the top of his head, ruffling his damp hair. "And I know you want to move forward with the water tower thing, but I'm seriously torn, Ro. The thought of disappointing my parents again if we get caught is really too much. It would devastate them."

"Hey, no pressure on the tower," I say and am surprised to realize that I actually mean it. "We can just hang out."

He grins at me. "So, what you're telling me is that I've finally officially won you over?"

I blush and feel like I'm sailing over the edge of that cliff again. "Something like that," I say, and then I freeze because I've just now realized what road we're on.

We reach a dramatic curve, and I slow down and abruptly turn down a side street on impulse.

The lions are thrilled.

"Where are we going?" Hayes asks, his voice thick with suspicion.

"You'll see." After passing a few culs-de-sac, we come to a row of small, two-family homes. I say, "Remember that guy who wouldn't...stop when I told him to?"

"Yes." Hayes sits up, grabbing the dashboard and looking out the window.

"I don't remember much about him." I point to a weathered brick duplex at the end of the row. "Except that his nickname is Turp, and he lives right there."

"And now you're finally ready to do something?" I see the flicker of rage reignite in his eyes.

I shrug. "I was thinking about what you said. I know I didn't deserve that. Maybe a little payback will give me some closure."

Looking up to the second-story windows of Turp's

bedroom, I can practically smell the wave of turpentine that permeated his bedsheets. He was incredibly arrogant for a guy who reeked of brush cleaner.

He was supertalented, but he had zero interest in studying art history or working on craft exercises. He seemed to believe he could become truly great based solely on his natural painting abilities. Like everything he churned out was genius, including the shits he took.

Plus, he thought the sniveling masses were too ignorant to appreciate high art. His snobbishness was off-putting, but I was blinded by his talent. Particularly the large, red painting hanging over his bed.

In it, Turp had created a perfect juxtaposition of color and light, and the thing was honestly close to brilliant.

We were already mostly naked when I realized that hooking up with Turp again felt all wrong. I thought having sex with him a second time would validate the first time, make it not a mistake. But it was a mistake. And doing it again was just going to mean two mistakes. Suddenly, I'd wanted to leave.

I was clear about changing my mind.

He definitely knew my no meant *no*.

I lick my lips and look over at Hayes sitting rod straight beside me. "Stay in the car." I shut off the engine.

"What are you planning to do?" Hayes reaches for his door handle.

"I've got this. Seriously. You wait here."

"I can't just sit here in the passenger seat, twiddling my thumbs."

"Hayes, I want you here with me. I appreciate your moral support, but I can't get you in trouble, and trust me, this is something I need to do *on my own*."

Stealthily walking around to the back of my car, I pull out a can of silver spray paint with a special tip that allows for small precision lines. I give it a few quick shakes and move toward the black Ferrari parked in the driveway. It's Turp's car.

I've always thought of rape as a back-alley-with-a-stranger sort of affair. I've held that what happened to me did not resemble a violent crime in the least. I never fought back. Heck, with some of the defensive moves my dad has taught me, I'm sure I could've taken the guy.

Instead, I just lay there, trying to lose myself in that amazing red painting.

I actually convinced myself that Turp's talent made everything okay. As if artistic genius can be transmitted via jizz.

I've been pretending it didn't really matter, but now that I'm back here, I realize I've been pissed off all along. *Extremely* pissed off.

The heavy panting of my lions is nearly audible as I finally have a place for all my fury to land.

Moving steadily, I reach his shiny car and hear a crunch of footsteps behind me. Whirling around, I'm face-to-face with Hayes, boldly following me with his shoulders back, a look of controlled rage on his face.

I hiss, "Seriously? What are you doing?"

The fabric of his T-shirt sleeves chokes his biceps as he crosses his arms. "I'm just here to support you, like you said. This is your vendetta. What are you going to do?"

With a sigh, I motion for him to follow me. "You'll see."

I move to the wide hood of Turp's car, and with another quick shake of my can, I begin writing my message of revenge.

Warning, ladies!
The guy driving this car is selectively deaf.
He can't hear the word NO.
Proceed with extreme caution or prepare to be FUCKED.

I step back and consider a moment, tilting my head from side to side. I hold a *wait* finger up to Hayes as I move past him and jog back to my car.

Opening the back hatch, I rifle through my small collection of loose cans, flinching as they clink loudly against each other.

Finally, I find what I'm looking for—a can of hot pink.

I dash back to the front of Turp's car and am just finishing up my drawing when I hear the front screen door of the duplex fly open.

The guy is better-looking than I remember, and I grin at him. "What's your expert opinion of my work?" I point to the hood of his car. "I realize it's a *lower* art form and perhaps a bit vulgar for some tastes, but I think I've captured the shape and quality quite nicely."

His eyes widen in horror at the penis I've drawn below the silver lettering.

He doesn't have time to recover before Hayes is directly in his face. "You think raping girls is some sort of fun pastime, art boy?" It's as if a switch has been flipped, and I don't recognize the raging Hayes in front of me. *Holy shit.*

Turp holds his hands up in defense. "Listen, buddy. I don't know what your girlfriend told you, but she wanted it. I swear."

Hayes raises his arm reflexively, and I drop my pink spray can to grab him.

"Come on, he's not worth it." I try corralling Hayes toward my car, but it's like attempting to move stone.

Turp harps, "You two can answer to the cops. I called them as soon as I saw you pull up."

Hayes and I look at each other.

I'm mentally calculating how long we've been here and dividing it by the notoriously fast response time of our police force. The realization that my dad is on duty and could easily be on his way to this location gooses me into action.

"We need to go *now*," I say firmly.

Hayes still has his eyes locked on Turp, but the sound of distant sirens finally unfreezes him. He presses his pointer finger into Turp's left cheekbone. "You called the cops because you *know* what you did."

I yank his arm hard, and Hayes finally turns away.

"So, she's fucking you now?" Turp mocks. "Better get tested, because that bitch's pussy is—"

He doesn't finish his sentence on account of the fact that Hayes's punch knocks him out cold. He just lies there on the ground, face up and unconscious, with one arm flung across his body.

"Holy shit," I say. Hayes and I stand there in shock, looking down at the unmoving Turp. Finally, I give a huge smile. "That was *awesome*."

But when I look over at Hayes, his face has gone white. He holds up his fist and stares at it as if it's a foreign object he's never seen before.

"Come on." I grab his forearm and feel it's trembling. The siren is getting louder by the second. Dragging hard on Hayes's arm, I finally manage to get his attention. "We need to leave. Now."

He and I run back to my car like we're costars in some frustrating dream where we look like we're sprinting but we're actually moving in slow motion.

When we finally reach the hatchback and dive in, I start the engine, hit the gas, and do a doughnut on the lawn, leaving two muddy streaks in a circle on the grass.

As I speed back down to the winding road, a police cruiser comes around the bend and heads straight toward us, lights flashing and siren roaring.

I try to duck down in the driver's seat as the screaming car blows past, but not before identifying the officer who's driving.

Officer Juchem has known me for years, and I'm pretty sure he just saw my car.

"Fuck." I look over at Hayes. "That's one of my dad's men. He helped me once when I broke down and I'm pretty sure he recognized me. He'll probably tell my dad about spray-painting that asshole's Ferrari."

Hayes doesn't respond, so I add, "Don't worry. There's absolutely *no way* to tie you to *any* of this."

He remains silent, and when I look over, he's watching his fist open and close as if it's being controlled by a remote. Finally, he runs his other hand through his hair and says, "*God* do I want a drink right now."

I know enough to keep quiet. Offering to stop and pick him up a six-pack as a joke is not at all the proper response here.

When I pull into the driveway of his aunt's cabin, I see she isn't home, so I kill the engine, hoping he'll maybe invite me in to cool off and possibly fool around to unwind.

I'm pretty turned-on by him right now. I may not approve of violence, but I found his rage-y reaction to Turp's insult sexy as hell.

"Hayes Michael Mcallaster," I say, "you are *not* just some rich kid from the suburbs. *That* was straight-up gangsta action."

Unbuckling my seat belt, I angle my body toward Hayes, who still hasn't moved.

"Listen, you have nothing to worry about. I would never let you get into trouble."

He takes a deep breath and runs his hand through his hair again before going back to examining his knuckles. "I said I *really* want a drink."

"So you're having a craving. Isn't that normal for an alcoholic? To want alcohol?" I reach over and rub his neck. "Looking for a little distraction to take your mind off it?"

I expect this to get a small smile from him, but instead, he reaches up to the back of his neck, catches my hand, and drops it to the center console between us.

"I can't do this, Rory. I thought I could…" He looks at me with so much sadness, it makes me want to cover his whole face with both my hands.

I'm consumed with regret, and now the lions have all scattered to save their own stupid hides. Why am I so damn impulsive? I should've known stopping by Turp's couldn't end well for Hayes and me.

I swallow and look down at my hand still sitting on the center console. As if I'm the one who put it there.

I really am too broken for him. "I'm sorry," I say. "I fucked up."

After an unbearably long pause, he says, "It's just that I've been working so hard to change myself. You don't understand how one single drink could send me back to a life that I don't want. A life of addiction that will lead me to either prison or an early death."

"I promise, you're in the clear—"

"Why can't you see that I'm not worried about getting busted?" The anger that flares in my direction makes me sit up straighter in the driver's seat. He says, "I'm worried about how I felt back there. I lost my mind. I wanted to kill that guy for what he'd done to you. And it seems like I care more about you than you care about yourself. I'm frustrated that you didn't go directly to the police after it happened. Or at least to your dad."

I reflect Hayes's anger back at him. "Why can't you comprehend the reality that I don't have that kind of dad? He never sat around reading Narnia books to me. He hates me. I'm an artist just like my mom was, and she broke his heart in every possible way."

"Your father doesn't hate you, Rory." He looks at me and I watch the fight drain out of him. I want to tell that fight, *No, come back!* But it's gone.

And now I'm left with facing what I've done.

Causing him to break the law and risk everything. Completely undermining his desire to act less impulsively. I've drawn Hayes into my drama and let him down after he's tried so hard to help me.

But then, it's not like I ever asked for his help.

"So, I guess this is it, then?" I say. "You forced your way into my life just so you can check out as soon as things get messy?"

He sighs. "There's this saying that AA has to be a 'selfish program.' That's because as we look at ourselves and our past behavior and try to change, we really need to make some hard choices. We need to choose our own best interests if we hope to get well."

Did he really just say all of that? I swallow the explosion of rage that wants to detonate right now. "Selfish program?" I say harshly. "Seriously, that's what you're going with as an excuse to blow me off right now? That you're in a *selfish program*?"

"I'm sorry. I didn't—"

"Yeah, well, in my experience, *selfishness* comes to people pretty naturally, but hey, good luck with your *selfish program*. Let me know how that works out for you."

I put my seat belt back on and restart my car's engine.

Hayes doesn't make a move to leave. "Listen," he says quietly. "I still think we were meant to be in each other's lives. Your lions spoke so strongly to me right away. The fact that I found you—"

"You were stalking me, remember?" I pull the elastic tie from around my wrist and gather my dreadlocks into a ponytail behind my neck.

"I really thought you and I could help each other find our ways." His use of past tense does not escape my notice.

"Yeah, well, painting that pink penis really did help. Thanks. Maybe I've found my calling as a vigilante artist, doling out spray-painted justice."

The hint of a smile plays at his lips, and I feel my anger subside. We shift so we're facing each other in the front seats.

He shakes his head. "I've loved my time with you, but after today, I know what I need to do. I'm walking out of the wardrobe, Rory. Your fantasy world is too real. I can't ever lose control like that again. When cops start getting involved, it's time to let go."

My body feels like it's made of wood. He's pulling the heavy wardrobe door closed and shutting me out.

I lean in and whisper meanly, "Narnia is a made-up place

that doesn't exist. Welcome to the real world where *everything sucks and we all get fucked.*"

Hayes opens the passenger door and steps one foot out onto the ground. "I seriously need to go call my sponsor."

He climbs out of the car, and before I can stop myself, I call after him, "Told you."

He turns back toward me, resting his forehead on both his hands as they grip the top of the car's doorframe. You would think he was purposely showing off the undersides of his biceps. "Told me what?"

"I told you there was nothing special connecting us together."

He closes his eyes a moment, then opens them and looks directly at me as he leans into the car through the open door. "There was always something special. And you know it. It's still here."

The truth of that hits me in the gut. He's right, and it knocks the wind out of me. I've never felt this connected to a guy before. This isn't just a *zing*; it's a *pow*.

Hayes goes on. "But my connection to you is going to destroy me."

My lions begin pacing. *He's* the one who woke up all these stupid feelings.

I snap, "That's what I do I guess: drive people to destruction. Cause havoc and ruin lives."

"Rory, I…"

"You're what? You're sorry?"

He stares at the center console and won't look at me.

"*Yeah*, well, I'm sorry too." I put the car in gear and start rolling forward, forcing him to close the passenger door.

Without even checking the rearview mirror, I can feel him watching me pull away.

So that's that, then. I just wish he'd never followed me in the first place. And that I'd never believed in some sort of Narnia world where people don't turn on you or let you down. Or abandon you for being too impulsive.

I wish I'd never let my guard down with Hayes.

Because rejection hurts most when you don't see it coming.

CHAPTER FOURTEEN

I'm dragged along through the following week like one of Kelly's soggy chew toys and find myself dropped on the lifeguard bench beside Scott one rainy weekday morning.

I'm severely awake due to the fact that I went to bed super early to avoid my dad. I started off reading Andy Warhol's book *POPism* about the sixties art scene, but I must've been pretty tired or depressed because I drifted off before nine o'clock.

My book was put away with my page marked when I woke up, so Dad obviously looked in on me when he got home. I picture him watching me sleep for a moment, probably trying to figure out if I was just pretending.

The upstairs hallway was still vibrating with his snores this morning as I snuck downstairs and slipped out of the house. It's too quiet there now, without Mom's videos playing.

Thankfully, my early wake up allowed me to work at my cabin for a few hours before beating Scott to the lake. When I did my rounds, the mist was still coming off the water like magic.

And now the promise of impending rain is pretty much a guarantee that nobody will come swimming today. I sort of love it when this happens. It's like the lake belongs to just us.

The ugly remaining dirt streak on my day is the fact that Hayes still hasn't responded to the text I sent him a few nights ago. I told Kat that things were over between us, but she felt like I should give Hayes and me one more chance.

I actually cringed at how vulnerable I felt as I hit Send on a text asking if we could talk about the way things ended.

He never responded.

I guess I shouldn't be surprised that my one attempt at developing a real romantic relationship not centered on sex drove the guy straight off a cliff. I'll be sticking with drive-by hookups from now on. They're the only guaranteed way to avoid rejection.

Scott and I sit silently underneath the giant yellow umbrella, watching as a light rain begins to dance across the empty lake. Small, rippling circles form on the surface at random. The tempo rises and falls, and I'm transfixed.

"You seem awfully quiet," Scott says beside me. "Something on your mind?"

I shove thoughts of Hayes underneath the raised bench we're sitting on. "Just digging the rain on the lake."

Scott bumps his arm playfully against mine and teases, "You afraid you're going to melt?"

I laugh. "Yeah, because you know I'm made of brown sugar."

Just then, the sky explodes, and I'm hit with sharp, cold drops of rain pelting my side.

Scott and I both hunch closer to the giant umbrella's pole, but the rain is coming sideways, threatening to turn our weak cover inside out. Finally, we hear the distant rumble of thunder. Scott calls, "Let's go," and stands up to close the umbrella.

I jump down and flip the sign on the back of our chair so it reads "Beach Closed." Just in case anyone mistakes this for a lovely beach day.

It only takes a moment for us to reach the changing shed at the back edge of the graveled clearing, but it's long enough for the rain to completely drench us both.

Rivulets of water are running down Scott's face, and he blows at the stream running from the tip of his nose. The spray hits me in my wet face, and I grimace and give a light laugh.

It feels really good to laugh.

Reaching up, I wipe the water from Scott's face with both my hands. I'm on automatic pilot, but when his expression shifts to obvious lust, it sparks a warmth in my cold, dank chest. He slowly reaches up with both thumbs and swipes the water dripping from my cheeks.

The moment feels so familiar. So separate from all the emotions I've been feeling. Like I'm finally back in control.

I turn away and pull my towel from my bag, burying my face in it a moment before flinging it over my head to pat my dreads.

When I've finished, I swing the damp towel around my shoulders and look at Scott. He's still watching me. Waiting for me to decide what's next.

Ignoring the water dripping from his hair into his wild eyes as they track me, it's clear *he wants me.*

And it feels so good to be wanted.

The lions are awake and hungry, and they're crying out with their need to be fed.

I jerk toward him, and in one smooth motion, the two of us come together and start kissing.

Scott tastes like rain and the trees with the slightest hint of minty salt. Or maybe it's more like salty mint. I'm distracted for a moment as I try to decide.

The forcefulness of his lips draws my attention back. A touch too eager.

Scott forges a trail of kisses down my neck and across my cleavage, and the sensations that ripple through me are helping me forget everything.

The lions are slowing their prowl.

Reaching up, I slide both straps of my bathing suit off my shoulders.

Scott draws back, looking at my chest as if he is dying of lust. He looks up at my face. "Are you sure?"

I don't speak, only nod, and with a smile, Scott bows his head.

I close my eyes and lose myself in the feeling of his hands sliding down my wet body.

I breathe in, but instead of the waft of cologne I expect, there is only the woodsy scent of pine. I'm picturing slicked-back, black hair, but when I reach up to grasp the back of his head, the texture is all wrong, and when I open my eyes, I'm surprised by Scott's wet, blond waves.

Scott continues kissing me, but I stop kissing him back.

I lift my chin, trying to get back into that bliss zone, but now every touch makes me think *not-Hayes-not-Hayes-not-Hayes.*

Angry at my mind for the way it is betraying me, I remind myself that he rejected me.

But it's as if I can feel Hayes's eyes watching sadly. *This isn't what I want.*

Scott has already partially disrobed and is easing me down onto the changing bench when I finally accept what I need to do. I need to stop this right now because I don't want to be with anyone who isn't Hayes.

I go rigid so suddenly Scott stops kissing my neck and looks up at my face.

When I shake my head at him slightly, he whimpers, "Are you seriously saying no *now?*"

I close my eyes and nod, and he groans like an agonized animal.

"Sorry." I shove a wet dreadlock back out of my eyes. "I'm just not into this."

His nostrils flare for a moment before he releases me. I move to the other side of the changing shed, and he weaves his hands together, placing them on top of his head. "Fuck, Rory. I never pegged you for a dick tease."

"I'm not a fucking tease, Scott. This just isn't right for me."

"Seriously? Unbelievable. You know you want it. It was just a matter of time before the two of us hooked up."

I've pulled one side of my bathing suit top back up and stop to look at him with one breast still out. "I was acting impulsive, Scott." I tuck myself away. "I'm trying to do better."

"So you're just shutting everything down right now? This is *so* not cool, Rory."

I feel ashamed for a minute. This doesn't seem fair to Scott. "I get the fact that my timing is, er, less than ideal." I gesture in the direction of his obvious expectation. "It's nothing personal. I've just been going through some stuff lately."

"'Lately' as in between the time we ran into this shack and started kissing and right now? What the hell changed, Rory?"

I launch across the small space to look Scott in the eye. My finger pokes hard into his chest, and he backs against the wall as I tell him, "The only thing that had to change, Scott. My. Mind."

With that, I grab my bag and towel and fling the door open wide.

It's still raining outside—except for in one small circle about five feet away where a red umbrella is blocking the downpour.

Underneath the arched red canopy, holding the curved handle in one hand, stands Hayes.

Scott moves in behind me, calling, "Rory, come on. I'm sorry."

He catches me around the waist at the door. The two

of us are both still flushed and breathing heavy, and I watch the comprehension wash over Hayes's face. Coming to all the wrong conclusions about what just went on inside this shed.

I want to tell him this isn't what it looks like, that what he thinks happened never happened, but I'm speechless.

Scott peers out at him and asks, "What the hell are you doing here?"

Hayes just continues standing under his red umbrella, watching me as the rain falls like a wall between us. Finally, he moves his eyes from me to Scott. "I was just asking myself that exact same thing."

He turns and starts walking toward the path that leads into the woods. I call, "Hayes, wait," and he pauses, lowers his shoulders, and walks back toward us.

When he reaches the open door of the shed, he holds out a package wrapped in a plastic bag. He says, "I finished my ninth step. Got you something to celebrate."

He looks up at me as if daring me to take the small, flat rectangle from his hand.

My breathing has slowed, but I can feel my heart still beating in my cheeks. My face is so warm, I imagine the raindrops that land on it turning into instant steam. I tell my cheeks to calm the hell down and stop acting so guilty.

I say to Hayes, "Nothing happened."

He just tightens his mouth and shakes the package at me in response.

I cross my arms, and with a sigh, he reaches forward and

tucks what is obviously a small, wrapped book into the crook of my elbow.

His eyes flick to Scott standing behind me and back to me for a moment before he turns on his heel so fast the rain on his umbrella runs off the back, drenching me.

"Hayes," I call, stepping out into the downpour.

But he just keeps walking away. Away from the beach. Away from me.

Needles of rain sting my eyes as I try to hold back the tears of regret. But they're determined, and within moments, my face is wet with a combination of tears and raindrops.

Scott is behind me. "Is that guy the reason why you stopped…what you were doing with me?"

I nod and start sobbing in earnest as he puts a consoling hand on my back.

Looking up at Scott, my breath hitches as I ask, "Are you sure you're not still trying to get into my bathing suit?"

"Your bathing suit would look *terrible* on me." He gives a small grin, and I can't help but to smile through my tears.

I look out into the rain and glimpse a red flash of Hayes's umbrella just before it disappears into the distant trees.

He's gone.

I'm shoving Hayes's gift into my backpack when my phone rings with a text from Kat. She's asking if I can take the last two hours of her shift at Danny's tonight.

That favor I owe her for kissing Ken must have been burning a hole in her Blue Q bag.

I tell her of course, even though it's fairly short notice and I really should be trying to find the loose shards of my life so I can glue them back together. Unfortunately, the Hayes-shaped fragment is lost forever now, and I'm pretty sure it's going to leave a noticeable empty space in the finished piece.

At least Scott realizes that a weeping girl doesn't want to be hit on, and he gives me the perfect blend of light attention and space for the rest of our shift. We play cards without comment for the next hour, while the rain gets softer and then harder and then softer again.

Likewise, I ride waves of regret as I picture that look of hurt on Hayes's face. How did things end up so wrecked?

Finally, Scott and I hear the laughter of small humans making their way toward the beach and emerge from the shed to find the sun has come out.

And just like that, it's a lovely beach day after all.

I turn the sign around, announcing the lake is open for swimming, and can't help but marvel at how quickly everything can shift. For worse or for better.

I just made a decision to listen to my inner voice, turned down sex midstream, and surprisingly, nobody's balls exploded. Anonymous intimacy wasn't really working as an escape for me anyway, and I can make choices that are not based on pure impulse.

I found that Scott is not a very good kisser, but he might

be a better friend than I thought. And I discovered that ignoring my feelings turns them into ravenous beasts that demand my attention. I cannot ignore my grief forever.

Oh yes. And only moments after realizing that I'm fully in love with Hayes, I managed to annihilate *any* chances of us ever being together. *Huzzah.*

"I'm so mad at myself for screwing things up in such an epic, Rory-like way."

I came in extra early to whine to Kat for a while before she leaves the store for the night.

As she moves about, getting ready, I notice for the first time that she's wearing a short, black skirt and her thick purple-and-turquoise Fluevog heels. "Wait a second."

She stands up straight and looks utterly guilt ridden for a moment before raising one of her artfully arched brows at me. "What?"

"Don't you use that fake-innocent voice with me. You're wearing your lucky Fluevogs. You have a date, don't you?"

Kat puts her hands on her hips. "It's not a big deal, Rory. It's just a late dinner and maybe a drink or two."

"I can't believe I've been over here going on and on about my nonrelationship with Hayes, and meanwhile, you're all dolled up, about to go out on an *actual* date. Who's the blessed guy?"

"First of all, you don't need to act as if me going out on a date is like some rare solar-eclipse event that only happens once every twenty years. I date. I just don't, you know, do it all that often. Or successfully."

"Do I know him?" My eyes grow wide. "Wait a minute, is it that guy who came in last week for neon poster board for his yard sale?"

"No, it's not neon-poster-board guy." Kat turns away from me.

"So then, who is it? Have I met him? Why are you acting so evasive?"

"I'm not acting *evasive*. I'm just trying to get this place straightened up before he shows up."

"Why on earth would your date give a crap about the way the store—" And I get it. "No. Way. You're going out with Ken?"

"Don't look at me that way. He's cute, okay?"

"You *just* called him an intergalactic freak last week."

"I meant he was acting like a freak. He's got that awkward, self-conscious thing happening that you know I find attractive."

I take her by the shoulders. "You are so much better than he is."

She grins at me. "I know that. And you know that. But most importantly, *he* knows that too."

Just then, the bell rings over the door and Ken pokes his pointy head inside. He usually strolls into the store with all the confidence of a douche-bag manager looking to bust some lady balls, but right now, he drums his twitching fingers against his khakis as his eyes dart around.

"Be ready in a minute," Kat tells him. "Just let me punch out."

Ken seems newly breakable as he watches her walk back to the stockroom. I hear him chastise himself under his breath, "I could've offered to just sign her out." He flinches as if he's completely blowing it, and the date hasn't even started yet.

This is not the douche-bag manager I've come to know and loathe.

I say, "Hey, Ken," and he recoils. I'm hit with a wave of sympathy and mean it when I tell him, "I hope you guys have a really good time tonight."

He takes a deep breath and seems to relax a moment. When Kat reappears, his face lights up, and his fingers start twitching again.

She moves back behind the counter to grab her purse, and I whisper, "I'm actually kind of rooting for you guys."

Kat smiles and mouths the words, *Me too*, before heading out the door with her twitchy date.

Things are usually slow at Danny's at night, especially this time of year, before the college reopens, but being alone in an art store is hardly what I'd call a travesty for someone like me.

As I wander up and down the aisles, I run my fingers over the delicious supplies. Charcoals and clay and wood and Mod Podge. Like old friends. Over the years, I've worked with nearly every medium represented here. I stop at the oil paints and can't block an image that rises to the surface of my memory.

It's a happy one, which is sometimes worse.

My mother is here, and I have all her focus. She's pointing to the small, white tubes of paint and explaining about color mixing.

I'm trying to concentrate on what she's saying, but my mind continually breaks away so it can marvel at how brilliant she is. I feel so lucky to have her for a mother.

I bask in the waves of intensity emanating from her gray eyes. Mom's tutorial on paints is interrupted when a clerk comes over to ask if she needs any help—an older woman who no longer works here.

Mom is dismissive and rude toward the woman, and I am glad. Can't she see that the two of us are sharing a moment here? Right here.

My mother gifting me with her love for making art. Projecting her creative essence into a fresh vessel, her daughter.

A part of me has an urge to start wrecking the display of paints right now. I picture myself dumping boxes of tubes on the floor and knocking down the shelves. Reminding myself I'd be the one stuck cleaning everything up, I continue down the aisle.

For the thousandth time I wonder, *Why, Mom? Why?*

Making my way to the counter, I reach underneath and pull Hayes's gift out of my backpack.

I drop the package on the counter with a solid *thunk* and stand, watching it. I picture his expression when he saw me with

Scott. The way his happiness at seeing me shifted when he saw I wasn't alone. And his look of hurt confusion as he put together the pieces of the puzzle all wrong.

I should've stopped him. Run after him. Explained everything and kissed him in the rain underneath his red umbrella.

But he was the one who was done with me after that Turp fiasco. He was afraid I was going to make him start drinking again, and so he rejected me. And I didn't want to be the reason he stopped trying to get better. I wanted us to be better together, but he acted like that was impossible.

Why wasn't he answering my texts? How was I supposed to know he'd show up at the lake? With a gift for me on top of it all?

Pulling off the plastic bag, I see that Hayes has actually gone to the trouble of wrapping my present properly. It's not a perfect wrap job, so it wasn't just done professionally wherever he ordered the book. He wrapped this himself.

I tear back the paper, expecting a book on loss or grieving or some version of *87 Steps of Bullshit Help for Messed-Up People*. Instead, it has a tan cover with a drawing of two girls riding on the back of a running lion. *The Lion, the Witch and the Wardrobe*. I look at the inside flap. Ages 8 and up. *Of course*.

He's written an inscription on the inside cover:

Rory,

Thank you for teaching me how to skip rocks. Skimming the surface seems to suit you. But

now, I'm hoping you'll come deeper with me.
As this story of Narnia shows, there is always
more happening beneath the surface. All we
need to do is keep our eyes open. I've been
keeping my eyes open, and now they can't
seem to stop looking toward you. Everything
has been leading up to this. Rory, I see the
depth in you.

As the book you are holding illustrates, "If
things are real, they're there all the time."

I want us to be real together.

Love,
Hayes

Okay, so the boy can write.

I turn to the first page and find a picture of the lion dancing with the two girls as the birds look on from the trees. The lion is wearing a ring of flowers around his neck, and I quickly close the book, trying to shake that disturbing image from my mind. Lions should never wear flowers.

Picking up the clipboard that holds Ken's task list for the shift, I see Kat has already drawn a line through each item. A glance beside the register tells me she's even restocked the pen collection. Going out with the manager has clearly improved my girl's work habits.

The rain outside starts up again and unless someone gets

a sudden flash of inspiration requiring immediate art supplies, there probably won't be any more customers for the night.

I pause a moment, reopen the book from Hayes, and begin to read.

Turning the pages, I follow four young children across a spare room, through a wardrobe, and into the land of Narnia.

Before I know it, closing time has long passed, and so I lock up, drive home, and mumble to Dad I'm turning in early.

And then I read a children's storybook long into the night.

CHAPTER FIFTEEN

"Wake up, Rory! You're burning daylight!"

Dad's calling from downstairs, using his favorite wake-up phrase of all time, a phrase I hate with the fiery passion of a thousand burning sunrises. I respond by moaning loud enough for him to hear me.

Pulling the covers over my head, I try to go back to sleep.

I finished reading *The Lion, the Witch and the Wardrobe* last night and finally drifted off just as the darkness started to lift and the first birds cleared their throats.

The next thing I know, my dad is at my bedroom door with the faithful family guard bitch at his side. "You don't need to talk to me, but you do need to respect house rules, Rory. Out of bed, right now."

"I was up late reading." I allow an adolescent whine to creep into my voice. When Dad gives me a look of disbelief, I lie automatically, "School assignment."

"Not buying it. And no daughter of mine is sleeping away her mornings on my watch. Now let's go."

"Five more minutes." I pull the covers up to my chin and try to look adorable. "Please."

Dad is apparently at zero tolerance. Taking three strides into my room, he reaches down and rips the covers off me in one sweeping motion. "Get your ass up, Rory."

The dog has moved to the foot of my bed like she's waiting for me to make a wrong move.

"Fine, fine." I drag my head painfully off my pillow, and with a dramatic waver, I sit up.

I give Dad a formal salute, and he gives one last look that drips with disapproval before finally turning for the door. He and Kelly walk away as one unit, leaving me alone in my room.

Grabbing my phone off the nightstand, I dive back under the covers and check my notifications.

I texted Hayes last night at nine o'clock to say sorry for the incident at the shed and that nothing happened, and then I wrote again later saying thanks I was enjoying the book.

Now I see that Kat texted me at 2:00 a.m. to thank me for covering her shift and to say that she had an amazing time. I smile. *Go, Ken.*

But there's still no message from Hayes. No response to my texts despite the fact that it shows he read each one right away.

I try writing to him again, telling him about Split Rock, an amazing place to swim that all the New Paltz locals know about, and asking if he wants to check it out with me later.

I watch as my text sends and the notice shows him reading it. The little bubble tells me he's typing a response, and for a full minute I don't pull my eyes from that little I'm-writing-you-back bubble on my phone.

The bubble closes, but there's no response and it takes a few beats for me to realize he's not writing me back after all. I keep watching, willing that stupid bubble to open again, but Hayes has clearly moved on.

I'm struck with an idea and open my end table drawer, pulling *The Lion, the Witch and the Wardrobe* from where I stuffed it last night. I'm still flipping through pages when Dad and Kelly reappear in my doorway. I gesture to the book. "Summer assignment, Dad. Give me a break."

He crosses his arms and I look down at the pages lying open in front of me. Of course I've turned to one of the spreads with an illustration. The drawing shows a crowd of Narnia's mythical creatures including dryads and naiads holding harps, a few centaurs, and a unicorn. At the center of it all are two leopards on either side of the best ever lion, Aslan.

"It's biology." I double down on my lie. "We're doing, er, mammals." I close the book before Dad can notice the horse has a horn spiraling from the center of his forehead.

"Whatever, Rory. But you're done sleeping in."

He heads back downstairs and Kelly stands, watching me, until I growl at her. "Traitor." Her tail gives a quick wag and she turns to chase after Dad.

I leaf back through the book and finally find the page I'm

looking for. Using my phone, I take a picture of a quote by one of the Narnia characters, Mrs. Beaver, talking about Aslan being good but not at all safe.

I send the picture with my comment, **Great story. But an awful lot of beaver talk for a kid's book.**

Again, I watch as Hayes reads my text and doesn't respond.

I drag myself out of bed, leaving my phone to sit blankly on the nightstand. If the one-two punch of a poignant quote followed by a solid beaver joke can't get a response, I guess I have no choice but to give up.

I've already showered and am getting ready to head to my cabin to work on my project when I notice Hayes has finally sent a photo back to me.

He must have another copy of the book at his aunt's house because he's sent me a picture that shows a section of C. S. Lewis's text as well. His quote talks about the realization that things can be both good and terrible at the same time.

He hasn't added a quippy comment to his photo. In fact, he hasn't bothered to write any comment at all.

When I get to the cabin, I spend hours organizing all my supplies, checking and double-checking colors, and planning the layers for the lion. I consider each step carefully, trying to cut unnecessary extras for maximum efficiency, but it's no use.

Trying to do the whole painting in one night on my own will never work. And of course, if I do only half the painting one night, I can count on the cops waiting to bust me when I head back to finish.

Even if I bring all the supplies up the night before and stash them somehow, it will only help me start in on an impossible mission a little sooner. It will also increase my chances of getting caught before I even begin spraying a single stroke.

I look at the practice wall that Hayes and I did together with his "dandy lion" cheerfully mocking me.

His cryptic text photo is still our last exchange, and I guess it's his way of telling me that I'm both good and terrible. As final words go, I suppose they could be worse. And better.

Giving a few metallic shakes to the can of purple paint in my hand, I draw a funny porn mustache on his cartoon lion. Then I turn my back to it.

I need to focus on my goal. Kat is so excited about my project that I know she's dying to help me out. Screen printing and jewelry making are more in her wheelhouse than spray-painting, but she has a ton of artistic talent and I know I can totally trust her.

I just can't *quite* picture her carrying backpacks filled with paint supplies while climbing up eighty-some-odd feet of narrow footholds on the water tower's legs. The image of her favorite chunky platform shoes poised on those rungs makes me shiver.

Hanging the first stencil will be the biggest challenge, and I really need some strong arms up on the tower with me. My mind spins as I try coming up with an alternative assistant.

Once again, my brain lands on that moment I opened

the door to the changing shed and saw Hayes standing there. The awful moment that I can't undo and the one that ruined all my chances.

I cringe again at the memory, but for the first time, my mind flips around to Scott standing behind me.

I wonder if I can convince *him* to help with some of the physical work. If I have Kat helping with the painting and him on stencil duty, it will still be tough, but we might be able to pull this monster off in one night.

Of course, after what happened, I'd rather not ask Scott for a favor. But now that I think about it, it's good for him to know that the friend zone is not a place of eternal damnation. It's a spot where boys and girls can support each other without expecting anything more than friendship in return.

And maybe just a little help committing one teeny minor felony.

I work in my cabin for the next few hours until I've nicked my fingers so many times they're just a combination of Nu Skin and Band-Aids.

I still don't want to stop, but my right hand is cramping up, and I decide I should probably take a break and go talk to Scott. Also, keeping all my fingers is important.

I swipe quickly at the blood that's dripped onto the edge of my stencil and head out the door.

Scott is almost always somewhere at the park, but he's

been repainting the trail markers this week, which means he could be anywhere. Unless he's on guard duty at the lake today, tracking him down could be a problem.

When I arrive at the beach, the place is fairly quiet, with only a few families milling about the pebbled shallow area. One amorous couple is treading water together in the deep section, and I try not to picture the day I dragged Hayes to shore in a headlock.

An older guard named Pete is perched on the lifeguard bench, scanning the water as if on high alert, although I'm pretty sure the two people kissing are watching each other pretty closely.

As I move to the front of the bench, I'm relieved to see Scott is sitting beside Pete, lounging in his usual position, twirling his whistle as he looks out over the length of the dock.

"Hey, guys," I say when I reach the chair. Scott sits up and says hello to me.

Without peeling his eyes off the water, Pete says, "Hi, Rory. You're off today. Did you read the schedule wrong or something?"

"No. I'm just here to have a quick word with Scott." When neither one of them makes a move, I add, "Privately."

Scott's eyebrows jump. "You mean in the *shed* sort of private?"

I roll my eyes. "No, over in those trees is plenty private."

"Kinky," he says under his breath, and I slap his ankle. He tells Pete, "I'm taking five. Can you handle the beach?"

Without looking up, Pete gives a thumbs-up. "Five minutes. Don't get lost."

I say, "Don't worry, we won't."

Scott follows me into the cool shade of the trees. When we reach a small clearing safely out of earshot, I turn, and he slides both hands around my waist.

"Couldn't wait to get back to this, could you?" He moves in for a kiss.

I punch him in the chest. "Are you kidding me?"

Scott's winded by my shot. After a few coughs, he says, "I figured that guy ghosted you after he caught us together in the shed."

"Hayes did not ghost me." *Did Hayes ghost me?* "Or, whatever, even if he did, that doesn't mean I'd come running to you. You and I are *friends* now, and I'm good on my own."

"Friends. Right." Scott rubs his chest where I hit him. "Sorry."

"Actually, I think I know of a way you can make it up to me."

"I'm listening," Scott says, although he's not listening as closely as he did when he thought we were about to make out.

I do manage to get his attention when I come right out and confess that I'm the one painting the graffiti lions around town.

"You *aren't* serious." His eyes go wide. "That newer one inside the fence by the swimming hole too?"

I nod proudly. "Yup, he's mine."

"Wow. I had no idea. You're really talented." He laughs. "I suppose your dad banning you from art had a bit of a rebound effect."

"I guess so."

A whistle blows and he glances back through the trees toward the beach. "So why are you telling me all this? Is this some sort of friendship pact? Or are you just feeling bad for breaking my heart?"

"You know I didn't break your heart. Just busted your balls a bit."

"Yes. I was there for that part." Scott grabs his crotch with both hands and feigns collapsing in pain. I shove his arm and he laughs.

"Listen, I was just thinking you'd maybe be interested in helping me out with a little painting project."

"Yeah right." Scott continues laughing. When he realizes I'm not kidding, he scowls. "Just because I won't turn you in doesn't mean I want to get involved with your illegal activity."

"Don't worry. You won't get arrested."

"Gee, promising I won't get arrested is not exactly turning this into a tempting offer." He reaches out to bend a branch on a nearby pine tree. Rubbing his fingers together, he examines the sticky sap that's come out.

"Listen, Scott. You know who my dad is. We'll be fine even if we get caught." Since I'm not sure how true this is, I repeat the part I'm certain of. "My dad's the sergeant, Scott. And with your help, we'll finish fast and get out before daylight."

He looks skeptical. "I don't know. How involved is this project?"

"It's pretty involved to be honest. But it will also be a good time. Doesn't your summer need a little risky adventure?"

He thinks for a few minutes, looking me up and down. I resist the urge to point my chest in his direction. My assets have nothing to do with our new friendship.

Finally he asks me, "Are you free tomorrow night?"

I give him a grin. "Yup, and I'm ready to start training you."

"Easy there. Slow down." He rubs a hand over his face. "The Ulster County Fair opens tomorrow night. I want you to come with me."

I put a hand on my hip. "You do not strike me as the fair-loving type. Do you even eat fried food?" I gesture to his toned frame. "Plus, we have a *lot* of work to do if you're going to help."

He crosses his arms and dips his head forward. "I have a surprise for you, my new *friend*. Something I think you'll really like."

"And your surprise for me is at the fair?"

"It will be." He grins. "I'll even treat you to a sack of fried Oreos."

I wrinkle my nose. "I'm more of a funnel cake girl, myself."

He laughs. "Of course you are. You got it."

"And if I come with you to the fair, you promise that you'll consider helping me with this giant spray-painting project."

"So now the project is *giant*?" He wrinkles his nose. "Just how *giant* of a project are we talking about here?"

I rub the back of my neck but drop my arm when I see Scott's eyes wander across my chest. "Well...let me put it this way," I say. "You don't have a fear of heights, do you?"

"Oh God. Forget I asked." Scott shakes his head, and we make arrangements to meet over at the fairgrounds tomorrow night.

He heads through the pines toward the lifeguarding bench but stops before he hits the clearing. "You know, I *am* on the lookout for more than just some random hookup."

"Yeah, I know the feeling." We smile at each other for a minute, and then I add, "You tell anyone my secret and I'll murder you."

"Being friends with you is going to be *fun*." With a grin, he crosses his heart and kisses his knuckle at me before stepping back out onto the beach.

I feel different as I retrace my steps back to my cabin. With Scott potentially onboard, this whole thing can really happen. After so much time imagining everything, I need to push down panic at the thought of actually going through with it.

My amazing Rory lion is really starting to come to life, and he's already scaring the shit out of me.

CHAPTER SIXTEEN

Opening night is insanely busy at the Ulster County Fair. My mother hated the fair, considered it "crass and common," but it's the sort of thing that everyone has to do each year, whether they're into it or not.

There's something so universally cheap and flashy and mildly depressing about the place that I can never get enough of it.

Last summer was the first time in my life I skipped coming.

The fair is blazing with so many lights, the twilight looks like midday when Scott and I walk through the front gate together with gloppy, green stamps on our hands stating we can ride ALL THE RIDES.

I inhale the airborne sugar, breathing the scent of things cooking in grease. You can find any treat imaginable here at the Ulster County Fair, most of them fried and covered in powdered sugar, from pickles to cheesecake to butter to dough. Everything's better after a quick dip in the fryer.

The sounds of games dinging and hucksters shouting harmonize with the distant screams of people on the rickety and roaring rides. The whole place is tacky, and I love it.

A rusty memory pings in my chest. I was about ten, and Dad and I had been to the fair twice in one week before finally begging Mom so much we convinced her to come along for a quick visit.

It had rained earlier that day, and so the three of us stepped carefully, trying to stick to the places where hay covered the gooey mud.

We didn't need to discuss where we were headed. We all knew. To the teacups.

When it was just Dad and I, we went on the most daring rides. The more ridiculous the better. Things that swung us around and slingshot us into the air. We'd spin until we could barely stand and our shared theory was there are worse ways to die than on a cheap ride at the fair.

But Mom would only ride the merry-go-round and the teacups, and they didn't have the teacups here every year.

Dad and I had already scoped them out and knew right where to go. There was a short line, and Dad put an arm around Mom while I pretended not to notice.

When it was our turn to ride, Mom selected a pink-and-yellow teacup, and Dad and I piled in on either side of her, protecting her from the exit.

I close my eyes for a moment and picture the way the three of us grabbed the silver wheel in the center. We spun and spun around until the rest of the world was a blur, and there was only the three of us, laughing and squealing and together.

I open my eyes, hugging the still-warm memory close for a beat like something fresh from the dryer.

I turn to Scott. "Okay, buddy. We'd better get our butts on some rides before you make good on that fried food promise. Riding after eating is no good; fried dough tastes way worse on its way back up."

Scott laughs and follows me as I stride past the barking invitations from the gaming alley.

"Step right up and beat the Guesser." "Try your hand at dunking Artie the Clown." And my favorite invitation: "Hey, that's a fine lady you've got there, young man. Toss the rings and win your girl a prize."

We walk over to the huckster, and Scott starts reaching for his wallet. I block him with my body as I pull out two singles. "I've got this round."

A few warm-up tries later, I manage to get a ring to stick and win a small plastic baggie holding a very sleepy goldfish.

Smugly, I turn and hand my glimmering reward to the small, dejected-looking boy who's been watching me.

His face brightens and I warn, "Don't get too attached. These things have a very short lifespan."

He announces, "I'm naming him Heaven," and runs away with his eyes glued to his new pet.

"Good," I call after him, "because that's where he'll be heading soon."

Scott smiles after the boy and I slap his arm.

"You know that was actually cruel of me, right? That fish won't live a week."

"I know," he says. "But that's how I got started with my first fish tank. My folks bought a small setup the day after the fair, and then the fish died a day later. They obviously had to buy me a few replacement fish, and now I've built up to a fifty-five-gallon tank."

As the two of us walk around the outer edges of the fair, I catch Scott checking his watch.

"What is this big surprise of yours, anyway?"

He grins. "You'll see."

I point from him to myself. "You have absorbed the fact that nothing is going to happen between us, right?"

He guides us toward the rickety scream rides. "Of course." He grins. "You can be my wingman tonight."

For the next hour, we go on ride after ride and laugh our asses off. "Time for me to wingman up," I say as we wait in line for a spinny ride with an arachnid theme. Only six of the ride's eight "arms" are working, and the other two are wrapped in red caution tape.

I spot a cluster of three girls looking around to see if anyone is noticing their cute outfits. They're half talking to each other as their eyes dart back and forth through the crowd. I recognize those looks. These ladies are *carousing*.

I turn and lean close to Scott's ear. "Okay, so, directly behind me, about twenty feet away, there are three girls standing by the fried dough stand."

He looks over my shoulder and nods.

"They're exactly what you're looking for," I say. "Odd number. Perfect combination of clean and classy but with a little touch of looking for excitement."

Scott squints at them. "How the hell can you tell all that from twenty feet away?"

"See the way they're barely listening to each other talk? And watch. I'll bet there will be at least one hair flip in five, four, three, two—"

"Ha! How did you do that?"

I shrug. "I speak fluent flirt."

"You never act that way."

"I'm a little more subtle." I look him in the eye. "But these girls seem perfect for you."

"How can you possibly know any of them are my type?"

I glance back over my shoulder at them. "Because they're pretty and you're a guy."

"That's a little insulting."

"Yeah, well, save your outrage. Do you want me to be your wingman or what?"

"Not if you're going to be this aggressive about it." Scott blushes. "I told you I'm looking for more than a fling."

"That's fine. But 'more than a fling' has to start someplace, right?" I grin at him. "Come on. Relax and have some fun."

"Can't I just relax and have fun with *you*?" I glare at him, and he quickly adds, "*Not* that sort of fun." He checks the time again.

"Listen, Scott, if the surprise you have for me is a way to try winning me over, you should know it's just not going to happen."

He widens his eyes with innocence. "I just want us to get to know each other better as friends, Rory. We've been working together all summer, and you want me to help you with this big *illegal* project, and I don't even know what your favorite color is."

I wink and hold up my stamped hand. "Toxic-sludge green."

"Nice." Scott grins. "Mine's green too, but more of a pine shade."

"Shocking," I say because it's not. In fact, Scott spends so much time with the trees it's no wonder he's not seeing anyone.

The spinning spider ride we're waiting to board slows down.

I tell him, "I'll feel better if you'll at least try talking to those girls. I'm not saying you should ditch me and get someone pregnant tonight, just maybe get a few seeds germinating, see what sprouts up."

"I guess you have a point." He looks at me for a beat and sighs. "You should think about writing a wingman guidebook."

I laugh. "*The Girlfriend's Guide to Getting Guy Friends Girls.* I like it."

The ride stops and the passengers unload with the sound of safety bars creaking open and excited chattering. Scott promises, "I'll talk to them right after we spin around until we want to puke."

As I slide into one of the ride's black cars, I look out to

the crowd and see the three girls making their way toward the kiddie-ride section. Scott doesn't notice. He's too busy buckling the ride's thick, black safety belt around both our waists.

The ride genuinely does scramble our guts, and when we get off, the two of us can't seem to walk in a straight line. I'm laughing and Scott is clinging to my arm as we push through the swinging exit gate, and I look out across the midway and... *Hayes.* I stop short.

He and I spot each other at exactly the same moment and his expression mirrors the shock of electricity I feel at seeing him here. His hair is slicked back and he's wearing a tight black V-neck T-shirt, and I'm rendered speechless.

Scott is oblivious as he continues laughing and almost falling down.

Hayes's eyes shoot to Scott and I see his jaw clench twice before he turns away. He says something to an older guy with long, thinning hair in a ponytail who's standing with their group of mismatched people displaying vastly varying ages and styles. I realize these must be his AA friends.

The guy Hayes is talking to sweeps his eyes around the crowd. They land on me and I resist the urge to shove Scott headfirst into the cotton candy stand we're passing.

Scott gives another drunken stumble, and I help him get quickly back on his feet, but I know how this looks. *Shit.*

I hate that the guy with the ponytail sets his lips into a line before putting a consoling hand on Hayes's shoulder. And I hate how mournful my lions feel right now.

I can't read lips, but if I could, I'm pretty sure I'd read his saying, "Forget about her, buddy. She's not worth the trouble."

Scott has regained his balance and finally notices I'm distracted. Following my stare, he stiffens up when he sees Hayes.

"Oh crap." Scott lets go of my arm. "Do you think he saw us?"

I turn away. "Oh yes. He saw us, all right. Come on. Let's get on the spider again. My guts aren't quite scrambled enough."

Scott knows I'm upset and tries to cheer me up by telling me a horror story about a puking incident he once witnessed on the Gravitron, but I'm so nonresponsive he finally gives up and we wait in the line together in silence.

I continue stealing glances at Hayes and his gang of rowdy friends, but he refuses to make eye contact again.

Finally, their squawking abates as they migrate down the row toward the Ferris wheel.

I look around desperately and finally spot the long-haired trio of girls just getting off the merry-go-round.

"How long do we have before this surprise of yours starts?" I ask Scott.

He looks at his watch. "Another half hour or so. Why?"

I grab his hand. "Come on." I pull him out of the line.

He doesn't protest as I weave us quickly through the crowd. When we reach the three girls, I put an arm around his shoulder.

"Excuse me," I say to them. "This is my good friend Scott, and he's recently had his heart broken. Would you girls mind taking him for some ice cream? His treat."

One of the brunettes flips her hair back and gives Scott a look of disdain, but the other brunette raises an eyebrow and the blond tilts her head at him and smiles.

I whisper in his ear, "Stop staring at me and go for the blond. I'll find you in a half hour."

He whispers back, "Fine. I'll be over between the pigs and the rabbits." He points toward the farm-animal area. "Don't be late."

I nod and, to the girls, I say, "He's in a tender place. Please take good care of him." I pat his chest.

The friendlier-seeming brunette turns to ask him his name, and I think, *You're welcome, Scott*, as I move toward the Ferris wheel.

I may not be able to transform my relationship with Hayes into something beautiful, but I cannot just leave it unfinished.

I have to at least try to rework this unique section of the terrifyingly out-of-control art piece known as *My Life*.

"Ready to take fate into your own hands?"

Hayes swings around to stare at me, and I point to the giant Ferris wheel he and his friends are waiting to board. One of the legs jerks violently with each turn of the wheel, as if the ride is having muscle spasms. I've jumped the line for the ride and can feel the glares on my back from the other people waiting.

With a sigh, Hayes gestures to the older guy with the ponytail standing beside him. "Roger, this is Rory." Roger is busy glaring at me as if line jumping is the least of my offenses. Hayes adds, "Roger's my sponsor."

He shakes my hand formerly, but Roger's voice is cold as he says, "Hayes has told me a lot about you."

The rest of their crew is staring at me in silence, and I resist the urge to turn and run into the arms of the fried dough man.

I wink at Roger. "Well, I hope he hasn't told you *everything*." My laugh morphs into an uncomfortable cough and I stand there, looking at my hands.

"Hey, I know you," a middle-aged mom-type says. "You work at Danny's."

I smile at her gratefully. "You come in for ink pads and stamps all the time."

She laughs. "Creative outlet, right, Rose?" The older woman beside her nods, and she adds, "Scrapbooking is my new drug of choice."

I don't know how to respond, so I smile and nod and go back to looking at my hands. The line jumps forward and Hayes finally breaks the awkwardness by saying, "I guess you can ride with me."

Roger opens his mouth to say something, but Hayes holds up a hand. "It's cool. I've got this."

I aim my smile up at him, but he doesn't look at me. We don't say anything more until we're safely locked side by side on the decrepit ride.

Clutching the bar tightly, I turn to him. "Your friends seem...um...nice. And I'm really happy for you finishing your ninth step."

"Yeah. Working on that step brought up a lot of stuff for me."

The ride lurches forward, and with a grunt, he quickly grabs the safety bar.

"You're not nervous, are you?" I ask.

"Why would I be nervous?"

"Because you're on this antique ride that is definitely not up to code. With me." He looks at me and then glances toward the car behind us. Like I'm abducting him in a Ferris wheel.

"I'm fine." He sighs. "Roger wasn't exactly onboard."

"I could tell. Do you keep him after you're done with all your steps?" *Please say no.*

"Of course. Roger's great. He lost his marriage and family due to his drinking. I was lucky I hit my bottom so fast and so young."

"I, personally, prefer my bottoms fast and young."

"Very funny." Hayes doesn't laugh.

We're quiet as our car climbs to the top of the wheel and stops. Together we watch the squealing park blanketed in blinking neon lights below. It feels like we're looking at a scene that we're not actually a part of.

The ride lurches forward again, and I give a small squeal. We both grab the bar and then laugh at our overreaction as our car begins to free-fall down the front of the wheel. I give another squeal as we swoop backward along the bottom.

Our car begins to climb up the back of the wheel again and I look over at Hayes. He's watching me.

My stomach and chest trade places.

Our eyes stay locked on each other as we drop and we rise. Finally, I whisper, "What does finishing your ninth step mean? For us."

"About us…" Hayes runs a hand through his hair, mussing up the perfectly slicked-back top.

I resist the urge to reach over and smooth back his hair. I'm not sure I could stop myself from kissing him if I did.

He takes a deep breath, thinks for a full rotation, and starts again. "In AA, we finish every meeting by saying the Serenity Prayer."

Hayes recites a prayer about accepting things that he's not able to change and about having enough courage to change what he can.

"That's nice," I say, confused.

"The last part of the prayer is about figuring out what I can change and what I can't. That's the part that matters. Letting go of the things I can't control is the only way to truly achieve serenity."

I feel a sickening feeling in my stomach that has nothing to do with the ride gliding around the top right now.

Hayes shuffles his feet against the metal floor of our car. "Rory, I can't change you."

A tremor of anger runs through me. I want to lash out, but I just calmly say, "So you need to ditch me."

"I mean, come on, Rory. You're here at the fair with your lifeguard partner." He says it like an accusation.

"Yeah, Scott and I are friends." I hate being treated like this. "I'm sorry for how things looked, but nothing happened between Scott and me. Well, I mean, not *nothing*, but you know—"

"Actually, Rory, I *don't* know. And I don't even need to know. The two of you are here together now." He shifts away from me.

"But it doesn't mean anything."

He looks angry. "And *that's* the problem. You don't think it means anything but *everything* means something."

"I'm just trying to explain that Scott and I are friends."

"It didn't look that way the other day in the rain."

"I understand what it looked like." I'm getting frustrated. "But I'm telling you how it was."

"And I'm supposed to, what? Just believe you?"

My inner lions stir. "You're not being fair," I say. "And besides, you said things between us were over and then you didn't respond to my texts."

"I was writing my response in the book," he says. "But you probably thought my inscription was just corny anyway."

"I didn't know if I was ever going to hear from you again." My voice rises. "And your note was actually the perfect degree of corniness." Thinking of his words soothes my lions, and I add more calmly, "Hayes, I *do* want to delve beneath the surface with you."

He looks me in the eye. "That wasn't meant as an offer for us to drown together."

I gasp with surprise that morphs directly into rage. My

lions pounce. "Are you serious?" I practically roar. "So you have basically hunted me down and pried me open and made me trust you so you could just abandon me?"

"Rory, I didn't—"

"You weren't kidding about that *selfish program* of yours." I poke him in the chest, and he glances over the side as if one of his AA friends will swoop in from another car to help him.

But I have him cornered and alone.

"Is that really what you anonymous alcoholics do?" I growl in his face. "As soon as things get too real or hard or out of control, you run away?"

He looks frightened, and I think, *That's right. I'm not the prey here. YOU'RE the prey.*

He opens and closes his mouth. "I just... I can't... Rory, I can't change you."

"I never asked you to change me!" I'm bursting with rage. "So go ahead and *hide* in your safe, little, selfishness circle and *shit* your creamy, smooth *serenity* out your *butt* because *I don't need you.*"

He stammers as if my jaws are on his throat, but I release before the kill. I lean against the side of the car. Away from him.

I can feel him watching me as we go weightless again and again, free-falling under the swinging shadows.

I've caught my breath by the time the wheel starts to slow down.

We slide into a rough landing at the bottom of the ride and the bar is ripped out of his hands.

Hayes doesn't move, and so I leave the car first, stepping down and refusing the help of the red-haired guy working the ride.

The ramp gives a metallic rattle under my feet as I stride toward the exit gate, and I can hear Hayes step onto the ramp behind me but don't glance back until I'm all the way in front of the Zipper.

He's shaking his head as he rejoins his alcoholic friends. They greet him with open arms, seeming relieved to have him back. As if they were all afraid I'd get him drunk during the ride or something.

Roger reaches up to put an arm around Hayes and turns to give me a long, sad look.

I have no idea how much Hayes has told Roger about me, but I can tell one thing. I know that look. He knows about my dead mom.

With a deep breath, I lift my head and stride away from the group that is clearly busy pitying me. The group that thinks I'm incapable of changing.

Too late, I think. *I already have changed.* But if Hayes won't give me the chance to prove it, he doesn't deserve me.

It feels as if my scrambled guts are being scooped out with each stride, and I suddenly want to go home and wash away the filth of the fair.

I pass the rabbit barn, looking for Scott, and wonder if he's made a connection with one of the girls I set him up with. And if he'll be giving my surprise to her instead of me.

I'm fine with that, to be honest.

The rabbits' cages are stacked from the floor to eye level, and I bend down to look at a big, black, lop-eared bunny wiggling his nose at me from his cage. I lean in close to get a better view of his adorable, fuzzy face.

A snuggly pet bunny would be perfect right about now. But then I think of Kelly and realize that nothing good in my life will ever be safe from the risk of bloody carnage.

As I walk away from the bunnies, I hear the loud whirr of a chainsaw coming from the direction of the pig barn. The chainsaw's motor revs a few times and then cuts off. I notice a crowd gathering around a sectioned-off space between two barns. The whole area is as bright as daytime, and as I draw closer, I notice the strong smell of cedar chips.

In the center of the clearing stands a guy wearing a sleeveless flannel and holding up a chainsaw as he gestures to a thick, five-foot-tall log beside him.

The guy's arms are oiled to emphasize his muscles, and he's wearing sunglasses, large headphones, and an orange baseball cap. He's shouting something to the audience, but I can't make out what he's saying.

I draw closer and get to the very edge of the crowd before I realize, *It's Scott.*

He's clearly about to perform some feat of power-tool wonder, and this audience is eating it up. I say a quick prayer that he's not about to start juggling chainsaws because (a) I care about him and, by extension, his extremities and (b) I seriously need his help on that water tower.

God, do I ever need to paint that lion now.

Scott calls out, "Gentlemen, start your engines!" and an old rock song blasts out from the gnarled overhead speakers. He restarts his chainsaw, and after a few revs of the engine, he launches himself at the log, holding the spinning blade at odd angles so he can carve rounded chunks off the top.

A cloud of sawdust rises up, and the music blares, and Scott grimaces as he works on the log.

It's hard to tell just what he's carving, but it doesn't appear to be one of the eagles or bears standing in random positions around the clearing. Leave it to the Ulster County Fair to introduce folks to the fine art of chainsaw sculpting.

I've always thought of Scott as purely a nature guy and am surprised to see him carving wood with a chainsaw. I never realized he did any form of art.

Mom once pulled me away from a guy on the sidewalk in the city who was making quickie paintings that featured dolphins flipping through space. I can still hear her scolding me that it was not "real" art, and it's easy to imagine her turning her nose up at this performance.

But I'm fascinated by unconventional forms, and right now I'm mesmerized by Scott's emerging sculpture. This takes some serious skill.

Making something in front of an audience is basically the opposite of what I do.

It isn't until he's been working quickly for a good fifteen minutes that I realize what Scott's carving. A lion.

I wonder if his surprise to me is the fact that he's doing the lion special after hearing about my graffiti lions or if the big surprise is the fact that he's a freaking chainsaw sculptor. I'm thinking it's a bit of both.

As the rough lion-ish shape begins to take a sharpened focus, I work my way up closer to the safety ropes. By the time the music stops and Scott turns off his saw, I'm directly front and center in the crowd.

Scott pulls his sunglasses off and looks around. The lower half of his face is covered in sawdust, and it breaks into a smile when he spots me. I wave and he gives me a thumbs-up.

It is like he's a different person in front of this audience. One who probably doesn't need me to be his wingman after all.

Searching the crowd, I notice that the girls I tried setting him up with are nowhere to be found.

He's using a long-bristled brush to dust the sawdust off the lion's head, and I wonder how his skills are going to translate to spray-painting a giant lion onto the front of a water tower.

Scott calls out, "Thanks for watching, folks. This sculpture will be auctioned off tomorrow night during the Ulster County Fair closing judging ceremonies, and the proceeds will be donated to help fund arts education."

I mentally tell my mother, *See that? Arts education. Take your snobby attitude toward quickie chainsaw sculpting and shove it up your...* I stop the thought since I maybe don't want to start talking back to my dead mother in my mind.

When Scott has finished absorbing his applause, he hands

off his saw and gear to a girl wearing cut-off jean shortie shorts. She holds up a hose, and he rinses the sawdust off his arms before he gestures for me to meet him at the ropes.

He walks up while drying off with a towel, and I say, "I can't believe you've been hiding this crazy talent." I gesture to the banner that reads "Masters of the Chainsaw" with three cartoon lumberjacks wielding chainsaws and logs in various states of being carved.

"This wasn't actually the surprise," he says. "I usually wow the crowd with a classic bear design. I'm sort of known for it." He gestures to the lion and imitates the wide-open mouth.

"So you did the lion just for me?"

"You and *arts education*, of course." He grins.

"Thanks, really. It's pretty amazing." I look back up at the banner. "What got you started with all this?"

"Working up on the mountain, I got pretty handy with the chainsaw. Turns out, I have an eye for picking out the right pieces of wood, seeing the animal inside and setting it free."

"That explains why you like going out walking the trails so much."

"I do find a lot of great logs at work, but I also just love those woods."

"I hear that." I smile for a beat too long and redirect our conversation. "Hey, what happened with those girls?"

He holds up his empty palms. "No common interests with the only girl who seemed interested."

I reach across the ropes to give him a light punch. "Being

interested *is* a common interest, stupid." He shrugs and I wrinkle my nose at him. "If I would have been there, I could've made something happen. Sorry I failed you as wingman."

"It wasn't you. It was me."

"Ha. Most famous breakup line ever. Thanks a bunch."

He laughs and slides under the rope to my side of the barrier. "What happened to the guy you ditched *me* for? Not looking to make a commitment?"

I shrug. "Let's just say it did not go well."

Scott puts an arm over my shoulder. "Can I interest you in a sack of fried fritters to help you forget your heartbreak and sorrows?"

"Everything's better when it's fried."

"No arguments here," Scott says. "Let's go."

He guides me toward the crackling sound of hot grease. I don't bother moving his hand off my shoulder, even though I'm pretty sure Hayes is still here, walking around the park with his friends.

I touch a finger to my lip and think of how much I hoped for one final kiss from him on that Ferris wheel.

"Extra powdered sugar," I tell Scott quietly as we step up to the line side by side.

I wonder if tossing my heart in the fryer would make it any better.

CHAPTER SEVENTEEN

As I approach the front door, I hear the strains of a familiar voice flowing from the living room.

"Being an artist is the most import aspect of your identity. You are an artist first and everything else flows from that. Never forget it. You are not human or female or even my daughter. You are an artist."

It's my mom. Dad must be listening to one of the videos on the laptop because everything about this speech sounds familiar.

I stand for a moment with one hand on the doorknob, listening. I never realized how melodramatic Mom was when she talked about art. Telling me I'm not even *human*? Seriously?

As soon as I walk in the front door, Dad slams the laptop shut, but we both know I've caught him in the act.

I could swear his eyes look like they're actually shining. Like he's tearing up at Mom's passionate speech.

Kelly runs from the foot of Dad's recliner to where I'm

standing at the door and sniffs me all over. She continues sniffing up and down my whole body so thoroughly and for so long it starts to get awkward.

Dad's brow furrows accusingly, and if it wasn't for Kelly's comical enthusiasm for the smell of fried dough, I'd probably be pissed at him for assuming the worst.

The dog's fuzzy snout digs into my side, tickling me, and I can't help but squeal with laughter.

I gesture to the dog and explain, "Fair's in town."

Kelly's tail is wagging like crazy, and Dad gives a chuckle of relief.

I point to the closed computer on his lap and ask with false casualness, "Whatcha watching?"

His expression tenses again. After a pause, he nods and says, "I was thinking I would maybe give your mom's videos back to you."

This was not what I was expecting and I'm stunned into silence.

"I still don't like you watching them all the time, but they were meant for you." He sighs. "I didn't really have the right to take them away."

He holds the closed laptop up to me and I move closer to take it, stuffing it quickly under my arm like a book.

We stand for a minute, both looking at the other's feet. Finally, I turn mine in the direction of the stairway.

Drawing a quick breath, he asks, "So, how much crap did you eat at the fair?"

I turn back. "A funnel cake the size of my head, plus a few fried Oreos."

"What? No pepper steak?"

"Well, of *course* I ate a pepper steak. That's not crap though."

He laughs. "Do they still have that horrific Zipper ride you always loved so much and made me go on?"

"*Me?*" I point a finger at him. "*You're* the one who loved all the wild rides."

In an instant and for a moment, I am his daughter again.

I think of him trying to connect with me in the stockroom at Danny's. He's not always the easiest guy on the planet to get along with, but I have to admit to myself that he probably doesn't really hate me.

Sliding the laptop onto the coffee table, I walk over and sit on the arm of his chair.

Dad sets his phone aside and absentmindedly pulls at the crease on his jeans.

"Thank you for giving me back the videos," I say.

He clears his throat and nods. "You know, I really am sorry I didn't tell you about Linda earlier."

I shrug. "Our first meeting might not have involved flying food if it had been planned a little better."

"You seem to have inherited your mother's explosive personality."

I cross my arms. "We prefer the term 'artistic temperament.'"

Dad sighs. "I know that becoming an artist is a way to

keep her alive." He reaches up to put his hand on my shoulder. "But are you able to see how it destroyed her?"

"You're wrong, Dad." But he's building into one of his anti-art rants, and I regret letting my guard down.

"Your mom was wrong in that video, Rory. You need to be a person first and an artist second. Your art will never love you back."

"You just don't understand."

"Then help me understand, Rory. Because I cannot lose you too."

On the word "too," his face breaks in a way that makes my heart lurch.

I look at how much he's aged in the past year. I see how afraid he is and recognize that he has no idea how to deal with feelings of fear.

All his training as a cop has taught him to be strong and wrestle the bad guys down to the ground. He sees art as the bad guy, and he's determined to eradicate it from our lives.

But I can't just change who I am. I can't give up on the part of me that is crying out to paint—the lion that is inside that needs to come out. It's so huge it might not even fit on that water tower, but I need to try.

I sigh. "I'm sorry, Dad. I know you miss her too."

He pulls me down into his lap like he did when I was little and wraps his arms around me like two big paws that hold me still. I submit, trying to ignore the awkwardness. Dad and I are not huggy people.

Finally, Dad releases me, leans back, and says, "I know making art kept you connected to her and maybe someday you can go back to it. I just feel better—"

"If I let it go for now," I finish his sentence for him, and he goes in for another hug.

The lion inside me is having a hard time enduring his embrace, knowing that I'm lying. That it still has to come out and have at least one last roar.

I know I can't just leave that water tower alone.

Artists make art, and I've come too far to give up being who I am just so my father will be less afraid. But for right now, in this moment, I can offer him what he needs.

I give him a kiss on his forehead and wrap my hands around his neck like I did when I was little. "Don't worry," I whisper. "I'm going to be fine."

There has been a gaping canyon between the two of us, and I realize he's been trying to build his imperfect bridge in his own damaged way to reach the side where I'm standing alone.

And now I'm building my weak and splintering way toward him as I move to sit down on the coffee table across from his chair. We start slow by sharing memories of Ulster County Fairs gone by with their fried fritters and rickety thrill rides, and while we don't discuss Mom, we allow space in the room for her memory.

Even Kelly lies down and rests her head on her front paws as she listens to our uneven laughter. It's okay to relax a little for just a moment.

By the time we finally head up to bed, Dad and I have managed to hang a perilous string bridge across the chasm between us.

Swinging dangerously high, our bridge's unfinished planks threaten to draw blood with the wood's sharp edges. And neither side is quite secure. The whole thing could easily plummet into the bottomless canyon, especially if Dad ever finds out about my graffiti lions.

But I trust us enough to believe it will eventually become crossable. Because we are clumsily building our rickety-ass string bridge

with unbreakable strands of love.

CHAPTER EIGHTEEN

The bell over the door at Danny's is still reverberating from my entrance when I walk up to the register and ask, "You ready to hit this thing with me next week?"

Kat stands up from behind the counter where she's busy working on a bright-pink display sign.

"Yes, absolutely." She picks up her sheet of neon poster board and slides it onto the counter. "What are we hitting again?"

I look around to make sure nobody is in the store before I hiss, "*The tower.*"

"Oh my God, of course." Kat points a thick marker at me. "The tower mural is going to be *epic*. Can't wait to stick it to those Sparkle Soda assholes!"

"That's right. This is an act of social rebellion. We are sticking it to those Sparkle jerks."

Kat leans across the counter so she's close to my face. "Listen, I know you've been going through some stuff with your dad. I was just wondering…if we happen to get caught…?"

"He and I are...well, we're trying to reconnect."

She grins. "That's awesome."

"Well..." I squint at her. "He *may* have the impression I'm done making art."

"And why might he think that?"

I shrug. "What can I say? I'm trying to make peace and the guy hates art."

She laughs. "So I'm assuming this means he *won't* help us out if we get nailed."

I bow my head. "I mean, I don't think he'll make things any *worse* for you, but it will be bad for me. Like, really bad."

When I look back up, Kat is watching my face. "You need this, don't you?"

I nod vigorously. "More than you know."

"So then, let's make sure we don't get caught."

We grin at each other, and I tell her, "I found a replacement for Hayes."

"What happened to Hayes?" she asks.

"It's—"

"Wait. Don't tell me. It's complex."

I nod. "But my buddy Scott is in. He's not experienced with painting. But he's pretty artistic, and he can help move supplies and do some climbing and lifting. I think with his support, you and I will be fine."

"Are you sure we can pull it off with just three people?"

"I was originally trying to figure out how to do it alone." I shrug. "This is going to be a piece of cake."

Kat sniffs me. "I'm detecting a light scent of... What is that?" She waves her hand toward her face as she inhales my aroma. "Oh yes, icing-covered *bullshit*."

I laugh. "Okay, so it's *slightly* impossible. But I'm still working on a few ideas for shortcuts, and if we go down, we're gonna go down spraying."

"That a girl," Kat says.

I tell her I just need a few more days of prep work and grab a sheet of paper to start going over my plan. The two of us are so distracted by our discussion, I practically leap when the bell rings over the door.

"What are you two ladies plotting?"

Kat's face lights up with a smile, and I turn to see Ken striding into the shop. He looks somehow more confident and in charge than usual. And maybe just a few inches taller.

I crumple up the page I've been writing on, but Kat looks purely happy to see the guy who could ruin everything. I hiss, *"He can't get suspicious."*

"Well then, I'd better act natural," she whispers back. Louder, she says, "Hey, Ken. There's something I wanted to show you *back in the stockroom*. Rory, you don't mind keeping an eye on the store?"

"Oh, sure. No problem." My shift technically doesn't start for another half hour, but I slip behind the counter while the two of them stride calmly yet purposefully toward the swinging door to the back room.

The image of them together feels like a collage of

contrasts. Kat's fiery-red hair probably shouldn't get too close to his flammable-looking comb-over, and her piercings and tattoos clash hard with his pleated kakis.

Great. Nothing like having my second-in-command acting like she's some schoolgirl with a mad crush. I'm hit with a pang of loneliness and think of Hayes and what a mismatch he and I were.

My mind wings back to the two of us making out in my cabin. His arms around me, hands pressing into my back as he eases me down onto my art table. The way his lips felt against mine and how our bodies fit together... Okay, so maybe we weren't a *total* mismatch.

I shove that image underneath the counter and smooth out the sheet I've crumpled up. It has a list of supplies divided into sections representing the backpacks we'll be carrying up. If the three of us each strap a pack on our front and one on our back, it will make for tough climbing, but we should be able to get everything up to the tower with just Scott making one extra trip down and back up.

With him doing all the heavy lifting and Kat and me spraying like crazy, we might actually pull off this project before the sun fully rises. As long as Kat doesn't get distracted with trying to paint each section perfectly, and Scott can work as quickly with a spray can as he does with a chainsaw, and if maybe I can manage to move at the speed of light, then the three of us are totally going to nail that water tower.

No matter what, after this, things will never be the same.

The rest of the week flies by as I focus obsessively on each detail of my roaring mural. I don't hear from Hayes, and I don't reach out to him again.

As much as it sucks, I get that his sobriety is his priority now.

Still, I can't help but wonder if, despite my last outburst, he'll maybe visit me in prison if I get busted.

My lifeguarding shifts with Scott go by more quickly now that he and I can talk about inspiration and craft and creativity. Not to mention plans for our giant, clandestine collaboration.

Dad and I still seem afraid to rock our timid string bridge too much. We've kept our conversations generic and avoided any heavy subjects that might unravel our progress.

I realize that Linda has probably been helping him to cope more than I ever could, and when he asks if I'll come out to dinner with them in two weeks for her birthday, I agree.

He says, "I told her you're usually not prone to violence, but she said to tease you that she's wearing a catcher's mask to the restaurant just to be safe."

I laugh politely and swallow down the lion that's clawing to leap out and up onto that water tower as soon as possible. It feels like it's going to rip me apart from the inside if I don't release the beast soon. I wonder if this is the way my mom felt all the time.

And then, finally, when I don't think I can stand to wait another day, it's time.

The sun is just beginning to set on a perfect, clear day as Scott and I wait in my car for Kat to arrive. All the supplies are divided neatly into eight backpacks with the lightest two saved for Kat.

It's getting late, and I'm starting to wonder if maybe Scott and I should just go ahead and get started. We'd only need to make two trips each.

"You're sure she's coming, right?" Scott's so nervous he's making my entire car vibrate, and it's getting me pretty worked up.

"She'll be here. Don't worry. Are you sure *you're* up for this?"

Scott gives me a strained smile. "I'll be fine. I just want to get going."

I send Kat a text asking where she is and she says she just had to pick someone up. I write back: **Your invitation did not have a plus one!**

She doesn't respond, but within moments, her pickup truck is pulling into the twilit clearing where Scott and I are just climbing out of my car.

Opening her door, Kat calls out, "Please don't be mad," before I can see who is with her. Typically, conversations that start with a person begging, "Please don't be mad," are not good conversations.

When Ken steps out though the driver's side door behind Kat, my first thought is, *Awwww, how sweet he was sitting shotgun right beside her.*

My next thought comes out loud, and it goes more like, "What the *hell*, Kat? You brought our *boss*. The whole point of keeping the graffiti-painting mission from him was to keep the graffiti-painting mission from him!"

"I know, I know. And helping you trick him was what finally got the two of us together. But I just couldn't leave that deception hanging there between us. A relationship can't be built on lies, Rory."

She puts an arm around his shoulders and the two of them look at me imploringly. They're dressed in head-to-toe black like a pair of matching twin ninjas except one ninja is larger than the other and the big one is wearing bright-red lipstick.

I'm caught between thinking Kat is adorable for being so open and honest with her new boyfriend and thinking she's an idiot for being so open and honest with her new boyfriend.

"Ken, I'm sorry, but it is *really* important that my dad never finds out about me painting graffiti."

Ken holds both of his hands up. "Listen, Rory, I'm totally onboard with this mission. Kat's had me reading old issues of *Adbusters*. It got us talking about the buying and selling of ad space as an infringement on our freedoms."

Kat says, "*He's* the one who mentioned this obnoxious soda ad."

Ken laughs. "She was practically bouncing up and down in her seat and couldn't help sharing your plan with me."

"Classic Kat." I sigh. "Well, it's too late now." I open my

hatchback and start pulling out the packs. "At least we'll make it up the ladder in one trip with an extra person carrying supplies."

I'm handing backpacks to Scott and Ken when the passenger door to Kat's truck opens up. In the growing darkness, I hadn't realized there was someone else still in the car.

I look at Kat, and she holds up her hands and repeats the phrase, "Please don't be mad."

The pack that I'm holding slips to the ground when I see him.

Hayes.

"Hey there, Rory." Hayes stuffs his hands in the front pockets of his jeans and straightens his arms so his shoulders rise up and press together.

I scramble to pick up the bag I've dropped. "What are you doing here?"

"I stopped by the art store because I needed to talk to you. I could tell right away something was up by the way Kat was acting."

Kat says, "Rory, I swear, he was so worried about you, he was a wreck. And then he came right out and asked me about the water tower project."

"It wasn't hard to put together." Hayes gestures to Kat's outfit. "The woman is dressed like she's about to commit a heist."

She says, "I had no choice but to admit to Hayes that tonight's the night. The moment he heard, there was no way he wasn't coming along. He would've gotten a ride here anyway."

Hayes has stepped closer, and he reaches to take the bag from my hand. "Aslan is on the move, huh?"

It's a saying from the Narnia book about the great lion king, but Hayes being here is all wrong.

"You can't be here now," I say. "I need to paint this lion, and there's no way you're talking me out of it."

"Believe me, if I thought there was any possibility of convincing you to stop, I'd try," he says, looking up the long ladder toward the tower above us. "But, right now, you need my help more than any of my extremely rational arguments against this adventure."

"I don't need your help."

"Actually, I'm familiar enough with your plan to know that you very much *do* need my help." He looks at me.

"We need his help, Rory," Kat calls over.

I ask Hayes, "Why on earth would you put yourself at risk? I thought your *selfish* program meant you don't help anyone but yourself."

"It turns out, after step nine, there are still three more steps that are much less self-centered." He laughs. "Roger helped me see I was maybe embracing the selfish thing a little too hard."

I don't even crack a smile.

He sighs. "I'm supposed to keep an inventory of my wrongs and to promptly admit them. I'm trying to admit my wrongs here. *Promptly.*"

"Prompt is one thing, but do you really need to do this

right now?" I look over to where Scott is holding the lighter knapsacks up to Kat and Ken.

"You have to admit, this timing feels like fate, doesn't it?" When I don't answer, Hayes goes on, "Cutting you out of my life wasn't just excruciatingly hard for me, Ro; it was wrong of me too. I should've given you another chance."

He spreads his hands toward me pleadingly, and I feel the pull of familiarity. Like he belongs here with me. But I don't know if I can ever trust him again. "Why should I give *you* another chance?"

"Because I get why you're here tonight," he says. "And I believe in your artistic vision. And because you were right about what you said at the fair. My life needs to be more than hiding from reality and shooting serenity sundaes out my ass."

I cover my mouth to hide my small grin at that. Finally, I say, "We could end up in a ton of trouble."

"Please give me the chance to prove myself. I won't abandon you again."

I look around at Kat, Ken, and Scott shifting their weight as they listen. When the three of them realize I'm watching, they turn toward each other and immediately start talking all at once. Like they're having a very intense and obviously make-believe conversation.

Hayes pulls my face back toward his, so I'm looking directly at him. "I was so focused on avoiding anything that could hurt me that I couldn't see how much I hurt you. I'm sorry."

I still feel that *zing* when our gaze connects. "Um, okay,

so congratulations." I drop eye contact and study his high-tops. "You did that step. Apology accepted. No need to risk your probation." I pat his arm without looking at him and turn to go.

"You don't get it." He pulls the bag I'm holding from my grip. "I have to make this up to you. It's part of my recovery to help make things right when I mess up."

I just stand there, staring at him in the twilight. In spite of everything, if I'm not willing to give him another chance and risk being hurt again, I'm doing the same exact thing that he did to me.

Finally, he holds his hands out to the sides. "There's really no way you can stop me from helping you."

Kat says, "You should really let him help, Rory."

I look around at my mismatched crew, the guys all shuffling their feet back and forth in anticipation as Kat widens her eyes at me as if to say, *Come on, already.*

The energy is so thick it's almost visible, and I smile at the realization that they're all anxious to help me make my lion roar.

I can feel time spinning by too fast, and I finally take control and announce, "Okay, so this is happening, people. Let's get a move on."

While Hayes is still swinging the bag he took from me onto his back, Scott steps forward and thrusts the huge knapsack filled with the folded-up stencil into Hayes's chest. The force of Scott's throw drives him backward.

"Be careful with that," Scott tells him.

Hayes repositions his stance and straps the backpack onto his front as two of them stare each other down so hard they may as well bare their teeth. *Great.*

At least having another extra person means I won't even need to stress Kat out by making her carry two packs of supplies like I'd planned. Which is probably best, considering her perfect law-breaking outfit does not extend to her choice of footwear. She's wearing chunky pink heels.

I un-bungee the small extension ladder attached to the roof of my car and set it up to reach the rungs that begin above our heads.

Before I've had time to position it properly, Hayes launches up the ladder, wearing the oversize packs on his front and his back.

Both ladder legs shift under his weight, and I grab the closest side firmly, calling out, "Easy! We are not taking any unnecessary risks here tonight."

Hayes doesn't look back as he climbs up to the blue rungs above.

Not to be outdone, Scott tightens the straps on his front pack and scurries up after him as soon as I have the ladder better situated.

And just like that, we're off to a solid start.

Standing in the shrinking light, Ken steps up to the rungs and looks at the ladder as if the thing has just started trash-talking his mother. I give Kat a look, asking if he's going to be okay.

"He has this little tiny thing about heights." She reaches out to rub Ken's back. "He's terrified of them."

"And so you thought you should bring him here on a date and make him climb eight stories straight up?"

"He'll be fine. Won't you, hon?"

"What?" He shakes his head. "Oh yeah. I can *do* this." He sounds like he's telling this more to himself than to us. "Wait, did you say *eight* stories?"

"Well, I'm going to go on ahead of you two," I say. "If you can't make it, I'll send one of the guys back down for your backpacks, okay?"

I'm doing a quick inventory of the smaller bags the two of them are wearing, suddenly grateful Hayes showed up to pick up the slack.

He and Scott have already climbed so high they appear small when I look up, so with a "good luck" to Kat, I make my way up the ladder. When I reach the top wooden rung, I shift the bag strapped on my front to one side so I can see where I'm going, grab the first cold, blue rung with both hands, and climb onto the leg of the tower.

I hear Kat below telling Ken, "Let's pretend we're part of the Starship Enterprise crew and our mission is to get to the top of this ladder so we can transmit a warning signal to one of our allies."

As I rise out of earshot, I hear Ken laugh and announce, "Must contact the Klingon Alliance."

Kat responds with something about "Vulcan Ambassador Sarek," and I stop trying to listen.

My arm and leg muscles warm as I make my way higher, and it feels good to be taking real action. This lion is primed and ready to be released into the wild. And I'm ready to be free.

As I pull myself up the final steps, I find Scott and Hayes facing each other like they're involved in some meta-retro Wild West standoff.

Hayes has a strange look on his face that I'm unable to read. *What the hell did Scott just tell him?*

But this is no time to be thinking about my messed-up relationship with Hayes. The sun has dipped below the mountains, and the rosy glow of sunset has shifted to blue. As planned, the moon is half-full, so it will be dark enough to cover us but not so dark that we need to use the flashlights I've packed.

"You ready to work, or do you two need to hug out some feelings first?"

I grab the bag off Scott's back and drop it at my feet. Sliding off my own backpacks, I unzip them as Hayes lines up his packs beside mine.

Both boys kneel down and start helping me unload the massive number of spray cans.

"I've got this end," Hayes tells me, pulling the stencil out of his bag.

During one of my first planning excursions, I measured the distance between the two ladders running to the top of the tower. The huge stencil has been pieced together and cut to the perfect size.

"Or I can do it," says Scott.

"Thanks, guys." I look back and forth between them. "Actually, Hayes, I can really use you on the black paint. You remember that thing I taught you in my cabin about angling from below?"

"Yeah. I remember a *lot* about your cabin." Hayes is looking up at the obnoxious Sparkle Soda ad, so I can't see his expression, but I don't need to.

I'm trying to focus on the work we're facing, but my feelings for Hayes and history with him are wrestling for space inside my head.

I feel panicky for a moment over my loss of control. Mom never would've done a collaborative project like this one. She believed true artists worked alone. Maybe she was right.

I kneel down and finish unloading the final pack as I try to focus on the job ahead. I just need to block out everything around me.

Just then, Ken and Kat get within earshot.

"Holy hell, this is high up." Ken's voice is tight.

Kat answers, "Just don't look down. Keep thinking about how awesome the two of us will look at Nerd Con next month. Picture me in my metal Princess Leia bikini."

"Our *Stars* have aligned," Ken says. "Your *Wars* and my *Trek*."

"Did I tell you how perfect you are?" Even from this far away, I hear the dreaminess in Kat's voice.

They arrive, climbing through the opening in the metal catwalk to join us.

Ken is gripping the railing so tightly I imagine the metal will be imprinted with his finger marks when he finally lets go. *If* he ever lets go.

He's doing this for Kat, who is doing this for me, and their adorable nerd banter is making this memory better. It's making the whole thing better. I realize I'm glad I'm not alone.

Scott and I unfold the stencil and climb our way up the two side ladders as Hayes helps Kat and Ken unload their bags.

I tape my side of the stencil to the face of the water tower with thick packing tape and quickly make my way back down the ladder to where the rest of the group stands watching.

"A little higher, Scott," I call up to him.

He gives his corner a tug and the open area of the stencil moves into perfect position over the Sparkle model's cheesy, dimpled smile.

I hand one can of black paint to Hayes and reach behind him to tuck one snugly into the back waistband of his jeans.

I'm surprised by a whiff of the cologne he's wearing. It's still familiar yet not at all unpleasant, which must be a weird mind trick or something because I know for a fact that this boy's cologne stinks and I hate it.

I realize we're staring at each other and I finally unfreeze.

Grabbing another can of spray paint for myself, I use it to point to the lower right of the cutout lion. "Start there."

Hayes's voice is gruff. "Get the feet going right and the rest will follow, huh?" Which is another saying from the Narnia book he gave me.

The smile in my voice is obvious as I say, "Or something corny like that."

But I can't get distracted now. This is go time.

I get Kat situated on the lion's tail with a can of paint and explain to Ken about my organization system.

"I need you to keep an eye on these guys, and when they say they're running low, you get ready to hand them a new can from these here." I point to a collection of black spray cans with multicolored caps.

He nods his head and says, "Got it," as if the cans are filled with oxygen and we're all entering some high-altitude, life-threatening situation. I like Ken's attitude.

Handing him an unlit flashlight, I call out, "Okay, guys. We're going to try this without any lights. If you get a clogged cap or need to see better for a minute, just call 'lights,' and Ken here will shine on you from the base section. Best to not have too many moving beams." I pat Ken on the back. "You good?"

He flinches, but nods.

As I pass Kat on my way to Scott's ladder, I whisper to her, "That guy must be totally bonkers for you because he is scared shitless."

She stops spraying the tail to smile at me in the twilight. "Yeah, we clicked pretty hard. Thanks again for covering for our first date."

"Thank you for *this*. I owe you back about a thousand shift trades."

"Oh, I'll be cashing in on those." She laughs. "Ken and I have some serious cosplay prep planned for the future."

I climb the ladder where Scott is securing the upper section with more packing tape. I reach up and hand him a can of spray. "Nice work," I say. "Leave the edges for Kat, Hayes, and me, but I think you can handle some of the center fill to save us time."

I guide him in painting the inner portion of the lion's back haunches as I emphasize how important it is to keep the can constantly moving.

"What I mostly need from you is *no drips*." I poke him in the side to emphasize my words, and he twists away from me with a laugh.

Hayes coughs, and when I look down, he's watching Scott and me. He sees me looking, and he quickly goes back to working on the lion's feet.

I push away the urge to ask Scott what the hell he said to Hayes while I was climbing up the ladder. There's no time, and besides, this work area is a drama-free zone.

I make my way back down to the grated walkway and grab two more cans of spray, one black and one hot pink. Crossing over to the opposite ladder, I pass Ken, who continues holding the thin railing in a death grip while watching Kat expertly work on the tail.

As I pass by Hayes, I give a low, "Thank you for this."

His response of, "No problem," reveals absolutely nothing about what Scott told him.

Launching up the opposite ladder, I position myself to start on the head, and after taking a moment to savor the fact that this is finally happening, I attack the first layer of the mane's outline with the black paint.

My can's *pssssht* feels like it's coming from inside of me.

I've left the facial details open, so I can give our lion that special touch at the end, but I need to make sure I mask the Sparkle Soda ad.

My plan to incorporate some of the hot-pink color from the ad into the lion's mane will make the end result more forgiving. Not to mention it will emphasize the fact that the garish advertisement is being devoured by our giant lion.

I pause a moment at the word *our*.

I've never thought of any of the lions belonging to anyone but me. I look down at the figures moving in the darkness, or in the case of Ken, standing stock-still in abject terror.

I feel my lips pull into a wide smile as I turn my attention back to the lion's still-forming face.

Our lion's face.

CHAPTER NINETEEN

Things are running smoothly, and within a few hours, we've filled the first garbage bag with empty cans. The black bag rests at Ken's feet, and he's even let go of the railing...with one hand, anyway.

Ken has proven himself useful in directing the light where needed without flailing it about in a way that would call more attention to the tower than necessary.

Now that it's later, I'm feeling more relaxed about someone spotting us. I figure once we hit around 2:00 a.m., we'll be in the home stretch, since in my experience, folks who prefer the shroud of darkness are less inclined to be snitches.

As we gradually finish the initial foundation layer, I fire Scott from painting, since it turns out that a Venn diagram comparing the skill sets between chainsaw sculpting and graffiti painting would show very little overlap. That one commonality is the fast-moving pace of both art forms, but Scott has been layering on way too much paint, and it's a good thing I brought extra.

He makes himself useful running supplies back and forth to Hayes, Kat, and me. Before long, we develop a shorthand system whereby we call out "black" or "gray" or some other color, and no matter where we are, we have fresh cans of paint in our outstretched hands within moments.

A few hours later, we're finally ready to ditch the enormous stencil that's now covered in so many dripping colors it looks like it could be an abstract art piece on its own. Like, if Jackson Pollock had taken his action painting in a more random direction.

At my guiding, Scott and I climb our opposite ladders and get busy undoing the tape that holds the stencil between us. Everyone stands back and watches as the giant cardboard cutout floats to the metal catwalk below.

"Wow," Scott says, and we all stop to admire our mural so far.

The lion is still a faint, floating form, and big sections of his body need to be filled in. But he's ready to start moving from ghostly to lifelike.

Ken gives an amazed, "Nice," and in the dark, I nod my agreement.

Hayes is the first one to jump right back to work.

"Looking good!" Kat calls and shakes her spray can, making it clink happily.

Scott climbs down the ladder and starts gathering up the used stencil, while Ken kicks at it helpfully from where he stands, holding the railing.

Kat and Hayes and I are all working as fast as we can, but everything seems to be taking longer than I planned. I can't believe I ever imagined I could do this alone, but if things flow smoothly from here on out, we just may finish before sunrise begins.

But we might not.

With a deep breath, I shove that thought down and start in on the most important part of the whole thing—the details of the lion's face.

Kat bellows, "Orange!" to request a new full can, and in a hiss-whisper, she calls up to me, "This is *amazing*, Rory."

"I know, right?" I don't look away from the open mouth of fangs I'm carefully outlining.

A loud, metallic clatter explodes into the night, followed by an unhelpful round of shushing as we all turn to see what's just happened.

Scott stands beside Ken with his hands raised in surrender. Ken hisses at Scott, "I can't believe you just did that."

"What happened?" I ask.

Scott and Ken gesture to the scattered cans at their feet. Scott says, "I just kicked over a whole shitload of cans."

"Well, then, straighten them up." I turn back to the lion's mouth. "And pass Kat a can of orange while you're at it."

"No, you don't understand," Scott says. "There *is* no more orange. Or red or green and now we're almost out of black."

"What are you talking about?" Hayes growls from where he's standing on the ladder opposite me. "There was just plenty… Oh."

"What?" I'm annoyed by all the distractions at a point when I really need to concentrate. "Why are you guys just standing there looking down over the edge?"

"Because." Scott covers his forehead with the palm of his hand. "That's where half the paint just went."

"You kicked the cans of paint over the edge?" I resist the urge to wing the spray can I'm holding at Scott's head. But only because it's still half-full and apparently we're almost out of black. I desperately need black to shade in the rest of the face.

Hayes asks, "Was this whole thing not challenging enough for you?"

"It was an accident," Scott says. "I'm sorry."

"That's great. Just great." I scramble down the ladder to make a quick assessment of the damage. Looking over the cans, I'd say we've lost more than a dozen.

I glance up at our lion and catch my breath. It looks amazing. But we really do need those cans to finish. "*Shit.*"

"I'll go down, see if I can find them. I think they fell mostly off to the right." Scott heads for the ladder.

"No, we need you handing out what's left of the paint," I say. "We're running out of time."

Ken's voice is strong. "I can hand out paint." He stands staring at Kat for a moment, looking like he's telling his hand to let go of the railing while his hand refuses to let go of the railing. "You need orange," he says to Kat. "Will gold work?"

She smiles. "I can work with gold." And we all stand, watching with amazement as Ken bends down and picks up a can of paint with a gold lid. He stretches as far as he can toward Kat while still holding on to the railing and, finally, pulls himself away from it.

"Ken!" Kat stretches toward him.

Walking like a zombie, Ken stomps along the grated walkway, holding up the can of paint as if it's an Olympic torch. Like these are the opening ceremonies of some twisted tournament for the walking dead.

We all stand, watching speechless as Ken hands the can off to Kat in a slow-motion display of willpower and courage against overwhelming odds. We all break into whispered cheers of celebration at his triumph.

Ken has moved a grand total of about three feet.

"Nice," I say. "Now, everybody, back to work. Scott, grab a flashlight and go see what you can salvage."

"Already on my way." Scott grabs an empty backpack before moving to the ladder and quickly disappearing into the dark abyss below.

I look up at the blank expression on the lion towering over our heads, trying to come up with an alternate plan in case Scott can't find those missing cans.

"You okay?" Hayes asks from halfway up the opposite ladder he's been working from. He's holding a can of paint poised over the lion's still-forming back.

I look at him through the darkness, wishing I could shine a flashlight to read his expression. "Mistakes happen, right?"

"All we can do is keep on trying," he says.

I'm hopeful that he's not just talking about our mural as I make my way back up toward our lion's still-forming face.

Fortunately, Scott manages to get down and back up fairly quickly. Unfortunately, he only finds about half of the lost cans, and even more unfortunately, most of our black is now gone.

"It was hard spotting the black cans with the black caps in the dark." Scott holds open the pack, showing me the cans he's salvaged. "I am so sorry, Rory."

"It was an accident." I consider the remaining supplies and quickly map out a new plan in my mind. All my creative synapses are sparking.

Quickly climbing up the ladder where Hayes is working, I hand him the final two cans of black paint. "Finish up the back end with these as best you can. Then that's it for black."

He gives me a nod in the dark and continues working.

Moving to the front, I lean back, debating how I can make the rest of this work without black. I'll be forced to keep some of the underlying color from the Sparkle ad and use it for accent lines.

I picture the ways I'll incorporate the faded pink into the lion's mane and facial features, and realize that, no matter what, the lion will be more pink than I'd planned. And, of course, we have plenty of pink spray paint left too.

I think about Mom's approach to unplanned obstacles when she was making art.

I'm remembering an endless series of different pieces that she trashed when she was unable to get things just right. In particular, a beautiful clay bowl that she pounded down until it was just a useless lump because she couldn't make it perfect.

Maintaining her artistic vision was what mattered.

I sigh. I'm way too stubborn to be a true artist because I don't give a shit if he's dripping and deformed and his colors are all wrong, wrong, wrong; this lion is going to freaking *roar* at the break of dawn.

I'm working on the lion's right eye and just noticing how tired my arm muscles are getting when I hear a faint beeping sound coming from below. It sounds oddly familiar but I can't quite place it.

"What the hell is that?" Kat shout-whispers.

"Where's it coming from?" I call down and see Ken already riffling through the empty supply bags.

The sound gets louder as Ken holds up a lit smartphone. "It's someone's cell phone. Who has the red-and-black case that says OBEY?"

OhmyGod. "Turn it off. Turn it off." I race down the ladder toward him as fast as I can while my phone continues to stroke out with a frenzied alarm.

"What's your passcode?" Ken is swiping at the face of it.

"No, I mean Shut. It. Down!"

I reach him just as he swipes right to turn off my phone

and I see the notification for only a split moment before it disappears. But I don't need to read the notification to know what just happened.

My screen goes black too late. My dad has just traced my cell phone and locked in on this location.

And I don't need any notifications to know a few other things too. He's already pissed and he's heading this way.

Everyone is frozen, watching me. I realize my lungs are empty, and I slowly inflate them.

Stepping back until the railing presses against my butt, I take the flashlight from Scott and sweep it from top to bottom, over our full design.

It's definitely looking very lionlike. But it's not quite done yet. And we're completely out of time.

The mission has failed. I look from face to face, all watching me.

I have to at least try. "Okay, guys. That was my dad tracking my phone. I need you all to clear out. Now." Nobody moves, and I shout, "The cops are coming!"

A harmony of groans rises up, and Ken lets out a panicked squeal as cans rattle and everyone moves quickly toward the exit ladder.

I start shaking my spray can, and Kat looks back and asks, "What the hell are you doing?"

"I'll be fine. I should have time to at least finish most of the details on the face before my dad gets here."

Everyone turns to look at the design, and Scott says, "The

body looks like his fur is molting or something. There are too many unfinished places. I can't believe I fucked up so bad, Rory. I'm sorry."

"It's not all your fault."

"Just *mostly* your fault," Ken chimes in.

"I way underestimated how long things would take," I say. "It'll be okay. I'll get as much done as I can before my dad climbs up. He'll have to handcuff me if he wants to stop me from painting."

"He is going to straight-up arrest your ass," Kat says.

"You don't know that," Scott says. "He might not arrest his own daughter."

Hayes turns to me. "We can't let you take the fall for this whole thing."

"Well, I won't forgive myself if you guys get into trouble."

Ken says, "Maybe we can block his way or something? Make it so he can't come the whole way up here?"

"And what?" I say. "You think he'll get bored and go away? You have clearly never met my dad. He'll have a task force surrounding the tower and helicopters buzzing around our heads."

Scott says, "Maybe your dad didn't get a lock on your phone before Ken shut it off."

Kat turns back to the lion and begins spraying again. After a moment, Hayes moves back into position and stretches out his arm. The sound of their cans *hiss* into the sprawling night. Our big, crazy night that will all be over very, very soon.

"Come on, guys. You're running out of time. You need to clear out. Leave the rest to me."

Between spray strokes, Hayes says, "Not. Leaving. You."

Kat stops spraying a moment. "Accept it, you're not getting rid of us."

• I look back and forth from Scott to Ken. "You guys should really get out of here."

Ken looks at Kat and says, "I'd rather spend the night in jail than walk away from what is happening up here tonight."

Kat turns around and strides directly up to him. Grabbing the back of his neck, she kisses him firmly before releasing him to go back to painting.

Scott and I look at each other with raised eyebrows, and he smiles. "Well, I'd like to stay and see how all this plays out."

"Are you sure?" I ask. "This really goes above the friend-zone pay grade."

He gives my shoulder a light punch. "Depends on the friend." He grabs a new can of silver paint and heads up the ladder toward a big section that desperately needs to be filled in. My eyes shift immediately to Hayes.

He was watching us but turns his attention back to the portion of the lion's chest he's been working on and starts spraying again. It's looking really good.

Kat says, "Get your fine ass back to work, Rory. Time's running out."

She doesn't need to tell me twice.

I call out, "You guys are *all* my favorite. Seriously!" I fly up the rungs to finish work on the lion's face, hoping it comes out well enough to express even half of the feelings churning inside of me right now.

We are working double-time and things are finally coming together with calls of, "Finished the back!" and "Done with the haunches!" coming at a more rapid pace.

The tiny hope that my dad didn't get a lock on my location is just starting to grow into a midsize hope when I hear the faint, far-away crunch of tires driving on gravel.

Hope dissolves in acid.

I lean over the railing, looking far below, and in the glint of moonlight, it's clear that the car is a squad car.

The roof lights aren't flashing, which would be a good sign except that the headlights are also turned off completely. Which must be bad.

Is my dad planning to pull off some sort of sneak arrest?

The sound of the car door slamming shut floats up to us, and I call, "Look alive, people."

Ken has moved the garbage bags filled with empties, so they cover the opening where the ladder joins the catwalk, and he's piled all the bags and remaining supplies on top. It's not the best blockade, but it should delay my Dad enough to buy us a moment or two.

And right now, every single moment counts.

This lion needs to look fierce, but he still has a touch of amusement in the eyes that I can't seem to get rid of. I've never had this much trouble with a lion's expression before.

As sections have been finishing up one by one, Kat and Hayes have been moving closer and closer to the face that I'm frantically trying to get right.

The two of them are directly below me, working on the mane, and I feel a hand brush the inside of my knee. I look down to see Hayes is focused on the stream of paint emanating from his can as he holds on to the ladder rung between my legs.

I swallow against the tightness in my throat just as my dad's voice comes floating up from below. "Isn't it a little past your bedtime, kiddies?" He's wearing his zero-tolerance voice.

With a panicked growl, I reach out with my can and quickly outline the lion's eyelids with pink. *There's that inner angst that's been missing.*

Hayes is still just below me on the ladder, leaning so far across he's practically horizontal. I see he's using dark gray and ask him for the can, telling him he can switch to using my pink for that section of the mane.

We're very nearly finished.

The sound of metal cans shifting against each other rings out over the valley as Dad starts making his way through the makeshift blockade.

Kat announces her section is *"Done!"* and she moves back down the metal catwalk to where Ken and Scott stand watching Hayes and I work together.

We are seamless, passing our cans back and forth, moving as one. My heart is beating fast as I hear my dad grunt with the effort of shoving our big garbage bags of empties out of his way.

"Almost there," I say, giving Hayes my hand so he can pull himself up to the rung just beneath me.

I wrap an arm around him and stretch myself as long as I can, adding just a touch of white underneath the lion's eyes one at a time. The can slips from my fingers and I lunge for it without thinking, losing my center of balance for a split second.

Without hesitation, Hayes grabs me and pulls me back so I'm standing upright beside him on the ladder. I suck in a breath as he wraps both arms around my waist and shakes his head disapprovingly. But he doesn't release his hold.

Everything else disappears. My dad and my friends and even our lion. There is only Hayes. I stand there, still one rung above him, so I'm taller, gazing down at his face.

His look of concern over my near fall melts as the two of us look at each other. A mass of *zings* ricochet between us, and I imagine him rising up on his toes to kiss me.

Judging by the look in his eyes, I'm pretty sure he's imagining it too.

He does stand up straighter, moving closer and biting his lower lip as if he doesn't trust it not to kiss me. He whispers in my ear. "You did it, Rory."

I let my gaze shift over to our lion.

And realize the thing looks *fucking amazing*.

The hugest smile spreads across my face, and I have tears in my eyes as I say to Hayes, "No, *we* did it."

I lean over and yell down to the rest of the gang. "*We did it!*"

They hoot and holler, and Ken and Scott give each other an awkward high five.

Kat calls out, "Suck on that, you Sparkle Soda assholes!" And Ken moves to give her a dramatic dip and kiss that is eight hundred times smoother than his high-fiving.

"Sorry to interrupt." My dad's voice booms over the celebration sounds. "But I believe you are all *trespassing* on private property right now."

I untangle myself from Hayes's embrace and call down, "They did it all for me, Dad. I'm the only one who should be in trouble here."

Dad is looking up at the lion with his hands on his hips. After complete silence for a full three minutes, he finally gives a long, low whistle.

I've always thought that my dad's angry voice is the scariest sound ever. His yell could send a chill up the most hardened criminal's spine. But for the first time, I realize that Dad's angry voice is nothing compared to his whistle.

Because the sound of that long, low whistle is *terrifying*.

CHAPTER TWENTY

I tap Hayes on the shoulder and gesture for him to go down the ladder to the landing so I can pass him. It will mean he needs to move closer to my dad. Hayes widens his eyes and shakes his head—the universal signal for *no friggin' way*. But with a quick nostril flare, he smooths a hand through his hair and heads down ahead of me.

When he reaches the catwalk, my dad turns, so the two of them are looking eye to eye. Dad gives him an up-and-down look that would have most guys wetting their pants, but Hayes doesn't flinch.

"Sorry, sir," he says. "But it had to be done."

Dad looks back up at the lion as I reach the bottom of the ladder. "It was all my idea. Honestly, Daddy. Please don't arrest anyone else."

He turns to me and raises an eyebrow. "Oh, so now I'm *Daddy*?"

I hear Scott give a soft, "Oh shit," under his breath, and my dad must hear him too, because he looks over his way.

"Little Scotty Tomlinson? Is that you?"

Scott tries to hide his face too late. "Hey, Sergeant Capers," he says in defeat.

Dad looks at Kat next and says, "From Danny's, right?"

Ken stands up straight and moves his body so it's covering most of Kat's. "I'm the manager there, sir. And I assure you, Kat and Rory are outstanding employees."

My dad gives a sarcastic laugh. "Oh, yes, I'm sure they are. Just *outstanding*."

Ken starts shifting his weight from side to side until Kat reaches over to put an arm around him and stops his rocking.

Dad turns his attention back to me, inspecting the can of spray paint in my hands. If it wasn't empty, I'd consider using it on him like a can of mace and yelling for everyone to *run*. Except that Dad's the one who taught me how to effectively mace an attacker, so it wouldn't really seem all that fair.

Plus, like I said, the can is empty.

After what feels like three eternities, he calls out, "Have any of you chuckleheads been drinking tonight?"

We all mumble assorted versions of *no* and *no way* and *we're not crazy.*

Dad leans into my personal space and gives my breath an obvious sniff. Leaning back, he says, "So those garbage bags are filled with empty *spray paint* cans only?"

Everyone nods enthusiastically, and I feel a wave of annoyance at the way my dad is toying with us. "You can't arrest any of them. They were all just supporting me." I point my thumb at Hayes. "And Hayes shouldn't be accused of violating his probation just because he was doing me a favor."

Hayes moves closer and hisses in my ear, "I don't think you're exactly helping things here."

"Honestly, Dad. You know this is between you and me. Please let my friends go."

Dad looks around, considering each person in turn.

Finally, he calls out, "Okay. This is what is going to happen. I'm ordering each of you sixty hours of community service. It can be whatever you like, working with stray dogs or picking up garbage. Hell, I don't care if you're all helping at the blood drive. You will get your hours documented, and you will report them directly to *me*. I see no reason to involve the courts, unless any one of you should choose to not comply."

The collective exhale is audible.

We give one another smiles and nods. None of us will let the others down.

Dad goes on in his commanding voice. "Now I need you all to climb yourselves very carefully back down this ladder and clear off this property. Bring the cans with you."

I can't believe he's really letting us off.

We all start to move slowly toward the exit, afraid to make a sound and blow our good fortune. As I pass my dad on the catwalk, he gives an eerie chuckle.

"Rory?" he says in a voice so low I feel a tiny bit of pee come out. "You're staying."

Everyone looks to me with traumatized expressions.

My voice cracks a little when I tell them, "Don't worry. I've got this." They all stay frozen until I add, "You guys had better go, or it will just make things worse."

This gets the gang moving toward the ladder with a chorus of *sorry*s and halfhearted *good luck, Rory*s.

Hayes widens his eyes at me, giving my arm a squeeze as he goes past.

"Nice knowing you," I tell him under my breath.

Scott gives me a salute from across the catwalk and grabs one of the garbage bags on his way down. Kat rubs Ken's back as he straps one of the empty backpacks on his chest and haltingly disappears below the catwalk. Kat throws an empty backpack over each shoulder and follows him down the rungs.

Hayes looks like he wants to say something as he swings the final two garbage bags clanking with empties over one shoulder. He stands with the sacks, sliding his gaze back and forth between my dad and me. Finally, he gives a firm nod before disappearing.

I turn and lean over the railing, watching my crew make their way back down the ladder. Scott has nearly disappeared into the darkness, and Hayes has already caught up to Ken and Kat, who are moving slowly downward.

We should not be acting this defeated.

"Hey, guys!" I call down, and all four faces turn up toward me. I punch a fist in the air. "We fucking did it!"

"Yes!" Kat calls out. "We kicked ass!"

Hayes gives an earsplitting whistle, and Ken and Scott whoop and woot in response.

"You about finished?" Dad's voice is like cold water thrown over my head, but it can't stop me from grinning over our victory.

"Yeah, I'm done. What now? Boarding school? Lifetime grounding? Women's prison?"

He moves to stand beside me and rests his elbows on the railing, looking off into the still-dark sky.

My dad stands there a long time. Long enough that I can hear the garbage bags clatter loudly into the back of Kat's pickup truck. After an extended pause, I hear the truck doors slam and the engine start up, and I listen to it slowly pull away.

I imagine Kat will give Scott and Hayes a ride home before finding some way to reward Ken for the tremendous bravery he showed tonight. Nerd love at its finest.

It's so quiet, I can hear the crickets chirping far below.

Finally, Dad says, "You know I'm angry with her too." He doesn't need to tell me he is talking about Mom.

"We don't have to do this, Dad. Honestly, this was my final project anyway." I look over at him in the moonlight. "Were you surprised when you followed my phone here?"

Dad shrugs. "I already knew you were the one painting the lions."

"What?" I think back to the time my phone beeped

while I was working late at night. "You locked in that phone trace to my cabin?"

He looks at me. "You have a cabin?"

Shit. "Oh, I mean…" I cover my eyes with my hand. "Walked right into that one. Why don't *you* tell *me* what you know?"

Dad gives a chuckle. "I won't reveal my sources."

"Wait. Did Scott tip you off?" I dig through my mind and hit on a devastating thought. "Was it Hayes?"

He shakes his head. "It wasn't one of your hoodlum boyfriends, Rory."

"Well, I've been super careful. Did you have one of your officers tailing me or something? GPS tracker on my car?"

"Relax, sweetheart. I found one of your designs crumpled up in the trash. It was just a sketch, but the look of your lions is so distinct, I knew it immediately."

I knock on the side of my head with my fist. "I'm such an idiot."

"Once I realized, I went out this past week and I visited a few of the lions around town." He stands up straight and puts his hands on his hips. "Studying your work, I think I figured something out."

I pray that what he figured out isn't that I deserve to face felony charges.

He turns and looks at me a moment before going on. "I was afraid that you being an artist meant you'd be traveling down the same crazy track your mom laid. Like it was all just waiting for you. You'd never be satisfied with life."

I drop my head and consider the delicate catwalk running between our feet. I know what he means. But it's almost as if the nozzle of my spray can was spraying some of my own darkness along with the black paint tonight. Now there's less of it inside me.

"Before we painted this tower, I was afraid of the same thing," I confess.

"But looking at your lions, I could see it. I just knew." Dad guides me gently by my shoulders until we're both turned around and facing the water tower. The lion's fresh paint still glistens in places. Dad hugs one arm around me, and I allow my eyes to climb up the painting.

I meet the lion's fierce gaze, and it frightens me.

"Just look at that *strength*, Rory." Dad turns me so that I'm facing him now. "Your drive and determination. That *fight* in you? I realize now that has nothing to do with your mother. *That's* what you get from me."

He and I look at each other, and I feel the connection of our flimsy string bridge running between us.

"You are so much stronger than your mother could ever hope to be," he tells me. "All I had to do was compare your work to see it. Her art was so much more delicate and detailed."

I consider the contrast between her fine blown-glass sculptures and my rough and wild lions and laugh. "Well, she was a bit more of a perfectionist."

His expression stays serious. "But you also used your art to bring others around you." He gestures to the ladder where my friends descended. "Rory, you proved art doesn't need to cause isolation."

It feels good to finally have everything out in the open. "I know that me being an artist scares you," I say. "It was the one thing that bound me and Mom together." I feel the tears starting in my chest. "I miss her so much."

"I miss her too." Dad's glistening eyes search the sky. "And I'll be in love with her for the rest of my life."

Swinging around so I'm leaning over the thin railing, I look toward the moonlit valley.

I imagine each lion I've painted turning its head upward, looking back at me. Waiting.

Holding my breath, I envision them opening their mouths and beginning to roar all at once. In my mind, they are so loud the whole town of New Paltz starts to quake.

The air is filled with the sound of all my anger and confusion and pain. And rage.

Finally, I let it explode out of me with the loudest "*RAAARRR!*" I can manage. The next thing I know, I am screaming and yelling and roaring into the night.

A treeful of birds alights from below, looking for a quieter neighborhood.

My snarling voice echoes over the valley, rolling back toward me, hitting my face, and flowing straight through my chest. I roar and scream again and again, until all the lions are overcome by my passion.

They roll over and submit, showing their soft bellies and whimpering at my torment. I am the only lion now. Even the towering one behind me bends down to nuzzle my cheek.

Comforting me.

My voice breaks, and the tears start. I bend forward, clinging to the bar.

Dad has stiffened beside me, and I'm sure I'll be getting a psych evaluation in the very near future. Or maybe I'm going straight to a padded room in jail.

Either way, I'm definitely heading someplace with a lock on the door.

Dad wants to leave now. I can sense it. But I can't move.

Clearing his throat, he throws his head back and lets loose with an earsplitting, all-out, "*RAAAHGH!*"

I'm so startled I stop crying. Swiping at the tears on my cheeks, I take a shaky breath and call out again. "*Aaaaagh!*" It's practically a scream ringing over the valley and harmonizing with Dad's deep, thundering howls.

He and I go back and forth like that for a time, taking turns roaring, releasing so much pain and anger into the cool night air, it's amazing we don't set the pine trees on fire.

Our roars grow more and more hoarse until I'm wrapped in giant, soft paws, held still. I am spent and realize Dad and I are hugging each other while crying. The roaring has silenced into sobs. From both of us.

We stay like that for a long time. Everything is quiet.

Maybe the two of us are huggy people after all. Finally, Dad asks, "You ready to head home?"

"I hate that place," I confess. "It's like Mom is everywhere."

Dad kisses the top of my head. "And here I thought you

were the one who didn't want to leave. I was planning on selling that house the day after you go to college." He looks at me. "You thinking what I'm thinking?"

"You just want me to help you move all your crap," I say.

He tousles the top of my dreads. "See that? I told you the two of us were alike. We even think the same."

I reach over and tousle his hair right back.

He laughs. "Come on, let's call it a night before the cops show up."

"Wait, so you're going to just pretend you still don't know who's painting all the graffiti?"

Dad looks up at the lion and shrugs. "I never thought that ad was in the best interest of our town anyway. Your public form of peaceful protest is duly noted. Now let's get the hell off this tower."

He heads for the stairs, and I pause, looking into my lion's eyes. It has resumed its position, sitting up and roaring intensely over the valley.

I search in my chest for that familiar cocktail of rage and pain and grief, and find that the texture of it has changed. It still feels tender and enormous and beyond my control, but the edges are more defined. The size and weight and density of it all, somehow…bearable.

I don't know if this means I'm done painting lions or if it means I'm done painting altogether, but either way, I want to have a life. I don't need to be tortured or isolated or any of the things Mom taught me a true artist needs to be.

Dad has already disappeared down the ladder, and I move to follow slowly after him.

I'm ready to get back to work on my true masterpiece. The one titled *My Life*. And I'm thinking it's an even more expansive piece than what I'd first envisioned.

In fact, this project is going to be boundless.

CHAPTER TWENTY-ONE

I take my time climbing down, stopping to consider our lion from time to time. It looks different from the one I planned in my head, and yet it's as if he sprang fully formed from my wild subconscious.

As I near the ground, I can hear Dad talking below me. I'm still too far up to make out what he's saying and hope he's not talking to some other police officer who's onto us. I really don't want my dad getting into trouble.

Most of the cops he works with are cool, but I can think of a few guys on the force who are gunning for his position. They'd love to catch him trying to protect his daughter from getting arrested.

If it comes to it, I need to be prepared to take the fall.

Climbing the rest of the way down as quickly as I can, my heart drops faster than my descent when I hear the voice of someone talking to Dad.

I know that voice. It's Hayes.

I can only make out bits and pieces of their conversation, but Dad is saying something about "…over at the precinct…" and Hayes responds with "…call my probation officer…"

He must've stayed behind while Kat drove away with Scott and Ken.

And now my dad is threatening to arrest him.

I launch myself the rest of the way down the ladder and jump in between the two of them.

I hiss at Hayes, "What are you still doing here? What part of *clear the hell out* didn't you understand?" I spin around to face my dad, blocking Hayes with my body. "Dad, you can't arrest him. This whole thing was my idea, and he's been trying so hard to make good choices."

From over my shoulder, Hayes says to my dad. "As I was saying, *sir*…I'd love the chance to come in and speak at your D.A.R.E. workshop."

My dad gives me a look before turning back to Hayes. "Thanks. Your decision to turn your life around at a young age will have a real impact on those kids."

"Oh," I say. "Whoops." *Guess I read that situation wrong.*

Dad reaches past me to shake Hayes's hand. "Frank's been working probation for twenty years now. He has good instincts, and you have him to thank for this second chance. Please don't allow my daughter to talk you into any more illegal activity."

I narrow my eyes at my dad. "When did you talk to Hayes's probation officer?"

Dad leans over and kisses the top of my head again, which is apparently his new thing. He says, "I called him last week. You don't think I'd just sit around doing nothing while you went off gallivanting with some stranger who's on probation?"

"How did you even…?"

Hayes says, "I went to visit your dad at the precinct after we met that day in the restaurant." I'm staring at him, and he clarifies, "The day you were flinging plates against the walls?"

"You went to my dad behind my back?"

"I wanted to see what I could do to help. Finding him was easy once you told me your last name."

I think of Hayes casually asking for my last name while we were painting together. "That was a betrayal on so many levels." I turn on my dad. "And then *you* turned around and had him investigated?"

Dad looks at the ground. "All I did was talk to his probation officer. I had to protect you in case this guy was trouble."

I glare at Hayes. "Oh, he *is* trouble. And not the good kind either."

"Boy, did you ever step in shit," Dad tells him with a grin. He turns and heads toward his squad car. "Time for me to go feed Kelly. See you back at home, Rory?"

"Yeah, don't start packing without me."

"Don't worry. I won't. And, Hayes?" he says. "Keep up those meetings. That's a good bunch of folks you're with."

"Thank you, sir." Hayes gives an enthusiastic wave to my dad before looking at my expression and dropping his big grin.

I say, "You do know that my dad liking you makes you *infinitely* less attractive to me now."

"Ah, yes." Hayes laughs. "Parental approval. The kiss of death."

"What possessed you to go to him behind my back?"

"Sorry for meddling, Rory. I just really wanted to try to help you two." He slides a dreadlock off my face. "What are you guys packing for anyway?"

"We're moving out of that house," I say. "Just... starting over."

I turn and watch my dad give a casual, open-palmed wave from the driver's seat of his squad car as he pulls out. I'm hit with a pang of deep-down love for him and sadness for all that he's been through.

When I look back at Hayes, he's watching me. He says, "Speaking of starting over, Scott told me what really happened when the two of you were alone together."

I rub my arms as the night breeze joins our conversation. "I've made a few missteps, and I know I hurt you," I say, "but when you wouldn't even give me a chance to explain, that really hurt me too."

"I see that, and I'm sorry." Hayes looks toward the leg of the tower a moment. "Listen, I've been dealing with my issues, but I still have a long way to go."

"That's true." I smile. "But I'm pretty sure I'm a little more messed up than you are."

"It's not supposed to be a competition." He shoves my arm playfully. "But yeah, maybe you win by just a little."

I shove him back and he catches my hand.

We look at each other for a beat, and I want to be vulnerable with Hayes. I want to go deeper than the flirty surface banter we enjoy.

I say, "I'd like us to try having one of those relationship thingies you've talked about. If you don't feel that, you should tell me now."

He dips his head down and steps closer. It's like I'm right at that moment when the elevator stops.

He whispers, "Yeah. I feel that."

The smirk on his face gets the elevator rising again.

He says, "Your friend Scott also told me that the reason you put on the brakes with him was because you realized you're in love with me."

"Yeah, well, my friend Scott needs to learn how to shut the hell up."

"I overreacted when I saw the two of you together because of how strong my feelings are for you, Rory."

"I can't blame you for thinking the worst." I hunch my shoulders and look up at him. "But I'm really glad you're giving us a second chance."

"Oh, wait," he says. "There's one other thing."

I straighten my posture, but before I can ask him what, he

grabs my chin and pulls me in for a kiss. I laugh against his lips, but he continues kissing me until that elevator starts again and I'm carried up, up, up along with him.

When we break apart, I follow his gaze upward to our amazing roaring lion and smile.

I ask, "Does it look like the lion you pictured?"

He squints up at it. "Not especially. But it looks like a Rory lion, which is even better."

"Thanks for coming tonight. I'm sorry I almost got you arrested."

"Well, after talking to your dad, I was pretty convinced he wasn't looking to bust you, even if he did, you know, bust you."

"Yeah, he's not so bad, I guess."

Hayes laughs. "The two of you are a lot alike."

I shake my head and two dreadlocks fall in front of my eye. I peek through them at him. "I'm like my mom a bit too."

Hayes pulls me into an embrace. "That may be true, but you are very much your own person, Rory." He looks up to our roaring lion. "With an amazing imagination. Does it look the way *you* pictured it would?"

I smile up at it, remembering the first moment I envisioned a spray-painted lion roaring with rage. I can still feel the rage that started it all, but it's no longer inside me. It's all right up there.

When I look back at Hayes, he's watching my face, and I answer, "No, it's all very different. But it's better this way."

I feel elated and scared and empty and full all at the same time.

My romantic visions of *ART* have been ripped to shreds,

and in their place is an image that's more real and strong and alive and kind of messed-up but true. Art isn't magic.

But making art can be.

Hayes's lips graze my cheekbone on their way to my mouth. As we kiss, I start to get that levitating feeling, my insides dipping and floating.

I'm pulled from my happy place by the sound of a ball bearing knocking about inside a can.

I draw back and realize the sound is coming from behind Hayes's back, where he's shaking a spray can. With a grin, he moves over to the closest leg of the tower.

Before I can say a word, he's painted a very stylized pink heart with *HM + RC* written inside.

"Classic corny new-couple logo." I laugh. "Nice work. I love it."

Tossing the can over his shoulder, Hayes moves back in front of me and wraps both arms around me.

I say, "You do know you just littered, right?"

Hayes scrunches his whole face. "I know. I was just thinking that. I was trying to be all cool." He turns and begins rooting through the weeds. "No more lawbreaking." He holds the can up in triumph.

I laugh. "Starting…*now.*"

He moves closer, putting both arms around my shoulders and drawing me close. And as the two of us kiss again, I swear I can hear our lion

breathe a sigh overhead.

ACKNOWLEDGMENTS

A huge thank-you to Ammi-Joan Paquette and the whole EMLA squad, including my agency-mates who are all so talented and generous and funny. To Katherine Prosswimmer, thank you for helping me make this book so much better, and to the rest of the Sourcebooks Fire team, especially Annette Pollert-Morgan, Todd Stocke, Aubrey Poole, Gretchen Stelter, Elizabeth Boyer, and special thanks to Brittany Vibbert for the amazing cover design.

To my writer people, especially Jessica Verdi for her superpowers of encouragement, Amanda Coppedge Bosky for her perfect insight and talent, Jen Nadol for her illuminating critique and my Lucky 13 girls and Binders for always being there. This journey would not be nearly as much fun without you all! To Dad, Mom, Ger, Jen, Zach, and extended loved ones: I am so lucky to carry each of you in my heart.

And most of all, thank you to my family who endured my working from the back of the van during our epic coast-to-coast road trip. Brett, Trinity, and Aidan, you are all my favorite—Go Team Crompton!

ABOUT THE AUTHOR

Laurie Boyle Crompton is the author of several YA books including *Blaze*, *The Real Prom Queens of Westfield High*, and *Adrenaline Crush*. She graduated first in her class from St. John's University with a BA in English and Journalism. Laurie has written for national magazines like *Allure*, survived a stint as a teacher at an all-boy high school, and appeared several times on *Good Day New York* as a toy expert. And yes, "toy expert" is an actual profession. When she was seventeen, Laurie and her best friend once spray-painted their names on an underpass in Butler, Pennsylvania in the middle of the night. Laurie later painted her first car hot pink using forty cans of spray paint. She now lives near New York City with her family and one very fuzzy "dog toy expert" named Baxter Bear. The last thing she spray-painted was a bunch of old lawn furniture. Visit lboylecrompton.com.